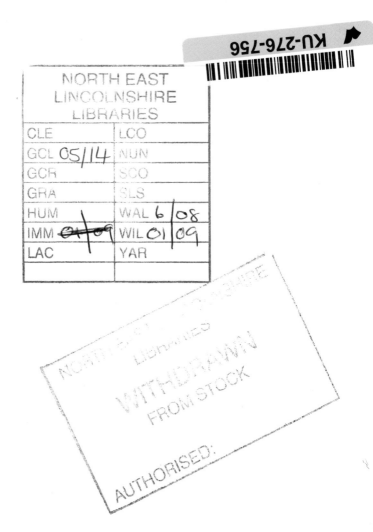

SOLDIER OF FORTUNE

The dashing Captain Daniel Rawson can charm a woman as well as he can parry a sword, and he proves himself invaluable to John Churchill, the Duke of Marlborough, and the Confederate forces as they head towards the ferocious battle of Blenheim. On the march across Europe, Rawson is pursued by Abigail Piper, with whom he enjoyed a brief flirtation in London, and by the murderous servants of the General Salignac, the latest man Daniel cuckolded. Their instructions are simple – kill Rawson and bring back proof. A simple order, but have they underestimated their target?

SOLDIER OF FORTUNE

SOLDIER OF FORTUNE

by

Edward Marston

Magna Large Print Books
Long Preston, North Yorkshire,
BD23 4ND, England.

British Library Cataloguing in Publication Data.

Marston, Edward
        Soldier of fortune.

        A catalogue record of this book is
        available from the British Library

        ISBN   978-0-7505-2823-8

First published in Great Britain in 2008 by Allison & Busby Ltd.

Published in Large Print 2008 by arrangement with
Allison & Busby Ltd.

Magna Large Print is an imprint of Library Magna Books Ltd.

Printed and bound in Great Britain by
T.J. (International) Ltd., Cornwall, PL28 8RW

PROLOGUE

Saturday, July 4, 1685

Daniel Rawson saw him at once. The boy was walking across a field with his dog, Tinker, at his heels when he caught sight of a lone horseman coming over the brow of the hill. He sensed that it must be his father and broke into a spontaneous run. Thinking that they were playing a game, Tinker chased after him, shooting past him then zigzagging crazily in his path. Daniel did not even notice the animal. His gaze was fixed on the rider and his mind was racing. It was almost three weeks since Nathan Rawson had left home to join the Duke of Monmouth and it had been the longest and most agonising time of the boy's life. Desperate to know how his father was faring with the rebel army, he had been fed on nothing but rumour, lies and tittle-tattle. At last, he would learn the truth.

Recognising his son, Nathan kicked his horse into a gallop then raised an arm in greeting. Daniel replied by waving both of his hands in the air and Tinker barked excitedly. By the time that father and son finally met, the boy was panting for breath but nevertheless able to blurt out a few words.

'Welcome back, Father!'

'How are you, lad?' said Nathan, reining in his

horse and dismounting to embrace him. 'Is all well here?'

'What news?' Daniel gasped. 'Have the royal forces been put to flight? Has the King been deposed? Have we won yet?'

Nathan shook his head sadly. 'No, Dan. Not yet.'

'But we *will* win – you promised me that we will.'

'And we may still do so in time.'

'Where's the army now?' asked Daniel.

'No more questions until we get home,' said the other, holding him by the shoulders to appraise him. 'Let me take a good look at you. I've missed you and your mother so much.' Tinker barked in protest and Nathan smiled wearily. 'Yes, I missed you as well, Tinker,' he added, patting the dog's head. 'I've missed you all.'

Thrilled to see his father once more, Daniel was at the same time distressed by his appearance. Nathan Rawson was a big, broad-shouldered man in his late thirties with the boundless energy that his son had inherited from him. There was no sign of that energy now. He looked tired, dispirited and much older than when he had left the farm to join a cause in which he fervently believed. In the eyes of a ten-year old boy who worshipped him, his father had shrunk in size and lost all of his buoyant self-confidence.

'Come on,' said Nathan, trying to conceal his anxieties behind a warm grin. 'Let's ride home together.'

'How long will you be staying?'

'Only until tomorrow – we've been granted furlough.'

'Mother will be so pleased,' said Daniel.

'Then let's not keep her waiting.'

Foot in the stirrup, Nathan mounted the horse then offered his hand to his son. Daniel was a sturdy boy but he was hauled up effortlessly to sit behind his father. With the dog scampering beside them, they began to trot across the fields in the afternoon sunshine, Daniel holding tightly on to his father with a fierce pride that was tempered by desperation.

Juliana Rawson was so delighted to see her husband return that she burst into tears and lapsed back into her native language. Since he could speak Dutch more fluently than his father, Daniel had a much clearer idea of what his mother was saying. As his parents threw their arms around each other, the boy realised that they needed some privacy. The most useful thing he could do was to stable the horse. It was only when he was unsaddling the animal that he noticed the ugly gash down one flank and the dried blood on its withers. His father had clearly seen action.

Set in the heart of Somerset, the farm was large enough to give them a comfortable living yet small enough to employ a mere five labourers and two domestic servants. Unlike some in the county, it had not been requisitioned by the rebel army nor had its livestock plundered to feed hungry soldiers. It was ironic. Nathan Rawson had abandoned his military career to get married and take up farming. In the hope of putting the Duke of Monmouth on the throne, he had now given up farming to follow the drum once more.

When he got back to the house, Daniel found his parents in the kitchen, sitting side by side at the table. The boy took a chair opposite them and hung on his father's words. Because of his experience in combat, Nathan had been promoted to the rank of captain and he was impressed by the men who served under him.

'They lack nothing in courage,' he told them, 'and they come from all parts of the West Country. We have miners from the Mendips, fishermen from the south, wool-workers from Devon, mountain men from the Quantocks, graziers from Bampton, wild marsh-men from Axbridge and hundreds of other stout-hearted fellows ready to take up arms to rid the country of a Catholic tyrant.'

'There's talk of deserters,' Daniel chipped in.

'Every army has a few cowards who turn tail when the first shot is fired. We're better off without them. Besides,' Nathan went on airily, 'we've recruited some deserters ourselves from the royal ranks. They'd much rather serve King Monmouth than labour under the yoke of King James.'

'But where will it all end, Nathan?' asked Juliana worriedly.

'That's in the laps of the gods, my love.'

'What will happen to *you*?'

'I'll give a good account of myself in battle, have no fear.'

'What about us?'

'You and Dan must pray for our success.'

It was not the reassuring answer that she needed and her face clouded. Juliana was a comely woman in her thirties with vestiges of the youthful prettiness that had first attracted Nathan Rawson. He had been fighting in the Netherlands at the time and they had been on opposite sides. It was different now. Their respective countries were at peace with each other and their marriage symbolised the fact. She did not want her happiness to be shattered by warfare.

'Have you killed anyone?' asked the boy, wide-eyed.

'Daniel!' scolded his mother.

'I want to know.'

'The lad has the right to be told,' said Nathan, subduing his wife with a hand on her arm. 'Yes, Dan,' he added, turning to his son. 'I killed a man during a skirmish at Norton St Philip and wounded two others. They attacked us hard that day but we repulsed them in fine style. It was an important victory.'

'Ralph Huckvale's father died at Norton St Philip.'

'We were bound to suffer losses.'

'Ralph went off to serve in his place,' said Daniel. 'He's only a few years older than me. Why can't I join in the fight?'

'No!' cried Juliana. 'I couldn't bear that.'

'You must stay here, Dan,' said his father.

'But you were a drummer boy at my age,' argued Daniel.

'That was different.'

'I need you here,' said Juliana. 'You must stay with me, Dan.'

'Listen to your mother,' advised Nathan. 'Your job is to look after her and the farm. When I go away, you're the man of the house. Always remember that.'

'Yes, Father,' said the boy disconsolately.

'We rely on you. Don't let us down.'

It was a heavy responsibility to place on someone so young but, under other circumstances, Daniel would have been glad to shoulder it. He never shirked a challenge and always did his fair share of the chores on the farm. The problem, in this case, was that he longed to be with his father, to join the rebel army that had been formed with such enthusiasm when the Duke of Monmouth landed at Lyme Regis. The bold and dashing James Scott was the illegitimate son of the late Charles II but his followers believed that he was the rightful heir to the throne. The idea of marching with the future King inspired Daniel. Life on the farm offered many pleasures but it could not compare with the excitement of battle and the feeling of taking part in a momentous event. Daniel yearned for glory. Seeing his disappointment, Nathan offered him recompense. 'If you'd *really* like to help us...' he began.

Daniel rallied. 'Yes, Father?'

'You can sharpen my sword.'

He indicated the weapon that lay across the other end of the table. Daniel snatched it up willingly and rushed off to the outhouse where the whetstone was kept. Watched by Tinker, he first cleaned the blade with an old rag then he carefully sharpened it until its edges were like razors. He was exhilarated by the thought that he was holding a sword that had killed an enemy and inflicted wounds on other men. When his work was done, he could not resist taking part in an

14

imaginary fight, parrying blows from an invisible foe before beating him back and thrusting the sword deep into his stomach. For a short while at least, he was a member of the rebel army.

Nathan decided to inspect the farm, going out into the fields to speak to each of his men and to examine his small dairy herd. Daniel and Tinker accompanied him. At first, the boy thought that his father was checking on what progress had been made in his absence but, when it was all over, another thought occurred to him. Nathan Rawson was taking leave of old friends, giving each of them a few kind words by way of a last memory of him in case he never saw them again. Victory was obviously in grave doubt. Daniel shuddered.

That evening, Nathan tried to bring some comfort to his wife and child. Seated in his favourite chair in the parlour, he talked to them between puffs on his clay pipe and long sips of cider. He praised the Duke's skill as a military commander and spoke highly of his deputy, Lord Grey of Warke, the only member of the gentry in his ranks. He also stressed their numerical superiority over the royal troops and county militias ranged against them. What he did not mention was that their supporters in Scotland had been routed and that the hoped for rising in Cheshire in the name of King Monmouth had failed to materialise. A rebel force that had once expected to reach London within a week was still pinned down in Somerset, licking its wounds and uncertain of its next move.

Cheered by what he heard, Daniel was still apprehensive.

'They say that the Earl of Feversham is a fine soldier,' he said.

'He *was* a fine soldier,' corrected Nathan, 'but that was before he was badly injured in a house fire. He took a blow to the head that left him half the man he was. In any case,' he continued, sitting up, 'the Earl of Feversham is a Frenchman. It says much of King James that he chooses as a commander-in-chief a Roman Catholic from across the Channel. That's something we fight against, lad – the prospect that England will be at the mercy of foreigners.'

'I'm a foreigner,' said Juliana.

'You're also a zealous Protestant, my love.'

'But I'm not English.'

'You're my wife and that absolves you of any blame.'

'Tell me about Lord Churchill,' said Daniel. 'You fought under him once, didn't you? He's reckoned to be a good general.'

'Give the man his due – he's the best of them.'

'Do we have anyone to match him, Father?'

'To match him and to put him to flight,' said Nathan before downing the last of his cider in one long gulp. 'You can forget Lord Churchill and the Earl of Feversham, lad. They are appointed to fight on his behalf while King James skulks in London. Our ruler – King Monmouth – leads his men from the front like a true soldier and that's why we'll prevail.'

They were stirring words to carry off to bed and they rang in Daniel's ear for a long time. Later, however, when he lay awake in his bed with Tinker curled up on the floor beside him, he

16

heard sounds from next door that were less heartening. His parents were talking and, though he could not pick out their exact words, he knew that they were having an argument of some sort. That, in itself, was such a rare occurrence that it troubled him. His father's voice became louder, mingling anger, bravado and regret, to be followed in due course by his profuse apologies.

They came too late to appease his wife. Juliana Rawson had sobbed throughout. As her apprehension grew and her reproaches came more freely, she could hold back her pain no longer. The last thing that Daniel heard before he fell asleep was the sound of his mother crying her eyes out and begging her husband not to leave her.

The attack began at night. Though he had greater numbers, the Duke of Monmouth knew that he could not win a pitched battle. While the royal army consisted of well-trained, well-armed professional soldiers, led by seasoned commanders, his own force was made up largely of willing volunteers with little experience and poor equipment. Many of them had no weaponry beyond scythes, sickles, pitchforks and staves. The only hope of success lay in a night-time attack where the element of surprise would be crucial.

The omens were good. The government had pitched their tents behind the Bussex Rhine, a drainage ditch that ran from the moor to the River Parrett. They had not entrenched their camp and reports came in that the soldiers were enjoying the local cider, a potent brew that made men sluggish. When a thick mist descended to cover any nocturnal manoeuvres, the Duke issued his orders. At eleven o'clock that Sunday night, the rebels set out to change the course of history.

Discipline was savage. Like other captains, Nathan Rawson warned his troops that if anyone disturbed the army's silent progress through the dark, he would be killed on the spot by his neighbour. The four thousand men who left their camp at Castle Field did not even dare to whisper. Instead of heading for the enemy in a direct line, they opted for a circuitous march six miles in length that would allow them to strike at the northern flank of the royal camp. Following the Bristol road, they reached Peasey Farm, where they left their baggage train, continuing their advance until they got to the Langmoor Rhine.

It was here that the plan faltered. In the swirling fog, the local man acting as their guide could not find the crossing that had been cut into the deep ditch. As he beat round in search of it, he was heard by an alert sentry on the other side of the Rhine. The man also picked up the sound of jingling harness and the shuffling of hooves in the grass. Firing his pistol to warn the patrol at Chedzoy, he galloped all the way back to the bank of the Bussex Rhine and raised the royal camp with shouts of 'Beat the drums, the enemy is come! For the Lord's sake, beat the drums!'

The battle of Sedgemoor had begun. When the alarm was sounded, the response was immediate. The royal army was not, in fact, lying in the drunken stupor on which the rebels had counted. It was ready for action within minutes. Seizing

18

their weapons, the soldiers deployed between the tents and the Bussex Rhine in good order, helped by the fact that tapes had been strung out in advance to act as guide ropes in the darkness. They met the sudden emergency as if they had been expecting it.

The rebel infantry was still a mile from the royal camp but the cavalry had no need to hold back. Thundering across the moor, they headed for the Upper Plungeon, one of the cattle crossings in the Bussex Rhine. On their way, they were met by a sizeable mounted picket as it fell back towards the royal camp. Outnumbered three to one, the regular troops fired with such speed and accuracy that they drove the rebel cavalry back and managed to secure the Upper Plungeon. When he saw that the vital crossing was impassable, Lord Grey, the rebel second-in-command, was forced to lead the bulk of his cavalry along the front of the royal position in the hope of finding another passage across the gaping Rhine. It was a disastrous move.

Enlisted as allies, night and the eddying mist turned traitor, obscuring from them the fact that the ditch was not, as they had assumed, water-logged after recent heavy rain. It was simply caked in mud through which they could easily have ridden. As it was, they presented themselves as irresistible targets for the Royal Guards who unleashed such a devastating volley that it caused utter panic. As they were raked by a veritable blizzard of musket balls that killed or wounded indiscriminately, the rebel cavalry lost all order and control. Terrified horses and frightened riders could think only of escape.

The first ranks of infantry hurried towards the Bussex Rhine, only to be buffeted and scattered by their own cavalry in headlong retreat. When the horsemen reached Peasey Farm, they called out to the ammunition-handlers that all was lost and that they should take to their heels. It was a calamitous start to the battle. At one stroke, Monmouth had been deprived of most of his cavalry, had his infantry dispersed willy-nilly and lost all of his reserve of powder and shot. From that moment on, the result was never in doubt.

The rebels, however, did not acknowledge defeat. With their infantry stretched out along the Rhine, they fired successive volleys at the enemy and pounded them with their four cannon guns. While the artillery caused some damage, their musketry was largely ineffective because the royal troops lay flat on the ground and let the bullets fly harmlessly over their heads as they waited for light to improve. In the early stages, the royal army had three glaring deficiencies. They had no artillery, they lacked a full complement of cavalry and as yet they had no commander-of-chief in the field. When these weaknesses were rectified, as they soon were, the government forces were invincible.

While he waited for dawn, the Earl of Feversham prepared to turn defence into attack, consulting with Lord Churchill and his other commanders. By the time the light strengthened, the royal infantry was drawn up in disciplined ranks with the cavalry on its flanks, its artillery continuing its bombardment of the rebels. Monmouth had seen enough. Spurring his horse from the field, he was followed by Lord Grey and the other surviving riders. On a command, the royal troops swarmed across the Rhine in a general assault, dipping their pike-points and plug bayonets in readiness. The cavalry, meanwhile, surged across the ditch to attack both flanks of the enemy.

It was all over. The rebel lines broke and ran. Braver individuals stayed to fight on but they were soon overpowered. The moor was littered with dead bodies and dying men as the cavalry pursued the fleeing rebels and cut them down with ruthless efficiency. Those not killed were captured and Nathan Rawson, having fought bravely to the last, was among the hundreds disarmed and roped together. The Monmouth rebellion had been crushed beyond recall, its army vanquished and its humiliated leader a desperate fugitive.

It was two days before Daniel Rawson found out what had happened to his father. When he heard that his uncle, Samuel Penry, had been shot in action, that his friend, Ralph Huckvale, had been trampled to death by fleeing rebel cavalry and that the massive Joseph Greengage, who owned a neighbouring farm, had been cut to ribbons during the rout, he began to fear the worst. He eventually discovered that Nathan Rawson was one of over five hundred prisoners crammed into St Mary's Church in Westonzoyland. Daniel was not allowed to see him and was dismayed to learn of the appalling conditions inside the church. Prisoners were unfed, wounds went untreated and those who died of their injuries were left

21

unburied. Captives seemed to have no rights whatsoever. By way of retribution, a few of them had already been summarily hanged.

Daniel was still gazing up the dangling figures on the gibbets when he felt a jab in the ribs. He turned to see the anxious face of Martin Rye, an older boy from the village near his farm.

'Go home, Dan Rawson,' he urged.

'But my father is held prisoner in the church,' said Daniel.

'Then there's no hope for him. My two brothers were also captured at the battle but the only time I'll get to see Will and Arthur again is when they string them up like these poor souls.'

'I feel that my place is here, Martin.'

'Go home while you have a home to go to.'

'What do you mean?'

'Haven't your heard?' asked Rye. 'If anyone took up arms in the name of King Monmouth, they're either burning down his house or seizing his property. Your farm won't be spared.'

'Can this be true?' said Daniel in alarm.

'Ask any of these guards and they'll tell you. But don't get too close to them,' cautioned Rye, gingerly rubbing the side of his head, 'or they'll give you a cuff to help you on your way.'

'When will the prisoners come to trial, Martin?'

'Forget about them. Go home – your mother needs you.'

It was a prophetic warning. Daniel had ridden the eight miles to Westonzoyland on a carthorse. On the journey back, he had to go across the battlefield, stained with the blood of the fallen and scarred by the cumulative brutalities of combat. The grim duty of burying the dead was still going on as putrid corpses were tipped into large pits to share a common grave. When he first traversed the moor, Daniel had been struck by the thought that his Uncle Samuel, Ralph Huckvale and Joseph Greengage all lay somewhere beneath that soil but he did not even accord them a passing sigh this time. His mind was on the possible loss or destruction of his home.

Old Nelly, the carthorse, had been bred for her power rather than speed and she could not be pushed too hard. Daniel nursed her along and only forced her into a canter when the farm at last came into view. Everything seemed exactly as he had left it. The house had not been torched and the livestock still grazed in the fields. His fears, it appeared, had been groundless. When he rode into the courtyard, however, his apprehension returned. Three horses were tethered to a fence and laughter was coming from behind the barn.

Dismounting quickly, he tethered Nelly and ran towards the noise. Tinker was barking now and the laughter increasing. When he came round the angle of the barn, Daniel saw two red-coated soldiers. One of them was lounging against the wall while the other was tossing a large twig for the dog to retrieve. Tinker had entered into the game with spirit but he lost interest the moment that he saw his master. Scurrying across to Daniel, he barked a welcome. The soldiers grinned and sauntered across to the boy.

'You must be Nathan Rawson's son,' said one of them.

'What if I am?' retorted Daniel.

'Then you're about to lose your father.'

'And your mother will have something to remember us by as well,' said the other soldier with a smirk. 'The sergeant is with her.' When Daniel turned instinctively to go, the man put a hand on his shoulder. 'You stay here, lad, until the sergeant has had his sport.'

Daniel was enraged. Pushing the hand aside, he ran towards the house. The soldier tried to follow but Tinker bit his ankle and refused to let go. After trying in vain to shake the dog off, the man seized a pitchfork that was leaning against the barn and used it to kill Tinker, jabbing away hard until his squeals of pain finally stopped. Daniel, meanwhile, had burst into the house. Guided by his mother's screams, he hurtled up the stairs and into his parent's bedroom. It was not occupied by his mother and father now. A distraught Juliana Rawson was lying on the bed, struggling hard against the soldier who was holding her down and trying to stifle her protests with guzzling kisses. He had already discarded his coat and lowered his breeches. Daniel's mother was about to be raped.

The boy did not hesitate. Grabbing the man's sword from the floor, he hacked madly at him until he rolled off his victim then he put all his strength into one purposeful thrust, piercing the ribs and going straight through the man's heart. The sergeant's eyes widened in disbelief for a second then he emitted a long gurgle before sagging to the floor in a heap. Juliana sat up on the bed and hastily smoothed down her ruffled skirt. She looked down at the dead body of her attacker with a mixture of relief and foreboding. Footsteps pounded up the staircase. Eyes blazing and sword in one hand, Daniel put a protective arm around his mother.

Major-General John, Lord Churchill was a lean, handsome, debonair man in his mid-thirties with an impressive military career behind him. The critical decisions he had taken at Sedgemoor, while his commander-in-chief was still asleep in bed, had saved the lives of royal troops and hastened the defeat of the enemy. He was entitled to feel proud of his contribution towards the quelling of the rebellion. While he admired their courage, Churchill had little sympathy for those who had taken up arms against King James. But their children were another matter.

'Sergeant Hoskins is *dead?*' he asked incredulously.

'Run through with his own sword, my lord,' explained the soldier before indicating Daniel Rawson. 'And this is the young villain who killed him.'

Churchill's gaze shifted to the boy. 'Is this true?'

'He deserved it, sir,' replied the boy stoutly.

'I didn't ask you about his deserts. I want simply to establish the facts. Did you or did you not kill Sergeant Hoskins?'

'Yes, sir.'

'And do you regret your action?'

'No, sir,' said Daniel firmly. 'I'd do the same again.'

'What's your name, boy?'

'Daniel Rawson.'

'His father is held prisoner at Westonzoyland,' said the soldier.

'There's no disgrace in fighting for a cause in which you believe,' said Daniel boldly, quoting his father word for word. 'Had I been old enough, I'd have joined the Duke's army as well. My father is Captain Nathan Rawson and he has great respect for you, sir. He served under you in Flanders.'

Churchill's eyebrows rose. 'Really?'

'That's where he met my mother.'

Juliana nodded sadly. They were in the parlour of a house that Churchill had requisitioned for his private use. Though he was not a tall man, he still towered over them. They stood before him with the armed soldier beside them. The bloodstained sword belonging to the late Sergeant Gregory Hoskins lay on a table nearby. His mother was cowed by the presence of so distinguished a man but Daniel met his searching gaze without flinching. Churchill looked from one to the other before glancing at the soldier.

'There's something you haven't told me,' he said quietly.

'I gave you a full report, my lord,' claimed the other. 'Sergeant Hoskins went into the house to inform this woman that the property would be seized from her in due course. She reviled him and the sergeant tried to remonstrate with her. While they were arguing, the boy rushed in and killed him.'

'And he did so with the sergeant's own sword?'

'Yes, my lord.'

'It was very foolish of Sergeant Hoskins to hand the boy his weapon,' said Churchill wryly. 'A lad of this age is no match for a veteran soldier. Whatever possessed the sergeant to be so reckless?'

The soldier licked his lips. 'He had put his sword aside, my lord.'

'How do you know? You were not present at the time.'

'It's the only explanation.'

'Very well,' said Churchill courteously. 'You've given me your version of events and I daresay that your companion at the farm will tell the same tale. Now I would like to hear what *really* happened.'

'I've already told you,' insisted the man.

'Let the others speak – they were actually there. Now,' he went on, looking at Daniel, 'where did this distressing incident take place?'

'In the parlour, my lord,' said the soldier.

'Hold your peace,' advised Churchill, making it more of a polite request than a brusque command.

'It was in my parents' bedroom, sir,' said Daniel quietly. 'He had no right to be there and to be doing ... what he was doing. If you don't believe me,' he added with a hint of truculence, 'you can come to the farm and see for yourself. The bed sheets are covered in blood.'

'A visit will not be necessary,' said Churchill. 'You came to your mother's aid as any good son would do in that situation. You are to be commended, Daniel Rawson.'

Daniel and his mother exchanged a glance of surprise.

27

'He killed Sergeant Hoskins, my lord,' argued the soldier. 'He must pay the penalty for that. I say that he should hang beside his father and be left to rot.'

'Fortunately,' said Churchill suavely, 'sentence will not be left to you. Indeed, you are more likely to be facing justice than dispensing it. If I learn that you condoned the actions of Sergeant Hoskins, you and your companion will answer to me. I'll not tolerate rape or pillage. I saw enough of both in Tangier to last me my whole life. Men who serve under me have a code of honour and I'll not let one of them besmirch that code.' He pointed a peremptory finger. 'Wait outside.'

'We had no idea what the sergeant was doing, my lord.'

'I gave you an order!'

'Yes, my lord.'

Drawing himself to attention, the man mumbled an apology then left the room quickly. Daniel and his mother could not believe what they had just witnessed. On the way there, they had been warned by the two soldiers to say nothing at all because they would not be believed. The least they could expect, they were told, was lengthy imprisonment. Instead, Daniel had been listened to and exonerated. Churchill had not merely understood what had happened at the farm, he had spared Juliana the embarrassment of having to recount it in detail.

'On behalf of my men,' said Churchill gravely, 'I owe you my profound apologies. You will be given ample time to gather your possessions together before you quit the property. I give you my word that nobody will harass you. As for you, Daniel,' he continued, picking up the sword from the table, 'I can think of only one way to reward your valour. Take this sword as your own and wear it with more honour than the man from whom you took it.'

In the ensuing days, two names were heard on every side – those of Major-General John Churchill and Colonel Percy Kirke. Nothing bad was spoken of the one and nothing good of the other. While Churchill had enhanced his reputation as a soldier and gentleman, Kirke had added to the long record of unrelieved cruelty he had compiled while stationed in Tangier. Kirke's Lambs, so called in ironic tribute to the atrocities they committed after the battle and in mocking reference to the Paschal lamb emblazoned on their regimental crest, consisted mainly of musketeers with a sprinkling of pikemen and grenadiers. Wherever they went, they left a trail of misery and destruction behind them, torturing and executing their captives at will.

It was not long before a third name was on everyone's lips and it soon eclipsed the other two. George Jeffreys was a notably handsome man with a flair for vicious cross-examination and a fondness for low company. Though still in his thirties, he had risen to the exalted position of Lord Chief Justice and was accordingly dispatched to the West Country by King James to supervise the trials of those who had dared to raise their hands against their monarch. Under the strict and merciless control of Judge Jeffreys, the Bloody Assizes commenced.

The circuit began in Winchester and the trial of Dame Alice Lisle was a stark warning of the horrors that were to follow. A widow of eighty, Dame Alice was accused of harbouring two rebels, even though she had no idea who the men were and had little sympathy for the Duke of Monmouth's cause. In a bruising six-hour trial, Jeffreys frightened and confused the old woman so much that she was unable to muster a proper defence. A reluctant jury was bullied into bringing in a guilty verdict and Jeffreys gleefully sentenced her to be burnt at the stake, the penalty for women convicted of high treason. Five days later, after an appeal to the King, she was spared incineration and was instead beheaded by an axe.

Everyone quaked when they heard the news. If an innocent old woman could suffer such a fate, what would happen to those who had actually fought beside Monmouth? The answer soon came. Gallows were erected successively in Winchester, Dorchester and Exeter as the judges continued their assize circuit. When they reached Taunton, Jeffreys and the rest of his judicial team had still not slaked their thirst for blood. With a blatant disregard for any evidence in favour of the defendants, Judge Jeffreys continued his reign of terror. Plagued by a kidney stone, he was sometimes in such agony that he turned into a ranting tyrant, moved to even greater extremes of savagery. Those who trembled in the dock before him did not realise how much money the Lord Chief Justice was making out of the Bloody Assizes by selling pardons and profiting from the traffic of those he sentenced to transportation. Suffering was a lucrative enterprise.

Nathan Rawson faced him with great courage and endured his cross-examination with calm defiance. His trial was brief. He was one of five hundred or more prisoners who were rushed through the court in a mere two days. Since Taunton was seen by the authorities as a hotbed of revolt, Jeffreys and the other judges were especially severe. Along with many others, Nathan was condemned to death. His wife and son were in the large crowd that gathered on the day of execution to watch their family members and friends being hanged. As her husband was taken up on to the scaffold, Juliana Rawson could not bear to look but Daniel did not take his eyes off the grisly proceedings. Most of the rebels showed fear and one pleaded aloud for mercy but Nathan Rawson met his end with fortitude, even managing a farewell smile to his son as the noose was put around his neck. Daniel had never felt so proud of him.

Later that night, when the guard had dozed off to sleep, Daniel cut down his father with the help of two friends and drove him away in the cart. They buried him with dignity in the churchyard of the village where he had been born. As dawn was breaking, Juliana and Daniel Rawson were driving away from the farm towards the coast. The cart was loaded with their possessions. Mourning the death of her husband, Juliana sat in silence with a shawl wrapped around her shoulders. All she could think about was returning to the safety of her native country.

As he drove the cart along the winding track, Daniel wrestled with a welter of emotions. He was hurt, sorrowful, shocked, indignant, vengeful and bristling with rage. Too young to understand the full implications of what had happened, he knew one thing for certain. He was no longer a boy. Indirectly, the battle of Sedgemoor had turned him into a young man. He had killed a soldier with the sword that had now been presented to him. It was a weapon he could not wait to hold in his hand again.

CHAPTER ONE

March, 1704

Daniel Rawson had always disliked Paris. As he rode through its streets in the gathering darkness, he was reminded why he hated the place so much. It was the noisiest, dirtiest, most foul-smelling city in Europe. It was also the most crowded. Broad avenues and magnificent public buildings had been introduced to give it status and splendour but they could not hide the fact that the majority of Parisians lived in tiny, squalid, ugly, vermin-ridden houses or tenements. But the main reason why Daniel loathed it so much was that it was the capital city of a country against which he had been fighting ever since he had joined the army. He was at the heart of enemy territory.

In his opinion, however – and it was an opinion

based on long experience – Paris had one re-deeming feature. It was the home of some of the most beautiful women in the world, exotic birds of paradise with wonderful plumage, gorgeous ladies who were steeped in the arts of love and eager to pass on their secrets to the select few. That was what had enticed Daniel to enter the city in disguise and to ride with an anticipatory smile of delight on his face. He had an assigna-tion.

Thoughts of what lay ahead did not distract him from the ever-present danger in the streets. Beggars had accosted him at every turn and pros-titutes had tried to lure him brazenly into hovels where he could be overpowered and robbed. When he went down a narrow lane and saw two ragged men ahead of him, therefore, he knew instinctively that trouble was at hand. Though they were lounging against a wall on opposite sides of the lane, they were not really engaged in casual conversation. They had been waiting for someone to fall into their trap. As soon as Daniel drew level with them, they pounced. One man seized the reins of his horse while the other tried to haul him roughly from the saddle.

They had chosen the wrong victim. A swift punch from Daniel broke the nose of the man who had grabbed him and sent him reeling to the ground with blood streaming down his chin. Slipping a foot out of the stirrup, Daniel kicked the other man so hard in the chest that he yelled in agony and let go of the reins, thudding against the wall with a force that knocked the breath out of him. Daniel urged his horse into a brisk trot

33

and left them to nurse their wounds and rue their mistake.

His destination was the fashionable Faubourg Saint-Germain, an area renowned for its countless inns and cabarets but replete as well with fine houses and imposing hotels. It was Daniel's second visit to the address so he had no difficulty in finding it. As before, he was met with a welcoming signal. A candle burnt in an attic window to assure him that the coast was clear. He needed no more invitation. Riding down the side of the house, he dismounted in the courtyard at the rear and tethered his horse beside the stables.

The maid was waiting for him. As soon as he reached the rear door, she opened it for him, her pretty face glowing in the light from the lantern in her hand. She looked at the visitor and exchanged a conspiratorial nod with him before leading the way up the backstairs. After shutting the door behind him, Daniel followed, blessing the day when he had first made the acquaintance of Madame Bérénice Salignac and learnt how often her husband was away from his lovely young wife.

The maid reached a landing and checked that nobody was about before she conducted him furtively along it. When she came to her mistress's boudoir, she gave a coded tap on the door then stood back. When he heard the expected three knocks from inside the room, Daniel dismissed the maid with a smile of thanks before opening the door and going through it. Bérénice had moved back to the middle of the room where light from the fire and from the flickering candelabra combined to show her at her best. Daniel feasted his eyes on her.

Removing his hat with a flourish, he gave a low bow before putting his hat on a chair and tossing his cloak over the back of it. When she offered her hand, he held it lightly between his fingers and bestowed a loving kiss upon it. Bérénice noticed his glove.

'Oh!' she exclaimed. 'That looks like blood.'

'It is,' he said, examining his knuckles, 'but you need have no fear, my love. It's not mine. It belonged to a man who was foolish enough to try to stop me reaching you this evening.' He pulled off his gloves and dropped them on a little table, holding out both hands for inspection. 'There you are – not a mark on them, as you see.'

Bérénice was fully reassured. Still in her early twenties, she was a shapely woman of middle height with exquisite features and complexion. Her blond hair, parted in the middle, fell down both sides of her head in ringlets. Though she was entertaining her lover, she was not wearing night attire in readiness. Her costly blue satin dress had a close-fitting bodice with a trained skirt worn open in the front. The sleeves were short to the elbows with turned-up cuffs and deep ruffles emerging from below. Hitched up at the back to give a bustle effect, the skirt revealed a decorative petticoat. Shimmering jewellery enhanced an already complete portrait of feminine beauty.

Daniel had learnt the rules on his previous visit. Bérénice Salignac liked to take her time and savour each moment. They began with wine, poured from a decanter, then sat beside each other on an ornate settee. Daniel kept up a steady stream of compliments in the fluent French he had taken pains to master. He was no longer the sturdy boy from a Dorset farm but a tall, slim, handsome, urbane gentleman, not far short of thirty, with a soldier's bearing that was offset by his natural charm and tenderness. He had courted Bérénice studiously for some weeks before she had finally succumbed to his advances.

'You have neglected me,' she said, pouting slightly.

'I'll make amends for that this evening,' he promised.

'Where have you *been?*'

'I told you, my love. I had business to attend to.'

'What kind of business?' she pressed. 'I know that you are a merchant with interests all over the world but your work surely does not take precedence over me.'

'Nothing could ever do that, Bérénice,' he said, taking the opportunity to plant another kiss on her hand. 'But let's not waste time talking about trade. The only person with whom I'm interested in having commerce at this moment is the one I adore.'

Her eyes flashed coquettishly. 'How do I *know* you adore me?'

'I could give you at least ten good reasons.'

'What's the first?'

'That would be telling,' he said with a teasing smile. 'And I'm not sure that you're in the right mood to hear them.'

She stamped an impatient foot. 'I want to be *told*, Daniel.'

'Let me refill your glass.'

'No,' she said, grasping him by the wrist. 'Stay here and recite these ten good reasons for me.' She lowered her voice to a purr. 'There may be a reward in store for you.'

He sealed the bargain with a laugh then he began. As he worked his way unhurriedly through the list, he was allowed to take a liberty each time, unhooking part of her dress or delicately removing an item of jewellery or even taking off a whole garment. At the end of his recitation, she stood before him almost naked, exuding a bewitching fragrance and making a visible effort to hold back her passion.

'Now, it is my turn,' she said, helping him off with his coat. 'I must tell you the source of my adoration for *you*.'

Bérénice did so with deliberate slowness, undressing him at intervals, heightening their mutual pleasure by delaying its release until they both reached a point of explosion. Daniel could wait no longer. Picking her up in his arms, he carried her to the bed and placed her gently down beneath its richly embroidered canopy. No more words were needed. Their writhing bodies continued the dialogue in a much more expressive language. Bérénice surrendered herself completely and he responded with characteristic vigour, kissing her, caressing her and filling her with the urgency of his love. She matched his ardour at every stage, letting out a cry of ecstasy when she reached the peak of her pleasure and taking him into Elysium with her. They lay panting happily in each other's arms.

'Your husband is stupid,' he said at length.

'Stupid?'

'How could any man spurn such joy?'

'Armand has not spurned it,' she said coldly. 'He is probably sharing the same joy with his mistress at this very moment. I am a wife in title only. My husband sees me as no more than an attractive piece of furniture.'

'Then he is blind as well as stupid.'

'It was so different when we were first married.'

'Were you happy then?'

'I was treated with respect.'

Bérénice omitted to mention that she had been the mistress of Armand Salignac before becoming his wife after the untimely death of her predecessor. The extravagant promises with which she had been showered beforehand wilted under the tedium of domestic life. As his lover, she had been mysterious, desirable and only infrequently available. As a wife, she was there all the time, diminished in every way by sheer familiarity. Her mystery had soon vanished.

'I should never have married a soldier,' she sighed.

'He's wealthy and highly esteemed at Court.'

'But he's never here to enjoy that wealth or to take me to Court where I can share his esteem. It's where I belong, Daniel – among the ladies at Versailles, earning smiles and glances from the King.'

'Even *I* cannot compete with King Louis,' he admitted.

She hugged him. 'You outshine any man!'

'Does that mean I can come here again?'

'Yes – as often as possible.'

'What about this blind, stupid, uncaring husband of yours?' he asked. 'He cannot stay away from the house forever. Surely, he will return to his wife soon.'

'If he does, it will only be to pack his trunk.'

'Is he off on another campaign then?'

'Armand will leave next month,' she said bitterly. 'Knowing him, I doubt if he will even bring me back a present from Vienna.'

'Vienna?' Daniel's ears pricked up. 'Why is he going there?'

'Armand swears they will capture it in a matter of weeks.'

'Indeed?'

'According to him...'

Bérénice talked about her husband with a candour she had never shown before. When she had first met Armand Salignac, she freely conceded, she had been impressed by his military prowess, his social position and his easy sophistication. He had been loving and attentive to her. Once married, however, he cared less about Bérénice and more about his career in the French army, subordinating her to the fringes of his life while he sought glory in the field. When the campaigning season resumed in April, he would desert her without a hint of regret.

Cradling her in his arms, Daniel listened intently until a more menacing sound was heard. It was the rattle of a coach, turning off the cobbled street and rolling down the side of the house to the courtyard. The lovers sat up guiltily. Without warning, Armand Salignac had returned home.

They leapt off the bed as if it had just been set

on fire. While Bérénice ran to the door to check that it was locked, Daniel went to a window that overlooked the courtyard. He watched in horror as the coach came to a halt and a servant rushed to open its door. A bulky figure stepped out. It was clear from the deference shown to him that he was the master of the house. Daniel did not hesitate. Snatching up his clothes, he dressed himself with a speed born of practice. A hasty retreat was his only option.

Bérénice reached for her own apparel, alternately cursing her husband and apologising profusely to her lover. When she glanced in a mirror, she saw how ruffled her hair was and trembled with fear. Her husband must not be allowed to see her in that state. Having put on his own clothes, Daniel helped her into her dress, trying to calm her and insisting that she was not to blame for her husband's unexpected return. The important thing was that she was not compromised in any way. He was still assisting her when there was a thunderous knock on the door.

'Bérénice!' shouted her husband. 'Bérénice – let me in!'

It was no time to stand on ceremony. Taking a last kiss from his lover, Daniel opened the window and clambered out on to the roof. As he searched for a way to get down to the ground, he could hear the cuckolded husband, pounding on the door with a fist as if trying to knock it down. Escape was his priority but it would not be easy. When he looked at the courtyard, now illumined by torches, he saw that ostlers were loosening the harness on the horses so that they could be led forward out of the shafts. Daniel's own horse had attracted the attention of a servant who was opening the saddlebags in the hope of identifying the animal's owner.

An alternative route was needed and that meant scrambling across a steep roof made slippery by vestigial frost. It was a perilous manoeuvre. If he lost his balance, he would plummet down to certain death. Picking his way over the tiles with extreme care, he went up to the apex and cocked a leg over it. Daniel was able to rest briefly and consider his best course of action. From his elevated position, he could see, in the gloom, the guttering that ran along the base of the roof. Long, square, cast-iron drainpipes conducted rainwater to the ground. He had to trust that one of them would hold him.

Taking his weight on his hands, he pulled himself forward along the ridge tiles until he came to the part of the house that overlooked the garden and which was obscured from the stables by a high wall. It looked like the safest place to descend. On a raw evening like that, he still faced hazards. A biting wind had sprung up and a sudden gust whipped off his hat before sending it downwards in a spiral. For an anxious moment, Daniel feared that it would land in the courtyard and be spotted by someone but, unseen by him, it swung sharply to the left and came to rest in a flower bed.

With the wind plucking at his cloak, he inched himself slowly back down the roof until his boot eventually made contact with the guttering. Daniel worked his way along it until he came to

41

a drainpipe then he knelt down and put a first tentative leg over the parapet. He did not dare to look down. Getting a grip on the drainpipe, he brought his other leg over then swung his body across. The drainpipe was old and rusted and, even with his gloves on, he could feel how cold it was but it had a brute solidity that cheered him.

Descent was slow and laborious. Even in daylight, it would have tested his mettle. Groping in the darkness, with his cloak flapping in the wind like a pair of oversized wings, he needed all his strength and concentration. It seemed to take an age and Daniel began to wonder if he would ever reach the bottom of the pipe. He clung on tightly and persevered, sweat oozing from every pore in spite of the cold. At long last, his toe finally brushed the ground. He let go of the pipe and stood there until the fierce ache in his limbs slowly subsided.

Accepting that he had lost his horse, Daniel searched for his hat then turned his mind to the problem of quitting the city. Before he loped off, he blew a farewell kiss up to Bérénice Salignac. He carried away fond memories of her. Though it had ended abruptly, his visit to the house had been, in more ways than one, very profitable.

Bérénice had waited until her lover had gone before she even thought of admitting her husband to the room. When she finally unlocked the door, he burst in and looked everywhere, opening wardrobes and even peering beneath the bed. It gave her time to recover her composure. Abandoning his search, Armand Salignac turned on his wife and glowered at her. Still wearing his hat and cloak, he was a big, heavy man in his forties with a neat black moustache and bristling eyebrows. He fixed an accusing stare on Bérénice.

'Somebody was here,' he declared. 'I can feel it in the air.'

'You are much mistaken,' she said with righteous indignation. 'And I resent the way you tried to batter down my door.'

'Had you opened it when I first knocked, there would have been no need to bang on it so loudly. Why did you keep me waiting?'

'For the reason I've just given you, Armand. I was annoyed. As your wife, I surely have the right to privacy in my boudoir without having someone attempting to break in.'

'You were not alone in here.'

'Of course, I was,' she retorted, taking in the whole room with a sweep of her arm. 'Do you see anyone else besides me? Would you like to look up the chimney to make sure that nobody is hiding there?'

'Do not trifle with me, Bérénice,' he warned.

'Then treat me as a husband should. There was a time when you begged me to spend a mere hour in your company and you were duly grateful when I did. Yet now,' she went on, 'you charge in here like a troop of cavalry and browbeat me as if I were guilty of the most unspeakable crime.'

'Infidelity is a heinous offence in my eyes.'

'You did not think so when you were married to your first wife.'

'*She* would never have betrayed me,' he asserted.

'No more would I,' said Bérénice at her most poised. 'When I took the solemn vows of marriage, I swore to abide by them. It is a pity that you did not do the same.'

'We are not talking about me, Bérénice. This concerns you and a secret visitor who entered the house this evening.' He took her by the shoulders. 'Tell me the truth, woman – did you or did you not receive a guest in this room?'

'No,' she replied calmly.

'You're lying!'

'Leave go of me, Armand.'

'I can see it in your eyes.'

'Let go of me!'

Pushing his hands away, she stepped back and gazed defiantly at him. Until that moment, she had not realised how much she loved Daniel Rawson. To save him, she would be ready to lie and prevaricate until her tongue turned black. Her husband could see that he was wasting his time. Doffing his hat, he removed his cloak and tossed it over his arm. He shrugged his shoulders apologetically.

'Excuse me, Bérénice,' he said with an appeasing smile. 'I think that I was misinformed. My behaviour was boorish.'

'It was unforgivable, Armand.'

'I will inflict myself on you no longer.'

'Thank you.'

Swinging on his heel, he went out of the room. Bérénice closed the door gratefully, turned the key in the lock then put her back against the timber and emitted a sigh of relief. They had survived. Daniel had escaped and she had withstood her

44

interrogation without a tremor. She and her lover would meet elsewhere next time.

Her sense of triumph was premature. Armand Salignac was a resolute man. Having failed to wrest a confession out of her, he sought the truth from another source. Discarding his hat and cloak, he went downstairs to the steward's quarters. Célestine, his wife's pretty maid, was cowering in a corner as she was being questioned by Gaston, the steward, a tall, thin, sharp-featured man of middle years.

'What has the creature told you?' demanded the newcomer.

'Very little,' said the steward.

'Has she admitted that someone was here this evening?' When the other man shook his head, Armand Salignac rounded on the girl with his eyes blazing. 'You'll tell me *everything*, Célestine, do you understand – every single thing!'

'There's nothing to tell,' she bleated.

'How dare you lie to me!' he roared. Turning to the steward, he snapped his fingers. 'Strip her naked and whip her until she talks.'

'No!' screamed the girl, shrinking back and covering herself protectively with both arms. 'Please don't hurt me!'

'Then stop deceiving me. I'll not tolerate it. What was the name of the man who visited Madame Salignac this evening?'

'I do not know his name.'

'Ah!' he said with a smirk of grim satisfaction. 'So there *was* somebody here. We are making progress. Go on, Célestine,' he coaxed. 'Tell me the fellow's name.'

45

'I do not know it,' she said, tears streaming down her face.

'You must know it. You let him into this house. Letters would have passed between them and you would have carried them. Forget your loyalty to your mistress,' he told her. 'You have a greater loyalty to me. I want his name and you can either yield it up to me or, as God's my witness, I'll flay the skin off your back with my own hand.'

Célestine was trapped. She had been a willing accomplice in the betrayal of her master and he despised her for it. Her only hope of mercy lay in telling him what he wanted.

'Well?' he said quietly. 'What is the man's name?'

'Daniel Rawson,' she whispered.

CHAPTER TWO

Holywell was the favourite residence of John Churchill, Duke of Marlborough. Situated near St Albans in Hertfordshire, it was a place of refuge from the rigours of waging a war, a country home where he and his wife, Sarah, could enjoy the domestic life that his military duties so frequently interrupted. When they first took full possession of the estate, they had rebuilt the house and laid out the gardens and walks, planting fruit trees in abundance and creating floral colour everywhere. While he was abroad, Holywell was rarely far from his mind and Marlborough was always sending gifts back to the house. As he and his guest dined that day, they had eaten off china shipped home by him years earlier from The Hague. They were now sharing a post-prandial drink.

'I begin to think they do not want us to *win* this confounded war,' complained Marlborough, toying with a glass of brandy. 'Every time I am in a position to deliver a telling blow, I am held back by the Dutch. I vow, Sidney, there have been many occasions when I've been sorely tempted to resign my command and be done with it all.'

'Far too much is at stake for you to do that,' said his companion seriously. 'The only way we will ever defeat King Louis is by having you to lead the armies of the Grand Alliance. With English, Dutch and Austrian troops at your disposal – not to mention practical support from elsewhere in Europe – you could conceivably mount a decisive assault on the enemy.'

'I could – but only if I am given a free hand.'

'I do my best to keep Parliament off your back, John.'

'They still hamper me dreadfully.'

'That's the penalty you pay for having a Tory government,' said the other with a shrug. 'The awful truth is that my fellow Tories do not believe in armed intervention on the Continent. Oh, they are happy enough to commit our naval resources to the war but they baulk at the notion of sending more troops and equipment to the Netherlands. They constantly bicker about cost.'

'Then someone should point out the cost of *not* engaging fully in this war,' observed Marlborough tartly. 'Do they actually *want* a Frenchman on the Spanish throne? Are they content to stand by while Louis XIV annexes Spain before threatening every country on their respective boundaries? It's madness!' he argued, smacking the table with a palm for emphasis. 'Politicians must be made to confront the enormity of the danger we face,'

'*I'm* a politician, John.'

Marlborough grinned. 'No, Sidney,' he said with affection, 'you're that contradiction in terms – a *wise* politician.'

Sidney, Earl of Godolphin, acknowledged the compliment with a smile. As Lord Treasurer, he was effectively Queen Anne's leading minister, and he brought acuity, experience and a tireless energy to the role. Five years older than his host, he was now well into his fifties and time had etched deep lines into his face. Though he kept it well-hidden, Godolphin harboured a secret sorrow, still mourning the death of his wife, Margaret, who had died in childbirth within a year of the marriage. Their baby son, Francis, had survived and grown up to wed Marlborough's daughter, Henrietta, thus bringing the two fathers even closer together.

It was a friendship that excited great envy and spite. Cynics always claimed that Godolphin's advancement was entirely due to his connection with the Marlborough family. Not only was the Duke much admired by the Queen, but his wife, Sarah, was her unrivalled favourite and thus able to exert immense influence at Court. Those who claimed that Godolphin owed his position to the triumvirate of Duke, Duchess and Queen ignored the fact that he had held high office under three successive kings and, over the years, acquired all the attributes of a statesman.

Marlborough was never flamboyant but, beside the sober garb of Godolphin, his own attire looked positively ostentatious. The Lord Treasurer was a quiet man in every respect, astute, thoughtful and in the habit of measuring his words carefully before he spoke. He had unquestioning faith in his friend's military capabilities and diplomatic skills. For his part, the Duke of Marlborough trusted Godolphin completely, relying heavily on his amity and good counsel.

'I am too old to lead an army into battle, Sidney,' he said.

'Nonsense!' protested the other. 'You will never be too old. There's no better captain-general in Europe. You've proved that time and again, John.'

'I've *tried* to prove it,' said Marlborough, 'but I've been dogged from the outset by Dutch circumspection. My hands are tied by the States-General. Instead of trusting me to take every decision in the field, they attached two Deputies to me to dissuade me from what they consider to be rash action. These men are *civilians*, for heaven's sake – what do they know about warfare?'

'Last year must have been very disappointing for you.'

'It was so frustrating, Sidney. I drew up a plan for converging movements on Antwerp, while troops would also move against Ostend in the north-west and against the Lines of Brabant.'

'Yes, it was a typically ambitious plan of yours.'

'Much too ambitious for our Dutch allies,' said

Marlborough, taking a sip of his brandy. 'Instead of obeying my orders, General Cohorn went off on a foraging expedition, would you believe! That was the first of two failed attempts I made to bring Villeroi to battle before Antwerp. How on earth can we defeat the French if we do not fight them toe to toe in a proper engagement?'

'Did you make that point to Grand Pensionary Heinsius?'

'I did more than that, Sidney. I gave him an ultimatum. I told him that I would never again take the field with such obstacles in my way and be forced to depend on the unanimous consent of his generals. Heinsius needs to knock a few senior heads together in the Dutch army,' added Marlborough soulfully. 'I would rather die than put up with anything like that again.'

'That should bring Heinsius to his senses,' said Godolphin. 'If we lose the Duke of Marlborough, we lose the war and the Spanish Succession will go unchallenged. France will be victorious yet again.'

He was about to expand on his comment when there was a tap on the door and a liveried servant stepped into the dining room.

'Excuse me, Your Grace,' he said. 'You have a visitor.'

'I was not expecting one,' returned Marlborough.

'The gentleman says he is here on urgent business.'

'Did he give you a name?'

'Yes, Your Grace – Captain Daniel Rawson.'

'Then bring him in at once,' said Marlborough,

50

getting quickly to his feet and sending the man out with a dismissive wave. 'I've been waiting for Rawson to turn up.'

'Who is he?' asked Godolphin.

'Remarkable fellow – I first met him after Sedgemoor when he was a lad of ten. His father had fought with the rebels and one of my men felt that he was entitled to violate the boy's mother by way of punishment. Daniel Rawson saved her honour by killing him.'

Godolphin blinked. 'A boy of ten killed a soldier?'

'Yes – with the man's own sword. I presented it to him as a gift. He's learnt to use it well, believe me. After his father was hanged, he and his mother fled to Amsterdam. Three years later, he returned here in the army of William of Orange.'

'So he was involved in the Glorious Revolution, was he?'

'From that point on, Daniel Rawson and I have always fought on the same side. I followed his career with interest. He was far too good a soldier to waste his talents in the Dutch army so I persuaded him to join a British regiment.' The servant showed in the visitor. 'Ah, here he is! Good to see you, Daniel.'

'Thank you, Your Grace,' said Daniel.

'Allow me to present the Earl of Godolphin.'

Daniel gave a respectful bow. 'It's an honour to meet you, my lord. I apologise for interrupting your meal.'

'Not at all,' said Godolphin, rising from the table and running an approving eye over the visitor. 'I hear good things of you, Rawson, and

51

praise from the commander-in-chief is praise indeed.' He glanced from one to the other. 'I'll leave you alone, gentlemen. I can see that you have need of private conference.'

'Don't let us frighten you away, Sidney,' said Marlborough. 'You're welcome to stay and hear what Daniel has to say.'

'After a splendid meal like that, what I most require is a walk in your delightful garden. At my time of life, a man must pay particular attention to his constitution. Pray excuse me.'

Godolphin left the room in a flurry of farewells. Marlborough came across to give Daniel a proper greeting by shaking his hand then he waved him to a chair and sat opposite him. He noted the dust on his clothing and the perspiration on his brow.

'You look as if you've been riding hard, Daniel.'

'I bring news that could brook no delay, Your Grace.'

'Then it must be from The Hague.'

'No,' said Daniel, 'it comes from Paris.'

'Paris!' exclaimed Marlborough. 'What were you doing there?'

'What else but gathering intelligence?'

'Go on.'

'It's as you feared, Your Grace,' said Daniel. 'They mean to strike at the heart of the Empire. When they won the battle of Speyerbach, they gained the fortress of Landau and seized two places on the Rhine that guarantee them secure crossings.'

'The towns of Brisach and Kehl,' noted Marlborough.

'In short, the French now have ready access to

52

their allies in Bavaria. Marshal Tallard means to exploit that advantage.'

'That's precisely what I would do in his position.'

'Vienna is their target. If they take that and put the Emperor to flight, it will be almost impossible to dislodge them.'

'Then we must ensure that they never get close to the Imperial capital,' said Marlborough firmly. 'How much did you glean in Paris?'

'A fair amount, Your Grace.'

'Tell me all.'

Clearing his throat, Daniel delivered his report. He had committed all the details to memory, knowing the folly of writing it all down and carrying incriminating documents on a mission behind enemy lines. If he were stopped and searched, such material would bring arrest, torture and probable execution. Locked inside his brain, the information was wholly safe. Marlborough was an attentive listener, letting him give his account in full before asking any questions. When Daniel had at last finished, he earned a broad grin of admiration from the Duke.

'How ever did you find all this out?' asked Marlborough.

'I chose my source carefully.'

'I'd be tempted to say that it was General Salignac himself for you seem so well-informed about his movements.'

'I spoke to someone very close to the general,' said Daniel.

'Then it must have been his mistress. In my experience, French officers rarely confide in their wives. It's when they lay their heads on the pillows of their paramours that they become more talkative.' He raised a quizzical eyebrow. 'Am I right?'

'Both right and wrong, Your Grace,' replied Daniel with a twinkle in his eye. 'The lady in question was once the general's mistress but is now his wife, a position with which she is not entirely happy. What she has gained in respectability, she has lost in other ways. In brief, she craves attention. I was able to provide it.'

Marlborough laughed. 'You always were a ladies' man and this is not the first time we've profited from the fact. I congratulate you, Daniel. You've learnt more from an hour in the arms of a woman than my other spies in Paris have learnt in a month.'

'Each man has his own methods of garnering information.'

'Yours is by far the most pleasurable.'

'I endeavour to give as well as to receive pleasure, Your Grace.'

'As any gentleman would,' said Marlborough. 'What you have told me confirms decisions I had already made. My plan of action must be an audacious one because audacity is the only way to succeed against the French. When I reach Holland again, I'll acquaint Grand Pensionary Heinsius with the notion that the army will head for the Moselle. I know that he favours the move.'

'He might do so,' remarked the other, 'but there's not enough daring in such a manoeuvre for the Duke of Marlborough. I fancy that you have something else up your sleeve as well.'

'You're a shrewd man, Daniel.'

'I have the advantage of having served under your command.'

'Then you'll know how I like to keep my true intentions to myself and reserve the element of surprise. At this point in time, only the Queen, the Lord Treasurer, whom you just met, and Count Wratislaw, the Austrian minister, are aware of my design.'

'Apart from the Duchess, that is.'

'No,' said Marlborough guardedly, 'I've not even told my wife what I have in mind. All that she knows is that I intend to go higher into Germany – which, of course, is the truth.'

'But not the whole truth, I suspect,' said Daniel

'Wait and see.'

Daniel inclined his head. 'I'm at your command, Your Grace.'

'Then my orders are that you get some food and drink inside you,' said Marlborough, indicating the table. 'If you've ridden all the way from Dover, you must be starving as well as exhausted. You can speak to our cook and order anything you wish.'

'That's very kind of you.'

'It's scant reward for what you learnt in Paris.'

'Will I have time for any leisure, Your Grace?'

'Yes, Daniel. We'll sail from Harwich at the end of next week. That will give you almost eleven days.' His smile was warm. 'Do you think you could find a way to amuse yourself in London for that length of time?'

Daniel chuckled. 'I'm certain that I can.'

'Then enjoy yourself while you can because

there'll be little opportunity for dalliance once the army is on the march once more.'

'I know.'

'When hostilities do resume,' warned Marlborough, 'you'll have to take great care not to meet General Salignac on the battlefield.'

'Why is that, Your Grace?'

'Put yourself in his place, man. He'll be eager to wreak a terrible revenge on the person who seduced his wife.'

'I have no worries at all on that score.'

'Really?'

'No,' said Daniel. 'The general has absolutely no idea who I am.'

Using their forged passports, the two men boarded the ship at Calais.

'We'll never find him,' moaned Seurel. 'It's a waste of time.'

'We *must* find him,' said Catto, speaking in faultless French. 'We've tracked him this far and we'll pick up his trail in England. The general will not condone failure, Frédéric. If we go back empty-handed, we'll pay dearly.'

'How do we know that he crossed the Channel?'

'I've described him to three different port officials and they remembered him clearly. Daniel Rawson may not have used his real name but he definitely sailed from Calais.'

'How could you describe him when you've never even seen him?'

'The general's wife has seen him,' said Catto with a snigger, 'and she was in a position to note

56

the most private details about the man. We not only know exactly what he looks like, we have his name and his occupation.'

'Didn't Madame Salignac say he was a merchant?'

'That was only a ruse. What merchant takes a beautiful woman to bed in order to ask about her husband's movements in the army?'

'I see what you mean.'

'As soon as he realised what had been going on, the general knew who Daniel Rawson really was – a British spy!'

Seurel cackled. 'A lucky one at that – *I* wouldn't mind spying on Madame Salignac. She'd set any man's blood racing.'

'Nobody would ever get close enough to her again,' said Catto. 'The general has seen to that. His wife might as well be in a convent.'

'Mon dieu! What a terrible waste!'

Frédéric Seurel made a vivid gesture with both hands to reinforce his meaning. He was a short, ugly, thickset man in his forties with dark hair and beard. He had been an accomplished thief in his youth but a harsh prison sentence had made him resolve to respect the law in future. Hardened by ten years in the French army, he had been invalided out when badly wounded in the thigh. He still walked with a pronounced limp.

Charles Catto, by contrast, was a tall, slender, lithe man in his early thirties with fair hair, a conventionally handsome face and a plausible manner. Born and brought up in England, he preferred to fight in a French regiment and it was there that he had caught the eye of General Armand Salignac. Because he was so alert, reliable and resourceful, Catto had been employed by the general in all sorts of secret missions, with an unbroken record of success. None of his assignments, however, had had the importance attached to the present one. Catto and Seurel had been left in no doubt about that.

There was a burst of activity aboard. Urged on by a stentorian voice, the crew hoisted the canvas, pulled up the gangplank, cast off and made ready to sail on the morning tide. Seurel was uneasy.

'I hate being at sea,' he said.

'Think of the benefits, Frédéric.'

'What benefits? Feeling sick, unable to touch food, spewing up my guts time and again? Where is the benefit in all that, Charles?'

'At the end of our voyage,' said Catto. 'We catch our prize.'

'I wonder.'

'Trust me. I know how to stalk a man.'

'We don't even know that he is in England,' said Seurel.

'Yes, we do.'

'How?'

'A spy will always run back to his paymaster,' said Catto, 'to pass on what information he has found out. My guess is that Daniel Rawson will have headed straight for the Duke of Marlborough. We know for certain that the Duke is still in England. He won't sail for Holland until next week at the earliest.'

Seurel was startled. 'Are you sure of that, Charles?'

'We have our own spies.'

'Yes, you've been one of them in the past.'

'I'm pleased to say that I have,' admitted Catto proudly. 'I've enlisted in more than one British regiment in order to gauge its strength and ferret out its marching orders. If they ever caught up with me – and I'll make sure they don't – I'd be shot as a deserter.'

'You're like me,' said Seurel, spitting over the bulwark then wiping his mouth with the back of his hand. 'You enjoy danger.'

'I thrive on it.'

The wind was freshening now and filling the sails. As the ship gradually picked up speed, it began to tilt and ride over the waves. A rhythmical creak set in as the timbers met the relentless force of the sea. Catto was interested to watch the sailors going about their duties but Seurel pulled a face and rubbed his queasy stomach. He tried to take his mind off his discomfort by renewing the conversation.

'There's something I never understand about you, Charles,' he said, brow furrowing. 'Why does an Englishman fight for France?'

'I prefer to be on the winning side.'

'Is that the only reason?'

'No, Frédéric,' replied the other. 'The French army has been the finest in the world for a very long time and it is a privilege to serve under its flag. What really appeals to me, however, is that I can fight alongside men of my own religion.'

'You are a Roman Catholic?' said Seurel in surprise.

'I joined the army for the pleasure of killing Protestants.'

'So did I. Each bullet I fired was in the name of the Pope.'

'My family was as devout as any in Rome. It did not make us welcome in England. We were persecuted because of our beliefs. My grandfather died in prison, my father was driven into exile when King William sat on the throne. Who can ever forget what that butcher did to the Catholics in Ireland?' he asked with sudden vehemence. 'Those who talked of toleration showed precious little of it during his reign. We were glad to leave England. We settled in Beauvais and I grew up there. I look upon France as my home.'

'Me, too,' said Seurel. 'I wish I was there now.'

'We're still in French waters.'

'I like to have solid ground beneath my feet.'

'You'll have that soon enough,' Catto assured him. 'As for the benefits I mentioned, just remember how much we'll be paid for this little adventure.'

'Only if we catch up with Daniel Rawson.'

'We will, I promise you.'

'What if he has left England?'

'We follow him wherever he goes, Frédéric.' He patted his purse. 'We are well-provided with funds. He can run but he will never escape us. Sooner or later, we'll find him.'

'And then?'

'We obey the general's orders to the letter. We kill Daniel Rawson and take him certain proof of the man's death.'

'To do that, we'd have to carry his dead body back with us.'

'There's a much easier way than that, Frédéric.'

Seurel looked blank. 'Is there?'

'We simply cut off his head,' said Catto. 'That will suffice.'

CHAPTER THREE

It was a regular pilgrimage. Whenever he returned to England, Daniel Rawson always found time to visit the county where he had been born and where his father had been executed for his part in the Monmouth rebellion. He reached Somerset that afternoon to find it gilded by the sunshine and scoured by a stiff breeze that blew his horse's mane almost vertical. Daniel was prompted by curiosity as well as by a sense of duty. He wanted to see how the farm they had once owned was now faring, and if anyone in the vicinity still remembered him. Most of all, he wanted to see again the fields, hills, woods, ponds and rivers he had known and loved as a boy.

As he rode along, he was struck by how different it all was to Holland. When he and his mother had sailed to Amsterdam, they had left rolling coun-tryside behind them and settled in a land that was uniformly flat and menaced by the sea. Only the ingenuity of Dutch engineers kept the waters at bay. Instead of farming the broad acres of Somerset, Daniel had moved to the busiest port in Europe, a clean, well-ordered, prosperous city that taught him to live another kind of life altogether. But he never forgot the joy of growing up in rural seclusion in England even though that joy had been rudely curtailed.

After visiting his old farm, he went on to Chedzoy and Westonzoyland, deliberately crossing the site of the battle that had led to Nathan Rawson's capture. It looked so peaceful and untrammelled now. Where scores of rebel soldiers had met gruesome deaths, cattle grazed unconcernedly. Thick green grass covered the mass graves into which brave men of the West Country had been tumbled after they had been shot or cut down in the searing heat of battle. Daniel could almost hear the thunder of the cavalry, the rattle of musket fire, the angry clash of weaponry, the roar of artillery, the frantic neighing of wounded horses and the heart-rending cries of agony from dying men. Sedgemoor would always be a field of slaughter to him.

It was ironic. Nathan Rawson had been hanged for fighting against a royal army that was led, in part, by the very man whom his son now served. Daniel saw no betrayal in that. John, Lord Churchill, as he had been at the time, had earned his respect by condemning the sergeant who had tried to rape Daniel's mother and by presenting the boy with the sword he had used to kill the man. Three short years after the battle, Daniel had returned to England as a drummer boy in a Dutch army led by William of Orange. King James II had been deposed in a bloodless revolution and Churchill, having fought in the royal army at Sedgemoor, had adroitly changed his allegiance.

Daniel had come to see it as a clever tactical move rather than the action of a traitor. Survival was all. Like any good commander, Churchill had known which way the wind was blowing. In fact, his military career had later stalled under William and Mary, only to be revived in spectacular fashion when Queen Anne came to the throne. As the Duke of Marlborough, he was now captain-general of the forces of the Grand Alliance, fighting against the very army in which he had once served. In waging a war against France, Marlborough could put into practice all he had learnt from his mentor, the great Marshal Turenne, during the war in the Netherlands. At his disposal were soldiers, like Daniel Rawson, drilled to a high standard and honed into professional warriors.

The journey stirred many memories for Daniel, his bitterness softened by nostalgia, his sadness lightened by the fact that he had been able to carry on from his father and achieve, in the army that had ousted the Stuart dynasty without firing a shot, what Nathan Rawson and his fellow-rebels had failed to do. Dedicating himself to military life, Daniel had now risen to the rank that his father had held at his death. One Captain Rawson had been succeeded by another.

Riding south, he soon came to the village of Durston, a small community nestling around an old parish church. It was here in his birthplace that his father had been laid to rest on the night after he had been hanged. Having cut him down from the gallows, Daniel and his friends had been able to do nothing more than bury him in an unmarked grave, hard against a wall of the churchyard and largely obscured by a yew tree.

Fleeing the country with his mother, the boy had prayed that nobody would discover the hasty, unlicensed grave.

Years later, when he was still in the Dutch army, he was able to return to the village and explain to the vicar what had happened. His plea fell on sympathetic ears and the bones of Nathan Rawson were disinterred and buried in a more fitting spot with a headstone to mark it. His father was not an interloper in the churchyard any more but a welcome son of Durston, occupying a legitimate place at last. The year before she had passed away, Daniel had been able to bring his mother back to England to visit her husband's grave. It had brought immense comfort to Juliana.

Tethering his horse, Daniel entered the little churchyard and picked his way through the crosses and tombstones, some encrusted by moss and bird droppings, others leaning over at acute angles. When he came to his father's grave, he first removed the large pile of twigs and leaves that had blown up against it. The headstone glowed in the sun, its chiselled inscription standing out clearly. Daniel removed his hat and looked down at the last resting place of Nathan Rawson, recalling happier times while not forgetting the horror of his father's execution. The boy's belief in the concept of justice had been shattered by the Bloody Assizes. George Jeffreys, the leading judicial butcher, had died a mere three years after the ghastly event but his name could still make Daniel seethe with fury.

Lost in thought, he stayed there for a long time

and was only jerked out of his reverie by the sound of a spade striking the earth nearby. Another grave was being dug. Another companion was coming to join his father. Daniel put on his hat. Having paid his respects, he felt somehow cleansed and exhilarated. It was time for pleasure.

'That's absurd,' said Dorothy Piper with a brittle laugh.

'You've not even known him for a week.'

'Had I known him but a single day,' retorted her sister, 'it would have been enough. I'm in love, Dorothy.'

'You don't even know the meaning of the word.'

'I do now. Since I met Captain Rawson, I've suddenly been filled with wonderful thoughts and thrilling new sensations. He's the best man in the world and I want you to be happy for me.'

Dorothy was blunt. 'Don't be ridiculous, Abigail. This is nothing but a passing infatuation. In a month's time, you'll have forgotten that Daniel Rawson ever existed.'

'I'll never forget him!' attested Abigail, stamping a foot. 'I love him and I want to share the rest of my life with him.'

'There's no earthly hope of that happening.'

'Yes, there is.'

'He's a soldier, you fool. He'll be abroad most of the time.'

'I'd follow him wherever he goes,' said her sister. 'Not that he's going anywhere at the moment. He's here in London and he's mine. And you've no call to rule out someone in the army. It was only last year that you became involved with Lieutenant-Colonel Masters. There was no talk then of a soldier being an inappropriate choice.'

'That was different.'

Abigail sighed. 'It always is.'

'My private life is my own,' said Dorothy reproachfully, 'and I'll thank you not to interfere in it.'

'You always insist in interfering in *my* private life.'

'It's my duty as an elder sister to protect you, Abigail. I'm trying to stop you from being badly hurt. Don't you see that?'

'All I can see is someone obstructing me because I've found the love of my life and she hasn't. That's why you're being so beastly to me, isn't it? You're insanely jealous.'

Dorothy spluttered. 'That's an outrageous thing to say!'

'It's the truth.'

'It's a poisonous lie and I demand that you take it back.'

'No,' said Abigail with a show of bravado. 'You've had romances and intrigues but that's all that they were – brief entanglements from which your admirers soon extracted themselves. My case is different. I have someone I wish to *marry*.'

'Be silent!'

Dorothy was so enraged by what her younger sister had said that she raised a hand to strike her. Thinking better of it, she let her arm drop to her side but she was still smarting. Abigail's accusation had more than a grain of truth in it.

Dorothy had had many *amours* but they all petered out sooner or later. Although she had met men who excited and amused her, she had never found one whom she was moved to consider as a husband or – and this piqued her – who looked upon her as a potential wife.

The sisters were in the parlour of their house in Westminster. The family mansion was near Warwick and their father, Sir Nicholas Piper, represented the town in Parliament. Both of his daughters preferred the social life of the capital to a more subdued existence in the country. Dorothy was in her early twenties, a tall, stately young woman with the kind of features and figure that appealed strongly to men. She also cultivated the wit and sophistication needed to hold her own in any civilised gathering, and had many accomplishments, not least as a musician. She prided herself on her self-possession.

Abigail, on the other hand, still had the bloom of youth on her. Having spent all her life in the shadow of her elder and more talented sister, she yearned for independence from her and for the opportunity to be taken seriously as a woman. Her childhood prettiness had evanesced into a porcelain beauty that turned heads but, until now, she had lacked the skills and confidence to exploit it. The arrival of Daniel Rawson had been a revelation to her. For the first time ever, she had aroused interest in a man with whom she was besotted.

'Let's not argue, Dorothy,' she said, trying to placate her. 'I'm sorry if I spoke out of turn – it was unpardonable of me. I know that you have my best interests at heart.'

'I do, Abigail,' said the other. 'My only wish is to help you.'

'Then the simplest way to do that is to leave us alone. When he comes today – if he comes, that is – I beg you not to spoil it for me.'

'You need me here as a safeguard, Abigail.'

'Against what – Captain Rawson is a gentleman.'

'He is, by your own report, a dashing soldier and I'll not have him taking advantage of my younger sister.'

'Nothing would be further from his mind,' said Abigail. 'On the two occasions we've met, Daniel – Captain Rawson, that is – has been kind and considerate to me.'

'It always begins that way.'

'Leave us alone, Dorothy – *please.*'

'I'll stay discreetly in the background.'

'How can either of us express our true feelings with another person in the room? It would be malicious of you to stay.' A distant bell rang and Abigail went into a mild panic. 'That's him!' she cried. 'He honoured his promise, as I knew he would. Oh, Dorothy,' she went on, taking her sister by the arm and leading her to the door, 'let me have some time alone with him, I implore you. I always disappeared obediently whenever your admirers called. The least you can do is to return the compliment.'

Dorothy pondered. 'Very well,' she said at length, 'but I'll be in the next room. If there's the merest hint of impropriety, you've only to call me.' She forced a smile. 'All I ask is that you don't expect too much or you could be cruelly disappointed.'

After giving her sister a token kiss, she left the room by the door in the far wall. Abigail, meanwhile, was staring at the double doors that gave access to the hall, straining her ears for the sound of voices or the clack of footsteps. She made a few last adjustments to her dress and to her hair before striking what she hoped was a dignified pose. There was a tap on the door and the butler entered.

'A Captain Rawson has called, Miss Abigail,' he said.

'Show the gentleman in at once,' she instructed, trying to keep the tremble out of her voice.

The butler stood aside and motioned to the visitor. As Daniel stepped into the room, she almost swooned. He was wearing his dress uniform and carrying his hat under his arm. When he greeted her with a little bow, she replied with a nervous laugh, quickly collecting herself as she struggled to master the situation. Daniel flashed the broad smile that had first stirred her passion.

'I trust that you got my letter, Miss Abigail,' he said.

'It came this morning,' she replied, having read it a dozen times. 'You implied that you had something to say to me, Captain Rawson.'

'I have many things to say to you, not least how beautiful you look today but any mirror would tell you that.' She gave a shrill laugh of gratitude. 'We've only met twice, I know, and our conversations were necessarily brief, but they were long enough for me to form the highest opinion of you.'

'Thank you, kind sir.'

'That's why I felt I had to tell you something that would have looked too cold and impersonal on paper. You deserve to hear it from my own lips, Miss Abigail.'

'Oh, please – do call me just Abigail.'

'That's a favour I shall cherish,' he said, taking a step towards her and making her blush slightly. 'I should perhaps have told you this before, Abigail, but I did not want it to cloud the delightful moments we spent together this week. The truth of the matter is this,' said Daniel, putting his hat aside so that he could take her by the hands, 'that I sail for Holland tomorrow.'

Abigail reeled as if from a blow. 'You're *leaving* me?'

'Duty calls, I fear.'

'But I've only just got to know you, Captain Rawson.'

'Daniel, please.'

'You can't abandon me now, Daniel.'

'It pains me to do so,' he said, 'but desertion from the army would carry a terrible punishment and that's the only means by which I could stay in London.'

'Where will you go?' she demanded. 'And for how long?'

'In the first instance, I'll be accompanying His Grace, the Duke of Marlborough, ready to fight once more against the French. Exactly where we'll go and how long the campaign will last, I cannot tell you.'

Abigail was alarmed. 'Will you take part in battles?'

'I mean to take a very active part.'

'Even though you could be wounded or even killed?'

'That's a risk every soldier must take.'

'I couldn't bear to lose you, Daniel!'

'Those sentiments are very comforting,' he said, squeezing her hands, 'but I shall do my very best to survive. I've been engaged in combat many times in the past fifteen years or so and I've always escaped with nothing more than bruises and scratches.'

'I hate to think of your suffering any injury.'

'Then put it out of your mind.'

'How can I?' she asked, her voice rising with apprehension. 'If I know that you'll be marching into battle, I won't be able to stop thinking about you for a single moment. I hoped so much that we could be friends, Daniel.'

'We *are* friends – that's why I'm here.'

'But you only came to tell me that I may never see you again.'

'Oh, I expect to be back here one day, Abigail.'

'When will that be?'

'Who knows?' he replied, releasing her hands. 'Our campaigns are usually limited to spring and summer. The roads are impassable from October onwards and the enormous food supplies on which an army travels are simply not available outside the growing season.'

She was devastated. 'You'll disappear until *October?*'

'At the very earliest, I'm afraid. In all honesty, I can't offer you any guarantee that I'll return to England then. Our captain-general may have other assignments in Europe for me.'

'I want you *here*, Daniel!'

Abigail was inconsolable. Before Daniel had arrived, she had been entertaining the most wondrous thoughts of how their friendship would develop. He had given her the firm impression that they had ample time in London on their hands. Yet she was now facing the possibility that she would not see him for six or seven months and even that timescale was fringed with doubt. As she watched her hopes crumble, she came close to desperation.

'I'll speak to my father,' she said, clutching at straws. 'He's a close friend of His Grace, the Duke of Marlborough. Perhaps I can get him to intercede on your behalf. Yes, that's the answer,' she went on, breath coming in short gasps. 'Father can help us. He can use his influence to get you relieved of your military duties.'

'But I don't *want* to be relieved of them, Abigail.'

She was shocked. 'You would rather go to war than stay here with me?' she said, eyes moistening. 'Do I mean nothing at all to you?'

'Of course you do,' he said earnestly, touching her shoulder. 'Why else would I be here? From the moment we met, I hoped that our acquaintance could blossom into something more. But any soldier is subject to the orders of his commanding officer. It's not a choice between fighting the French or staying here with you, Abigail. That's a false antithesis. My hope was that you would wave me bravely off in the knowledge that I'd return in due course to renew our friendship.'

It was not entirely true. What Daniel had really envisaged was that news of his imminent departure would prompt her to throw herself into his arms and spare him the trouble of a long courtship. He had met Abigail at a dinner hosted by the Lord Treasurer, his chance meeting at Holywell with Lord Godolphin bearing immediate fruit. Among the guests were Sir Nicholas Piper and his younger daughter. Daniel had taken an instant liking to her and contrived some time alone with Abigail.

She had made sure that he knew where she went for a walk with her maid every morning and, although it rained the following day, he was there for what looked like a casual encounter. In fact, her companion had been primed to drift away for a while so that the two of them could talk more freely as they sheltered under the trees. On his side, interest had swiftly moved on to frank desire whereas, for Abigail, it was a case of true love. Given her response to his news, it looked as if neither of them would get what they secretly coveted.

'You've let me down, Daniel,' she said, holding back her tears. 'You should have told me at the very start that you'd soon be leaving the country.'

'That would only have frightened you away,' he argued, 'and I could not bear the thought of that. It's happened before, you see. When young ladies hear that I'm in the army, they shy away from me because they know I must spend a long time abroad each year.'

'I was bound to find out sooner or later.'

'Granted – but by then, I trusted, we'd have

established a firm friendship, something strong enough to withstand the fact that we had to be apart for a little while.'

'I may not see you again until the autumn – if then,' she said despondently. 'That's far more than a little while. It's also more than I can tolerate. You do me wrong to raise my expectations then dash them to pieces like this.'

'We still have one whole day together,' he told her.

'What use is that?'

'Whatever use we choose to put it to,' he said, trying to soothe her with a smile. 'If I've hurt you in any way, Abigail, I'm deeply sorry. Tell me how I can atone for my treatment of you.'

He opened his arms in a gesture of apology that was at the same time a welcome invitation. Abigail was in turmoil, tempted to yield to his embrace yet held back by the anguish of losing him to a distant war. The conflicting emotions were too much for her. Unable to contain her distress, she let out a loud wail then fled from the room. Daniel instinctively tried to follow her but he found his way blocked by Dorothy Piper. Anger showed in her eyes at first but it soon vanished when she was able to study him properly.

'Good day to you, Captain Rawson,' she said, impressed by what she saw. 'I am Abigail's elder sister, Dorothy.'

'Delighted to make your acquaintance,' he replied. 'Abigail did not mention that she had a sister.'

She smiled. 'I begin to see why now.'

'Should I go after her and try to comfort her?'

74

'That would be pointless. She will already have locked herself in her room and will not come out for hours. I'll speak to her later.'

'Please assure her that I didn't mean to upset her.'

'I most certainly will, Captain Rawson.'

'Do you think she would permit me to call again – when I return from my duties, that is?'

'Whatever Abigail says, you have *my* permission to call.'

Her gaze was supremely confident. Daniel felt as if he were meeting an older version of Abigail Piper, equally beautiful and alluring but more experienced, more mature, more knowing. One sister had fled but another had taken her place. In the space of a minute, he felt that he had made more progress with Dorothy than he had done in a week with Abigail. The younger sister might be enamoured of him but it was the elder who held the greater promise. Daniel was content. When he was next in London, he resolved to call at the house again. He would have two excellent reasons to do so.

It was work that Charles Catto chose to do on his own. He had to visit places where Frédéric Seurel's nationality would provoke hostility. His friend therefore stayed behind in their lodging while Catto began his search, aware that Seurel would come into his own later when their quarry had been run to earth. Catto not only knew the London inns frequented by soldiers, he was able to pass himself off convincingly as a former member of the British army.

At the first two places he visited, he had no luck. The name of Daniel Rawson meant nothing to any of the discharged soldiers, carousing noisily and boasting about their military triumphs. All that they wished to do was to drink, smoke their pipes, play cards, sing out of tune and flirt with the resident prostitutes at the Drum, a lively tavern in Southwark, he had better fortune. The atmosphere was so boisterous that Catto had to shout in order be heard above the din but someone did eventually recognise the name that he mentioned.

'Captain Rawson?' said the man. 'Yes, I know him.'

'So he's a captain, is he?'

'That's right, sir.'

'What can you tell me about him?'

'I can't tell you nothin' with my throat so dry.'

'Let me buy you some more ale,' offered Catto, ready to pay for information. 'Take that seat in the corner and I'll join you.'

The man followed his suggestion. Though still in his twenties, he seemed much older and had good reason to curse his army career. In one skirmish against the French, he had lost an arm, an eye and all of his good looks. He was in constant pain yet his injuries had not dimmed his respect for Daniel Rawson.

'He was the best officer I ever served under,' he said when Catto brought two tankards across and sat beside him. 'The best and the bravest. See this?' he went on, pointing to his empty eye socket. 'And this?' He patted the empty sleeve of his coat. 'I got these when I joined Captain Rawson in a Forlorn Hope. Only six of us lived to tell the tale. Mind you, we killed a dozen Frenchies that day and broke through their defences. Captain Rawson fought like a demon. It was 'im who dragged me to safety when I got my arm blew off.'

'Do you know where he is now?'

'I might do.'

'There's money in it for you,' said Catto.

The man was suspicious. 'Why are you after the captain?'

'I have some good news to pass on to him.'

'What sort of good news?'

'That's private. Now, can you help me?'

'I could 'elp. I still have lots of friends in the regiment.'

'Which regiment is that?'

'The Duke of Marlborough's – so I get to 'ear all the gossip.'

'And what have you heard about Captain Rawson?'

The man took a long swig of ale before licking his lips. Catto slapped some coins down on the table and they were swept up quickly by the man's remaining hand.

'Well?' prompted Catto

'This is only a rumour but it's a strong one. The word is that Captain Rawson's sailin' from 'Arwich tomorrow with the Duke.' He took another swig of ale. 'Is that any use to you, my friend?'

He was talking to thin air. Catto had already left the tavern and was trotting back in the direction of his lodging, leaving behind him an untouched tankard of ale. Money and free drink

– the man was delighted with his bounty. It never crossed his mind that he might just have signed Daniel Rawson's death warrant.

CHAPTER FOUR

Something was amiss. As he watched them from the ship, Daniel Rawson was both puzzled and a trifle worried. Down at the quayside, the Duke of Marlborough was taking leave of his wife before sailing off to war. Daniel had witnessed such partings between them on previous occasions and been touched by the tenderness shown on both sides. There was little tenderness now. The Duchess was as striking as ever, wearing a cloak, hat and gloves to keep out the persistent breeze that came in off the sea. It was her manner that surprised Daniel. She seemed cold and distant. Though she permitted a farewell kiss, it was more of a token than a sign of affection. At the very moment that her husband was about to walk away, she took a letter from beneath her cloak and slipped it into his hand.

Daniel was perplexed. Whenever he had seen her before, Sarah, Duchess of Marlborough, had always been an imperious figure, a woman of grace, poise and real substance. Even in middle age, she had an extraordinary vitality. She was too loyal to let her husband down by not seeing him off but Daniel sensed that she was only there for the sake of appearance. He was reminded of his visit to Holywell when he had found Marlborough and Godolphin dining alone. Daniel knew for a fact that the Duchess was in the house. Why had she not joined the two men at dinner? Was there some kind of breach between husband and wife?

It was unsettling. Daniel had lost count of the number of times he had been alone with Marlborough and listened to him talking fondly of his wife. Having the firm foundation of a happy marriage meant so much to the Duke. It deprived him of any anxieties about his family while he was campaigning in Europe. That was important. The last thing that the Grand Alliance needed was a captain-general whose mind was distracted by marital problems. Daniel had fought alongside officers who were haunted by difficulties back home and unable to concentrate fully. A soldier with preoccupations could be a severe handicap to his comrades.

Marlborough was escorted on to the *Peregrine* by his private secretary, Adam Cardonnel. The captain was ready to welcome them aboard. When greetings had been exchanged, Marlborough stood at the bulwark so that he could wave to his wife as the vessel set sail. Daniel was close enough to get a good view of him. Whatever tensions there might be between Duke and Duchess, they did not register on Marlborough's face. He looked as calm and confident as he usually did. Now in his early fifties – an age when many commanders had retired – he carried his years well and had the sprightliness of a veteran soldier eager to return to the battlefield.

To Daniel's perceptive eye, the Duchess's performance was less convincing. She stood bravely on the quay, raising a hand when the ship pulled away and waving gently to her husband. Other wives who had come to watch their soldier-husbands leave were already dabbing at their eyes with handkerchiefs or blowing kisses at the departing vessel. The Duchess was apparently unmoved, fulfilling a duty rather than parting from a loved one who was off to a war that was fraught with danger. Marlborough waved with far more purpose. Significantly, it was his wife who turned away before he did.

When he finally stepped away from the bulwark, he caught sight of Daniel and beckoned him over. 'It's too breezy to stay on deck,' he said. 'I'll go below. Give me ten minutes to settle in then join me in my cabin, if you will.'

'Yes, Your Grace,' said Daniel.

'It feels so good to be back in harness again.'

'I agree.'

'We'll give King Louis a real shock this time.'

Marlborough patted him on the shoulder then went off along the deck. The crew were still unfurling the sails, each new spread of canvas catching the wind and increasing their speed. The *Peregrine* was a tidy vessel. Her mast was tall for a ship with a relatively shallow draught. She had a lengthy jib-boom, formed of two spars fished together and able to be hinged up when not in use. The rig was fore-and-aft with a square topsail and a topgallant fitted to the mainmast.

Glad that they were under way at last, Daniel was nevertheless leaving with some regret. Before he could reflect upon the competing loveliness of Abigail and Dorothy Piper, however, someone came across to him. It was Adam Cardonnel, the man who worked closer to Marlborough than anybody. Daniel had always liked him, not least because he was the son of a Huguenot refugee, who had fled from France in 1685 when the Revocation of the Edict of Nantes subjected Huguenots to vicious persecution. Many had gone to Amsterdam and Daniel had grown up with their children. Horrific tales of repeated French atrocities against religious minorities had strengthened his determination to fight against the rampant Roman Catholicism of Louis XIV's France. Adam Cardonnel was a living reminder of the horrors visited upon blameless Huguenots. In addition, he was a fine soldier and an engaging companion.

'Are you a good sailor, Daniel?' asked Cardonnel.

'I'm a far better soldier, sir.'

'We've seen considerable evidence of that.'

'Sea battles are a matter of broadsides,' said Daniel. 'I like to get close enough to an enemy to see his face, not fire at him from a distance with a row of cannon.'

'Artillery has a crucial place in land battles as well,' Cardonnel argued, 'but I take your point. You prefer close contact.' He smiled. 'From what I hear, you achieved that in Paris recently.'

'What I did was strictly in the line of duty, sir.'

Cardonnel laughed. 'I'm sure that it was.'

Daniel saw his chance to probe for detail. If anyone knew what Marlborough's real intentions

81

were, it would be his secretary. The Duke reposed full confidence in Cardonnel. Along with William Cadogan, the Quartermaster-General, he had been charged with removing some of the age-old abuses in the army. The two men had been so efficient that, as a result of their administrative and structural improvements, the army was better clothed, better fed, better paid and better led than Daniel could ever remember. Cardonnel deserved great credit for initiating much-needed reforms and implementing them.

'I cannot wait to be in action again,' said Daniel.

'The French will be happy to oblige you, I'm sure.'

'His Grace tells me that we'll head for the Moselle.'

'Then that is what we will do,' said Cardonnel impassively.

'I had the feeling that it was only part of the overall plan.'

'Did you?'

'It's not ambitious enough for our captain-general.'

'His Grace has never been allowed to give full vent to his ambition,' said Cardonnel carefully, 'or we'd have made greater progress against the French by now. Our allies are too cautious, especially the Dutch. It must be in their nature.'

'It's not in my nature,' Daniel told him, 'and my mother was Dutch. I've always favoured direct attack that stops just short of recklessness. I suppose I get that from my father.'

'Then he must have been a very brave man.'

'He was, sir.'

Daniel could see that he would learn nothing more about the plan of campaign. Cardonnel was far too discreet. On another subject, Daniel hoped, he might be forthcoming. He fished anew.

'I was pleased to see Her Grace, the Duchess, here today.'

'Force of habit,' said Cardonnel easily. 'It's happened so many times now. Each year they endure the same leave-taking.'

'Not quite the same,' noted Daniel. 'I fancy I saw reluctance for the first time, as if the Duchess were unhappy to be here.'

'Parting with one's husband for several months is never an occasion for happiness. Courage and understanding are required. The Duchess has borne her husband's long absences with equanimity.'

'Yet she seemed almost frosty today.'

'It's a cold wind, Daniel.'

'I was referring to her manner.'

'What you mistook for indifference,' said Cardonnel solemnly, 'was nothing of the kind. They are still suffering the effects of a family tragedy. A little over a year ago, you may recall, their son, John, died of smallpox. It was a bitter blow. John was their only boy to survive infancy and his parents had the highest hopes of him when he went off to Cambridge. At sixteen, he was dead.'

'I remember how shaken His Grace was by the event.'

'He was more than shaken, Daniel. To add to his grief, he had to leave for Flanders only twelve days after his son's death. He was unable to stay with his wife to share their terrible loss. That wounded him deeply. In some ways,' he went on, 'the Duchess has never recovered from the tragedy. She is still in mourning.'

'That would not explain her behaviour today, sir.'

'Then how do *you* account for it?'

'I wondered if there were some rift between husband and wife,' said Daniel. 'Not that it's any of my business,' he added quickly, 'but I was bound to speculate.'

'Then take your speculations elsewhere,' said Cardonnel with a note of rebuke. 'I do not trade in idle tittle-tattle and I feel insulted that you should imagine I did.'

Daniel was repentant. 'I apologise unreservedly, sir.'

'It's not your place to pry into the Duke's private affairs.'

'I accept that.'

'Never speak to me on such a matter again.'

Giving him no chance to reply, Cardonnel moved smartly away and left Daniel to chide himself for his folly in raising the subject. At the same time, he was not persuaded by the other man's explanation. He still believed that the Duchess had been showing her displeasure. That belief was reinforced when, minutes later, he found his way to Marlborough's cabin. After tapping on the door, he was invited in and entered the little wood-panelled room in time to see Marlborough hurriedly stuffing a letter into his pocket. There was no mistake about the anxiety and pain in the man's face even though it was swiftly replaced by a bland smile.

'Sit down, Daniel,' said Marlborough, indicating a chair. 'I've had more comfortable quarters in my time but these will suffice.' They both took a seat. 'I'm ready to put up with any privations in order to stop the French holding sway over the whole of Europe.'

'The same goes for me, Your Grace,' said Daniel.

'Then you will not mind going behind enemy lines again.'

'I'd be grateful for the opportunity.'

'It may well come in time,' said Marlborough. 'We have very few people as fluent in French and German as Daniel Rawson. You could pass for a native in both countries.'

'That's why I studied the languages so carefully.'

'With a helping hand from certain young ladies, I daresay.'

'There's nowhere better to learn the nuances of a foreign tongue than in the company of a beautiful woman, Your Grace.'

'You've been an apt pupil,' said Marlborough with a smile. 'Not that you've neglected your English lessons, of course. A letter I received from the Lord Treasurer told me that, when you attended a dinner at his house, you made a definite impression on Sir Nicholas Piper's younger daughter.'

'Abigail is a delightful creature.'

'Her sister is just as beguiling. The two of them are testimony to the fact that Nature can sometimes be defied. Sir Nicholas is positively ugly and his wife is extremely plain yet they somehow produced two of the most gorgeous daughters any man could wish to meet. If I did not know the parents so well,' he went on, 'I'd suspect witchcraft.'

'Miss Piper can certainly weave a spell,' said Daniel gallantly.

'To which sister are you referring?'

'I was thinking of Abigail.'

'She obviously caught your eye.'

'I found Dorothy just as captivating. Since it's so difficult to choose between them, I shall give them equal attention.'

Marlborough chuckled. 'You are incorrigible,' he said. 'Perhaps it's just as well that I'm taking you off to war again or Sir Nicholas would be unable to sleep soundly in bed, wondering which of his nubile daughters you would be pursuing.'

'Why did you send him on his way like that?' said Abigail Piper.

'I did nothing of the kind,' responded Dorothy. 'I merely told him that you would not stir from your room for hours and that there was no point in his waiting for you.'

'There was every point, Dorothy. I just needed to be alone to compose myself. As soon as I'd done that – and it took no more than twenty minutes – I intended to come back to resume my conversation with Captain Rawson.'

'It had already been terminated by you.'

'That's not true at all.'

'Put yourself in Captain Rawson's position,' suggested Dorothy. 'When a young lady flees from his company in floods of tears, he's entitled to conclude that she no longer wishes to speak to him.'

'But he wished to speak to *me*,' said Abigail. 'According to you, he tried to follow me as I ran out. You barred his way.'

'I could hardly let him chase you upstairs.'

'He wanted to console me. I was touched to hear that.'

'You acted too rashly in charging off.'

'I was deeply upset – what else was I to do?'

Dorothy put a sympathetic arm around her sister's shoulders. Abigail was still young and inexperienced but it was not the moment to school her in the subtleties of dealing with male admirers. In any case, now that she had seen Daniel Rawson, Dorothy was certainly not going to help Abigail to ensnare the captain. She felt that Daniel deserved a more seasoned woman, one who was well-versed in the elaborate rituals of courtship. In spite of the circumstances in which they had met, Dorothy wanted him for herself.

They were in the parlour of the Westminster house, side by side on a large sofa. Abigail was still fretting over the departure to Holland that day of the man whom she idolised. Her fear was that he had been estranged by her conduct and would dismiss her from his mind and heart. That was something Abigail could never do with him. Daniel Rawson occupied her every waking hour. She could not stop thinking about him, cherishing him, desiring him and constructing imaginary dialogue for the two of them to speak. In running away from him, she was afraid that she had made a fatal mistake.

'Do you think I should write to him?' she asked.

'I'd not advise it, Abigail.'

'But I could apologise for the way I behaved.'

'A young lady should never apologise,' said Dorothy loftily, 'least of all in writing. It could be construed as a sign of weakness. Besides, if anyone should issue an apology, it is Captain Rawson. He led you to believe that he would be in London for some time.'

'He admitted that and was very contrite.'

'I'm still opposed to the notion of a letter.'

'Why is that, Dorothy?'

'To begin with,' said the other, removing her arm from her sister's shoulder, 'there's no guarantee that the letter would reach him. When an army is on the move, correspondence with any member of it is bound to be difficult.'

'I thought of that,' said Abigail, 'and I believe I have the answer. I can ask Father to help me. Lord Godolphin will be in constant touch with the army, wherever it may be. Father will know how letters are sent and can prevail upon the Lord Treasurer's messenger to carry mine with him.'

Dorothy was impressed. 'That's a clever idea,' she said, 'though I still feel it would be unwise of you to write.'

'I have this urge to do so, Dorothy.'

'Then you must control it. On the strength of a week's acquaintance, you would appear very forward if you tried to begin a correspondence with Captain Rawson.'

'He might appreciate it.'

'Were that the case, he will write to you in the hope of eliciting a reply. Why not wait to see if he does that, Abigail?'

'I feel the need to make him aware of my feelings *now*.'

'Do not even consider it,' warned Dorothy. 'You must hide your true feelings until the proper time. In your present state of mind, you would commit things to paper that would make you look naïve and unguarded. You have to show maturity.'

'What should I say to him?'

'Say nothing at all, Abigail. It is up to Captain Rawson to make the first move and you must be patient. The campaign last year was long and exhausting. There's no reason to think that it will be any different this year. In other words, Captain Rawson will be very busy. If he can find a moment to write to you, then perhaps he will. When he does, you have an excuse to write to him.'

'But I may have to wait months,' wailed Abigail, getting up and moving restlessly about the room. 'What am I to do until then? How can I live until I know Daniel's true opinion of me? He's paid me many pretty compliments since we met but will he requite my love?' She came to a decision. 'I *must* write,' she announced. 'I'll do it instantly.'

'No,' said Dorothy, standing up to prevent her from leaving. 'I forbid you to do that, Abigail. Never show an admirer how vulnerable you are. If it will relieve your torment,' she continued, 'then put your thoughts in a letter – but do not send it.'

Abigail was crestfallen. 'You really think it unwise?'

'It's foolhardy in the extreme.'

'How can I let him know that I love him?'

'You must show forbearance. Captain Rawson will return one day – God willing – and he will be moved to learn that you have been steadfastly carrying a torch for him while he was away. That will impress him far more than a mawkish letter written on impulse.'

'Do you really believe that, Dorothy?'

'Yes, I do – bide your time, sister.'

'Is that what you would do in my place?'

'It's *exactly* what I'd do.'

After thinking it over, Abigail elected to take her advice. She gave Dorothy a kiss of gratitude on the cheek then went out of the room so that she could be alone with her thoughts. Dorothy was glad that she had dissuaded her from hasty action with regard to man on whom she doted. It left the field clear for her. Five minutes later, it was the elder sister who was penning a missive to Daniel Rawson.

They reached Harwich hours after the *Peregrine* had set sail and they had to wait the best part of a week before they could board a ship that would take them to Holland. As they made their way along the quayside, Frédéric Seurel was pessimistic.

'We'll never catch up with him, Charles.'

'Of course, we will,' said Catto, taking a more philosophical attitude to the delay. 'Armies do not march fast. We'll soon overhaul Captain Rawson.'

'How can we get to him when he is surrounded

by thousands of soldiers?' asked Seurel. 'It's impossible.'

'We'll lure him out somehow.'

'We do not even know where he'll be.'

'He'll be attached to his regiment and my guess is that it will never be far away from the Duke of Marlborough. There are Austrians, Dutch, Germans, Belgians, Danes, Irish, Swiss and even some renegade Frenchmen at his command but the Duke will always favour British soldiers.'

'They stand no chance against Marshal Tallard.'

'Do not underestimate him, Frédéric,' said Catto. 'The Duke is an astute general. He has not lost a major battle and he recaptured all the Barrier Fortresses from us. He began last year's campaign by seizing Bonn only two weeks after the first trenches had been dug. While the garrison was preparing itself for a lengthy siege, they were overwhelmed by a sudden attack. That was bold.'

'We'll soon capture Bonn back again.'

'I doubt that.'

'France has a bigger and better army,' asserted Seurel. 'We also have the support of the Elector of Bavaria. We must win.'

'I'm sure that we will – in time. But forget about the war,' Catto went on. 'That will take care of itself. Our only concern is the private battle we have with Captain Rawson.'

'Let it wait.'

'What do you mean?'

'My worry at this moment is *that*,' said the Frenchmen, pointing at the ship towards which they were strolling with their luggage. 'I'm scared, Charles. Sailing across the Channel was bad enough. The North Sea will be far worse.'

'We'll make a sailor of you yet, Frédéric.'

'The very thought of a voyage makes my stomach heave.'

'This is the last one you'll have to make and it's certainly the last one that Captain Rawson will have made. He'll pay dearly for his hour between the thighs of Madame Salignac.'

Seurel grinned. 'He may think it was worth it.'

'No woman is worth losing your life over.'

'I don't agree. I'd much rather be shot in bed with another man's wife than stabbed to death on the battlefield by a bayonet. At least I'd die with a smile of my face.'

They joined the end of the queue to board the ship. Proximity to other passengers made them keep their voices down. Seurel eyed the vessel warily then let his gaze travel up to the sky. It was overcast. A squall was in the offing. His stomach heaved more violently. He had heard many stories about how perilous the North Sea could be. People moved slowly forward, their passports examined before they were allowed aboard. Until now, the two men had spoken in French. As they edged towards the gangplank, Catto took the precaution of resorting to his native tongue.

'Have you been to Holland before?'

'No,' replied Seurel.

'It will be a novelty for you.'

'All I want is dry land.'

'Then you are going to the right place,' said Catto. 'The Dutch are very clever. They've reclaimed land from the sea by building dykes. When we disembark, we will, in effect, be walking on water.'

'I just hope to get there safely.'

'We will, Frédéric. We have an appointment with a great lover.'

Seurel was mystified. 'A great lover?'

'Yes,' said Catto, whispering in his ear. 'He's a man who lost his head over a woman.' They shared a grim laugh.

Dorothy Piper was pleased by the change in her sister. Ten days after Captain Daniel Rawson had left the country, Abigail seemed to have found some peace of mind at last. She no longer stayed in her room, pining for her missing admirer and scolding herself for what had happened when they had last met. Nor did she disdain food and drink any more. Abigail had somehow regained her appetite. She looked better, dressed more smartly and took a more positive attitude to life. Having locked herself away for so long, she now resumed her daily walk with her maid, Emily, a plump young woman who was very fond of her mistress and who responded to her every whim. Dorothy believed that the maid had been partially responsible for the marked improvement in Abigail and she thanked her.

Two more days elapsed and her younger sister's spirits seemed to lift even more. Dorothy could not understand it. No letter had arrived from Daniel Rawson and she was certain that Abigail had not written one to him. She decided to confront her sister next morning and find out exactly what had cheered her up so much. But when she came down for breakfast, there was no sign of Abigail. Thinking that she had gone for an early walk, Dorothy waited for a couple of hours before searching for her sister again. It was all in vain.

Unknown to her sister, Abigail Piper and her maid were sailing down the Thames estuary on a ship that was bound for The Hague.

CHAPTER FIVE

Daniel Rawson had every reason to dislike Henry Welbeck. In almost every way, they were direct opposites. While Daniel revelled in military life, Welbeck loathed it and never stopped complaining about its many shortcomings. Captain Rawson was a cheerful optimist but Sergeant Welbeck was a sour pessimist. The one took his pleasures where he found them while the other was a confirmed bachelor with a deep suspicion of women. Religion provided the other profound difference between them. Daniel was so committed to the Protestant cause that he was prepared to fight to the death for it. Henry Welbeck was an unashamed atheist.

Yet the two men had, improbably, become close friends. Welbeck was older, stouter and decidedly uglier than Daniel and he had a fiery temper that cowed the men under him. Fearless on the battlefield, he was a veteran soldier who had saved the lives of many of his own troops by prompt action. Most of his battle scars were hidden by his uniform but the long, livid gash down one cheek was a visible memento of the dangers of fighting the French.

'I hate the army,' said Welbeck disconsolately.

'Then why did you join it?' asked Daniel.

'I thought it would make a man of me. When the recruiting officer came to our village, I was a scrawny lad who'd never been more than ten miles from the cottage I was born in. I was stupid enough to like what I heard, Dan. The officer made it sound wonderful.'

'It *is* wonderful when you get used to it, Henry.'

'We were tricked,' moaned Welbeck. 'They fed us on arrant lies and as much ale as we could drink. By the time we were sober again, we found that we'd signed our lives away – and for what?'

Daniel grinned. 'The chance to meet me, of course.'

'I'd rather forego that pleasure and stay out of uniform.'

'What about the other delights of army life?'

'I didn't know there were any, Dan.'

'There's the satisfaction of serving your country.'

'Where's the satisfaction in being shot at, stabbed at, kicked at, sworn at and spat at by a load of greasy Frenchies and their allies? All I do is to give the enemy target practice.' He pointed to the scar on his cheek. 'How satisfied do you think I felt when I got this?'

'Very satisfied,' said Daniel. 'You killed your attacker.'

'He haunts me every time I look in a mirror to shave.'

May had brought warm sunshine and the army had assembled as regiments left their winter quarters to join the column of march. By the middle of the month, they had crossed the River Meuse near Ruremond on pontoon bridges. It was at this point that Marlborough joined up with his men. It was also an occasion for Daniel Rawson to meet his discontented friend again. As evening shadows dappled the field, they were standing outside a tent in the encampment. Their regiment was part of a formidable army, comprising 14 battalions of infantry and 39 squadrons of cavalry, supported by 1700 supply wagons pulled by 5000 draught horses.

'We'll give the French a drubbing this year,' Daniel prophesied.

Welbeck grimaced. 'It will be another wild goose chase.'

'I've caught a lot of wild geese in my time, Henry.'

'Well, they didn't speak French, I know that. We can never get these bastards to stand still and fight. And what the hell are we doing here, anyway?' he complained. 'Why did we get dragged into a war of the Spanish Succession in the first place? I don't give a damn who puts his arse on the Spanish throne.'

'You should do,' said Daniel.

'Why? It makes no difference to me.'

'Yes, it does. Spain itself may be weak but it still has its colonies and dependencies. Think of Mexico, Cuba, the Canary Islands, Sicily, Sardinia, Naples, Milan, bits of the Americas – not to mention the Spanish Netherlands. Do you want

96

France to control that empire? They'd go on to rule the world.'

'Let them – as long as they leave England alone.'

'But they wouldn't, Henry. If they conquer Europe, they'll look to overrun us next. Would you like to see French soldiers in London?'

'Yes – if they were hanging from a gallows.'

Daniel clapped him on the shoulder. 'We agree on something at last,' he said.

'I just want this war to be over,' said Welbeck sadly. 'I seem to have spent a lifetime running after French uniforms.'

'If we destroy their army – as we will one day – you'll be able to run after French women instead.'

Welbeck snorted. 'Women are more trouble than they're worth, Dan. That's why I keep well away from them. I've seen the damage they can create. One of the best things Corporal John ever did was to forbid whores to ply their trade among the army. The men didn't like it at all,' he recalled, 'but it made them better soldiers.'

'Our commander cares for his men,' said Daniel. 'That's how he got the nickname of Corporal John. He doesn't hold himself aloof. He knows how hard life in the ranks really is and he's done his best to improve the lot of the average soldier. Thanks to him, we always have plenty of surgeons travelling with us. Thanks to him, we always have provisions awaiting us when we camp.'

'I'd still rather be home in England.'

'Then why have you stayed in the army so long?'

Welbeck gave a rare smile. 'It needs me, Dan.'

Most officers did not consort freely with the ranks but Daniel was an exception to the rule. He was happy to spend time with people like Henry Welbeck and to learn what the men he commanded were thinking and feeling. Critics warned him that making himself so approachable would lead to a loss of discipline. It had not happened in Daniel's case. If anything, his men respected him even more.

'Where exactly are we going, Dan?' asked Welbeck.

'Put that question to our commander.'

'You spent time with him in England. What did he tell you?'

'Precious little,' replied Daniel. 'All I know is that he means to spring a few surprises on the French.'

'In his place, I'd be bored with this campaign. It goes on and on.'

'The Duke will bring it to a conclusion sooner or later.'

'Then it had better be sooner,' said Welbeck, wagging a finger, 'because he's not getting any younger. What about his family back in England? He spends so much time away from her that anyone would think he doesn't get on with his wife. Is that true, Dan?'

The question caught Daniel off guard. His mind went back to the quayside in Harwich when he sensed a rift between Marlborough and his wife. Something was troubling his commander and it did not bode well for the campaign. Fond as he was of Welbeck, however, he was not ready to confide his worries on so sensitive a subject.

'No, Henry,' he said, contriving a smile, 'it's not true. The Duke and Duchess are happily married. I can vouch for that.'

John Churchill, Duke of Marlborough was glad to be reunited with his army. The sight of massed ranks of soldiers always inspired him and he fervently hoped that this year he would be able to deliver the decisive victory that they deserved. When the messenger arrived in the camp, he had several letters for the captain-general, many of them from military allies requesting orders. The letter that claimed priority, however, was the one from his wife, Sarah, and he retired to his tent to read it in private.

He opened it with an amalgam of hope and trepidation. Before he had left England, his wife had accused him of having an affair and expressed her anger in the most forthright terms. Though she had agreed to see him off at Harwich, she left him in no doubt about her feelings of betrayal. As he read the familiar calligraphy, Marlborough's heart was pounding and he steeled himself against further unjustified allegations of adultery. They never came. Instead, Sarah's letter contained a heart-felt apology for misjudging her husband and begged him to forgive her. So eager was she to make amends and to attest her love that she offered to join him on the campaign.

Marlborough was overjoyed. His writing materials had already been unpacked so he sat at the little table to pen an immediate reply.

I do this minute love you better than ever I did before. This letter of yours has made me so happy, that I do from my soul wish that we could retire and not be blamed. What you propose as to coming over, I should be extremely pleased with; for your letter has so transported me, that I think you would be happier being here than where you are; although I should not be able to see you often. But you will see by my last letter, as well as this, that what you desire is impossible; for I am going up into Germany where it would be impossible for you to follow me; but love me as you now do, and no harm can come to me. You have by this kindness preserved my quiet and, I believe, my life; for until I had this letter, I have been very indifferent of what should become of myself. I have pressed this business of carrying an army into Germany, in order to leave a good name behind me, wishing for nothing else but good success. I shall now add, that of having a long life, that I may be happy with you.

When he had signed the letter, he read it through again then looked once more at his wife's missive. A huge burden had suddenly been lifted from his shoulders. He was now able to devote all his energies to the campaign. Reassured that his wife loved him once more, and that she had accepted how unfounded her suspicions had been, Marlborough felt capable of anything. He got up, summoned his secretary and began to work through the official correspondence with renewed enthusiasm. Sarah's letter had been a good omen. Not even the might of France could stop him now.

King Louis XIV had ruled for so long that he seemed a permanent fixture on the French throne. His dominant passion was a love of glory and he had pursued it enthusiastically on the battlefield and in the boudoir. It found its most visible expression in the building of Versailles, the sumptuous palace that became both the home of the Court and the centre of administration. In defiance of all advice, *Le Roi Soleil*, as he was dubbed, chose to live in the country, well away from the stench of Paris and its teeming streets. At immense cost, in terms of money and of the lives of many workmen who perished there, Versailles rose from the marshes to become the largest and most opulent structure in France. Because it had no view to please the eye, Louis had one created for him, surrounding the palace with gardens that were unmatched in size and splendour anywhere in Europe.

It was here that he lived in luxury, following an unvarying daily routine by the clock and conducting a war against the Grand Alliance while enjoying an endless round of balls, plays, operas, musical concerts and *fêtes*. Though he sported a magnificent periwig and wore the rich apparel befitting a French monarch, he could not entirely disguise the effects of age. Now in his mid-sixties, he was overweight and puffy. Since most of his upper teeth had been removed during an agonising operation almost twenty years earlier, his smile had a kind of sinister comicality to it – not that anyone would dare to laugh at him. The king was impossibly vain, single-minded and peremptory. He brooked no opposition.

He was in a private room at Versailles when Louis de Rouvroy, Duc de Saint-Simon, a leading courtier and trusted friend, discussed the conduct of the war with him.

'Let me remind you of the earlier counsel you were given, Your Majesty,' said Saint-Simon reasonably. 'At the very outset, your advisors were not at all sure that it was wise to provoke another war when our finances were stretched and our army was in sore need of more recruits.'

'I provoked nobody,' snapped Louis. 'They provoked *me*.'

'Your retaliation was a little hasty, Your Majesty.'

The king glowered. 'Do you have the gall to criticise me?'

'No, no,' answered Saint-Simon with an emollient smile, 'your word is final and I would never gainsay it. On the other hand, Your Majesty, we do have to consider the implications.'

'So do I, man,' asserted Louis. 'When the Dutch and the Austrians declare war on France, our country is under threat. *That* is the only implication I see. Bless me!' he went on, clicking his tongue in irritation. 'Queen Anne of England has also joined this alliance. Even a woman is taking up arms against me! Am I supposed to stand by and do nothing?'

'That's not what I'm suggesting, Your Majesty.'

'I'm not interested in suggestions.'

'As you wish, Your Majesty.'

'Do not question my ability to make the right decisions.'

'I'd never doubt them for a moment,' said the other tactfully.

'Do we not have the finest soldiers in the world?'

'Yes, Your Majesty.'

'And are they not led by the best marshals?'

'They are indeed, Your Majesty.'

'Then let's have no more bleating about shortage of money and men.' He was about to dismiss Saint-Simon when a messenger entered the room and bowed. 'Stay here,' he said to his companion. 'The news may be important.'

Beckoning the messenger across, the king took the despatch from him and broke the seal. As he read it, he frothed with indignation. He thrust the despatch at Saint-Simon.

'Read that!' he ordered. 'The Duke of Marlborough is leading an army towards the Moselle. Do you see what that means? He has the effrontery to invade France!'

'The Dutch would hold him back from such audacity,' said the courtier, scanning the despatch. 'They have always done so in the past. Yet this intelligence contradicts their former policy,' he went on, as he finished reading. 'If he is heading for Bonn, he must indeed be thinking of a strike towards the Moselle.' He returned the despatch. 'This is grave news, Your Majesty.'

'I'll draft new orders for Villeroi at once,' said Louis angrily. 'He is to intercept Marlborough and stop him from making any advance on French soil. I'll not have my territory invaded by anyone. It's a humiliation that will not be borne.'

'I heartily agree with you, Your Majesty.'

The king was shaking with fury. He was so accustomed to hearing good news from the battlefield that he believed his armies were invincible. The notion that someone would dare to encroach on French soil was anathema to him. He read the dispatch again before scrunching it up and hurling it at the floor. His lip curled in derision.

'Marlborough!' he growled.

The Confederate army moved in easy stages. Roused at four o'clock in the morning, they assembled in rank and file a quarter of an hour later. The march began at five and they pressed on until late morning, setting up their next camp before the heat of the noonday sun could take its toll. Afternoon and evening were times of rest. Marlborough had carefully planned ahead. Wherever they camped, they found ample provisions awaiting them. There was no need to scour the area for food. Corporal John had already seen to their needs.

At each stage of the march, Marlborough rode on ahead with his cavalry then waited for the infantry, artillery and baggage wagons to catch up with him. When they reached their destination for that day, Marlborough adjourned to his tent with his secretary. He unfurled a map and tapped it with a finger.

'We are right here, Adam,' he said to his secretary. 'We are poised to reach the Moselle.'

'How far will we go, Your Grace?' asked Cardonnel.

'Far enough to confuse the enemy. King

Louis's spies will have delivered their reports by now and Villeroi will be on his way to block our path into France. The marshal has no idea that our march towards the Moselle is part of an elaborate feint.'

'It's a brilliant conception.'

'The execution has to be equally brilliant. I've letters to write and orders to give,' he said, opening a leather satchel and taking out a pile of papers. 'There's never an end to correspondence.'

'It's one of the necessities of warfare.'

'I know, Adam, but it can get tedious at times.'

Marlborough's travelling table and chairs had already been set up for him in the tent. Quill, ink and paper stood ready. The two men removed their hats and set them aside before they got down to the business of the day.

'My wife never finds it tedious,' said Marlborough fondly. 'I had yet another letter from her today. The Duchess is pursuing me all the way across Europe.'

'Better to do so on the page than in person,' observed Cardonnel drily. 'An army on the march is no place for a lady.'

'Yet we have several following us in the baggage train.'

'Those women hardly come from the upper reaches of society.'

'That's where you are mistaken, Adam.'

'Oh?'

'One of them at least can boast of distinguished parentage.' Marlborough lowered himself on to his seat. 'Or, to be more precise, she will when she joins us. She's clearly a spirited young lady who is undeterred by the multiple discomforts of travel. It will come as a great shock to Daniel Rawson, I fear.'

'Captain Rawson?'

'Yes, Adam.'

Cardonnel was curious. 'In what way is he involved?'

'The oldest way of all, I suspect,' said Marlborough with a quiet smile. 'The youngest daughter of Sir Nicholas Piper is smitten by him. According to my wife's latest letter, Abigail was so distressed at his departure from London that she decided to follow him. As you can imagine, her parents are thoroughly dismayed.'

'The lady is *here?*' asked the secretary incredulously.

'She's certainly on Rawson's tail.' He chortled. 'We'll have to warn him about a possible attack from the rear.'

'It's highly dangerous for a woman to travel alone.'

'Her maid is with her, apparently.'

'Even so,' said Cardonnel. 'It's very reckless of them. I'd be very alarmed if a daughter of mine took such an appalling risk. They need an armed guard.'

'If they catch up with us, that's exactly what they'll have.'

'But they may never reach us alive.'

'Have more faith in the power of love,' said Marlborough. 'It can find a way past the most daunting obstacles. Abigail Piper is patently a young lady with tenacity and sense of purpose. I

106

fancy that Rawson will be seeing her before too long.'

The voyage had been a sustained ordeal. Sailing across the rough waters of the North Sea in a brig had been a rude baptism for Abigail Piper and her maid, Emily Greene. It was a supreme test of their mettle. They were sick, uncomfortable, soaked to the skin and very frightened. They were tossed around so helplessly by the surging waves, and lashed by such a violent storm, that they despaired of ever seeing dry land again. When it did finally appear, they were too weak to take any pleasure from the sight. They needed three days in The Hague to recover from the torments inflicted upon them by the elements and they were not cheered by the thought that they would one day have to make a return voyage.

Notwithstanding the many scares and setbacks, Abigail did not regret her decision to follow Daniel Rawson. She was soothed by dreams about him and lifted by hopes of what would happen when she finally caught up with him. She also derived a sisterly glee from thinking how dumbfounded Dorothy would be back in London. Abigail had looked ahead. To pay for horses, food and accommodation, she had brought a substantial amount of her savings with her. What neither she nor Emily was able to bring with them was much luggage. Travelling light was crucial.

Abigail was an accomplished horsewoman but her maid was an indifferent rider. When they bought two horses, therefore, Emily had severe misgivings.

'I'm not sure that I can do this,' she said worriedly.

Abigail was encouraging. 'Of course you can, Emily,' she said. 'The worst is behind us. If you can survive a voyage like that, you can do anything.'

'How do I know the horse will behave itself?'

'You'll ride the mare – she looks placid enough.'

'What if she bolts?'

'I'll be beside you every inch of the way,' said Abigail, putting a consoling arm around her. 'Come on – I'll help you to mount up.'

It took some time to get Emily in the saddle and she looked very unhappy about it. Their belongings had been stuffed into satchels that were slung across their horses. Knowing the dangers of travelling alone, they joined some merchants for the first stage of their journey. They had no difficulty in following the army. A body of men that large left clear evidence of their route. The weather was fine, the roads flat and their travelling companions were pleasant. Abigail was relieved to be on the move at last and Emily slowly became accustomed to the jolting rhythm of her mount.

'I could never have done this without you,' said Abigail.

'I wish you hadn't done it at all,' Emily admitted.

'You were keen to join me in my adventure at the start.'

'Yes, Miss Abigail, but that was before I knew what lay ahead.'

'Captain Rawson,' said Abigail, beaming. '*He* is what lies ahead. The captain is the sole reason we're here, Emily, and I'll endure any misery to reach him so that I can show my true feelings for him.'

'I hope he appreciates all the efforts you've made for him.'

Abigail was transported. 'Oh, he will – I *know* he will.'

Daniel Rawson liked to keep busy. When the army pitched camp for another day, he did not take the opportunity to rest. He checked on his men, practised his swordplay for an hour, then swam in the river. On his way back to his tent, he encountered Sergeant Henry Welbeck.

'It's too hot,' said Welbeck, sweat dribbling down his face.

'Do what I did,' advised Daniel, hair still wet. 'A dip in the river will cool you off nicely, Henry.'

'I can't swim.'

'Then it's high time you learnt. What will happen if we're cornered by the enemy and have to beat a hasty retreat across a river? Do you want to be drowned?'

'No, Dan. But, then, I don't ever expect to be in retreat. The Frenchies won't attack us. They'll simply observe from a distance. That's all Marshal Villeroi ever does.'

'He may be forced to do more than that this time.'

'Is that what the Corporal John told you?'

'No, Henry.'

'Then how do you know?'

'It's what I'd do in his position,' said Daniel. 'We've spent years trying to bring the French to battle and they've only obliged us with an occasional skirmish. I'm ashamed to say that my own countrymen, the Dutch, are to blame. They're more interested in protecting their own borders than launching a concerted attack on the enemy.'

'I always think of you as English – not Dutch.'

'I'm both, Henry.'

'That's impossible.'

'No, it isn't,' said Daniel genially. 'When I'm in pursuit of a young lady in London, I'm pure-bred English. When I'm doing the same in The Hague, I'm as Dutch as a windmill.'

'You always claim to be a churchgoing man.'

'So I am – I attend services every day here in the camp.'

'Does your religion allow you to chase so many women?'

'I always make sure that they're Christians,' replied Daniel with a wicked grin. 'I do it for sport, Henry, like every other soldier.'

'Not me,' said Welbeck, scowling. 'I can't abide women.'

'Then whatever do you do for pleasure?'

'I watch people like you getting into a tangle with the fairer sex. Seeing idiots led by their pizzle is always worth a laugh. They never learn. Your time will come, Dan, mark my words. Women will be the death of you in the end.'

'Every man is entitled to one vice.'

'Where does it say that in the Bible?'

Daniel chuckled. 'I can't remember offhand,' he said. 'But I'm surprised that an atheist like you has even heard of the Bible. If you had, you'd lead a more honest and God-fearing life.'

'There's no more honest man in the whole army,' said Welbeck, bristling. 'I don't need to fear a God in order to do my duty. And I don't need to pray for success in battle when I know that prayers are useless. Good commanders and well-trained soldiers win victories not someone up there in a place you call Heaven.'

'Don't mock, Henry. *You* may end up in Heaven one day.'

'I still won't believe it exists.'

Daniel burst into laughter. 'There's no convincing you, is there?' he said. 'Miracles happen every time we fight yet you still refuse to accept that there's a God.'

'The only miracle I want to see is an end to this war. Then we can all go home, put our weapons aside and lead peaceful lives.'

'That will only happen when we finally defeat the French.'

'Then where *are* they?' demanded Welbeck.

'Villeroi and his men are probably very close.'

'Watching and waiting.'

'There'll be plenty of action before too long,' said Daniel, giving him a playful punch on the arm. 'I feel it in my bones.'

When they crested the hill, the two men pulled their horses to a halt and surveyed the scene below. The camp covered a huge area, a small town of canvas nestling beside the river. Even from that distance, they could pick out the different colours of the uniforms. Charles Catto and Frédéric Seurel had caught up with their prey at last.

'There you are,' said Catto, 'I told you we'd find them.'

'How do we get to him?' asked Seurel.

'Leave that to me.'

'What do I do?'

'You can sharpen your dagger,' said Catto, taking a telescope from his saddlebag. 'It will soon be needed, Frédéric. You can have the honour of cutting off Captain Daniel Rawson's head.'

CHAPTER SIX

Long experience as a soldier had taught the Duke of Marlborough the importance of being a visible commander. The sight of their captain-general not only raised the morale of the men, it let them see that he was a flesh and blood human being and not some phantom who made vital decisions that marked the difference between their lives and deaths. Marlborough was therefore careful to be on show to his troops, riding through the camp on a regular basis so that he could inspect his men and allow them, in turn, to inspect him. A cheering word from their commander could have a big impact on the spirits of his soldiers, and they were touched when he remembered so many of their names.

Accompanied by Adam Cardonnel, he went through the camp that afternoon, noting every-thing with interest as he did so and dispensing pleasantries along the way. When he reached the area where Daniel Rawson's regiment were camped, he recalled the piece of news in his wife's latest letter. He sought the captain out and found him in his tent, playing backgammon with Richard Hopwood, a young lieutenant in the regiment. After chatting amiably with the two of them for a few minutes, Marlborough asked to be left alone with Daniel. Having already lost more money than he intended, the lieutenant was glad of an excuse to leave.

'I was just about to win another game,' said Daniel, indicating the board. 'Richard Hopwood is an obliging loser.'

'I'm sorry to interrupt you,' said Marlborough. 'I know how much you enjoy backgammon.'

'It's my most reliable source of income, Your Grace.'

'I'm sure it is. As it happens, I wanted a word about another game at which you excel.'

Daniel rubbed his hands. 'You've work for me behind enemy lines again,' he said, eyes igniting at the prospect. 'I was hoping you'd wish to deploy me.'

'That will come in time, Daniel.'

'I'm not to be sent on another assignment?'

'Not yet.'

'Oh.'

'I'm sorry to disappoint you,' said Marlborough, 'but this concerns another type of game altogether. It's just as dangerous in some ways, though seldom fatal.'

'I don't understand, Your Grace.'

'You will, Daniel. I had some letters from England today. Most of them were from people

113

like the Lord Treasurer who wish to be kept abreast of every development in our campaign. One of them, however, was from my wife.'

'How is Her Grace, the Duchess?'

'Extremely well,' said Marlborough with a pride and affection that banished all of Daniel's fears about marital difficulties between the Duke and his wife. 'The letter was full of interesting detail, one item of which relates to you.'

Daniel was taken aback. 'To me?'

'It concerns a lady of whom we've spoken before.'

'Then it must be Miss Piper.'

'Yes, Daniel. Has she, by any chance, been in touch with you?'

'She has indeed, Your Grace,' said Daniel. 'I received a letter from her a couple of weeks after we landed. It was unexpected but no less welcome for that.'

'In that case, you may already know what I have to tell you.'

'And what is that?'

'I was informed of the imminent arrival of Miss Piper.'

Daniel was thunderstruck. 'She is coming *here?*'

'You've made a conquest, it seems.'

'There was no mention of this in her letter.'

'She clearly intends to surprise you.'

'I am not so much surprised as astounded,' said Daniel, trying to take in the disturbing news. 'I only met Dorothy Piper once and we hardly exchanged more than a few words. When she wrote to me, I must confess that I was flattered but I never imagined that she would actually leave home to follow me.'

'Dorothy has not done so.'

'You just said that she had, Your Grace.'

'No,' corrected Marlborough. 'I told you that Miss Piper had sailed after you – without permission of her parents, I may add. The young lady in question is not Dorothy, however, it is Abigail Piper.'

'Travelling alone?' asked Daniel, immediately concerned for her welfare. 'What ever possessed her to do that?'

Marlborough gave him a shrewd look. 'We both know the answer to that, I think,' he said. 'Her maid is with her and I'm sure they will have the sense to find travelling companions on long, lonely roads where highwaymen might lurk.' He was amused. 'Well, this is a precedent,' he continued. 'I've never seen Daniel Rawson thrown into confusion by a woman before. If nothing else, Abigail Piper has achieved a singular response from you.'

Daniel was nonplussed. He was deeply moved to hear of the bold action taken by Abigail on his behalf but he was anxious for her well-being. With no knowledge of the country or its language, she and her maid were at a distinct disadvantage in the Netherlands. Even if they did arrive safely in Germany, there was the thorny problem of what to do with her next. Flirting with two sisters in London was a harmless enough exercise in his opinion. Being trailed by one of them during a campaign was a very different matter. For once in his life, Daniel was uncertain what to do in relation to a beautiful woman.

'I admire her courage,' said Marlborough, coming to his rescue, 'but I utterly deplore her lack of forethought. Does she not realise what happens on a battlefield? It's quite impossible for her to stay.'

'We can't force her to leave, Your Grace.'

'I agree. But, then, I don't believe that compulsion of any kind will be needed. Abigail is a delicate creature. When she realises that we rise before dawn and march at five, she may soon decide that army routine is not for her. At all events,' he continued, 'I'd like her out of the way for her own safety. Even without the danger of attack from the French, there's difficult terrain ahead – rivers to cross, forests to go through, mountains to climb. My own wife wanted very much to join us but I had to discourage her from doing so.'

Daniel was pleased to hear it. The fact that the Duchess had offered to travel with the army was confirmation that she and her husband had settled their differences. Marlborough could concentrate fully on the campaign. Daniel, on the other hand, could not. Eager for hostilities to start, he felt a responsibility towards Abigail Piper and could not dedicate himself to his duties as long as she was there. Somehow he had to make her feel that her journey was worthwhile yet ensure that she did not wish to stay long with the army. Marlborough put it more succinctly.

'Tell her what she wants to hear then wave her off.'

'Yes, Your Grace.'

'If she manages to catch up with us, that is,' said Marlborough with a frown. 'It will not be an

116

easy business. Abigail Piper and her maid are likely to meet all manner of hazards on the way.'

Until the horrors of the voyage, Abigail Piper had always considered herself to be blessed by good fortune. She was born into a wealthy family, had a social position and the relative freedom to develop her interests. As the younger daughter, she was inevitably at a slight disadvantage with her sister but she had learnt ways to circumvent Dorothy and to escape her vigilance. Throughout her life, there had been so many instances of sheer luck falling into her lap that she began to rely on it. The latest example was the crowning one. Fate had delivered the perfect man with whom she could fall in love. In her fevered mind, Daniel Rawson was the embodiment of good luck.

During her pursuit of him, chance favoured her at every turn. She and Emily Greene not only found amenable travelling companions whenever they needed them, the cavalcade invariably contained carts and wagons. The two women were often invited to tether their horses to the back of a cart so that they could travel with a measure of comfort. To someone like Emily, this was a godsend as her thighs and buttocks were already tender from the little riding she had done. Abigail, too, availed herself of the opportunity to get out of the saddle for a while. Progress was not fast but it was steady.

The inns at which they spent the night were serviceable if noticeably short of any refinements. Emily was amazed how quickly her mistress adapted to the meaner conditions. Having lived in comparative luxury all her life, Abigail had never had to sleep on a lumpy mattress before or wash in public or eat unappetising food. One night, they were even forced to sleep under the stars but there was no complaint from Abigail. Each day took her closer to the man she loved and that was all that mattered to her.

When they reached Bedburg, they parted company with one group of travellers and immediately found another, heading south towards Bonn. There were fifteen of them in all, making the journey in three carts or on horseback. The men were armed and there were enough of them to ward off a potential attack. Abigail and Emily hitched their horses to one of the carts and climbed aboard. The driver was a friendly man in his late thirties with a solid frame and a pleasant face fringed with a fair beard. His name was Otto and he knew enough English to have a conversation with his two guests. While Abigail sat beside him, Emily was in the back of the cart, perched on something that was covered by a tarpaulin.

'Why are you going to Bonn?' asked Abigail.

'I keep the promise,' replied Otto.

'Promise?'

'To my wife, I swear it.'

'Oh, I see.'

'Marthe, she was born there.'

'Are you going home to her?'

'No,' he said with a forgiving smile. 'I take Marthe there.'

Abigail looked around. 'But she's not with us now.'

'Yes, she is.'

'Where – is she one of the women in the other carts?'

He shook his head. 'I promise that Marthe, she will be in Bonn buried beside her mother.' He glanced over his shoulder. 'In the back, the coffin is.'

'Goodness!' cried Emily, jumping up as she realised that she was actually sitting on the dead body of Otto's wife. She moved further back to sit down. 'I'm so sorry, sir. You should have told us.'

'Marthe, she will not mind,' he said. 'A good woman, she was.'

It took time for the Abigail and Emily to get used to the idea that they were sharing the cart with a corpse. Otto was a talkative man. He turned out to have borne arms in a German regiment that had fought against the French the previous year, an injury to his foot ending his reluctant career as a soldier. Abigail pressed him for detail.

'Did you ever meet the Duke of Marlborough?' she inquired. 'Father says that he's the most brilliant commander in Europe. He has outstanding people under him. I don't suppose that you ever came across a Captain Daniel Rawson?'

'No, no,' said Otto.

'Captain Rawson is with the Duke of Marlborough's Foot.'

The German looked at her. 'But he has two feet, no?'

Abigail giggled. 'That's Captain Rawson's infantry regiment,' she explained, taking pleasure from saying Daniel's name for the third time.

'He's a very brave soldier. The Duke admires him greatly.'

'I did not like it, being the soldier.'

'Why not?

'From my wife, it take me away.'

'Did you kill any Frenchmen?' wondered Emily.

'The musket, I fire many times. Maybe, someone I kill.'

'How long do you think the war will last?' asked Abigail.

'For ever,' said Otto with resignation. 'France, she never stops wanting the more. Always fighting, her army is, always will.'

'The French could be defeated by British heroes like Captain Rawson.' Otto looked sceptical. 'They could,' she added stoutly. 'The Duke of Marlborough is resolved to win a famous battle against the French. I heard that from Captain Rawson himself.'

Otto was not convinced. He had the world-weary air of a man who had seen too many armies marching to and fro across his native land. Lapsing into silence, he drove on. They continued on their way, following the course of the River Rhine as it snaked southwards. It was late afternoon when the weather broke. After rolling along in the sunshine, they suddenly found themselves at the mercy of driving rain and a swirling wind. Since they had little protection from the downpour, they had to find the nearest shelter they could. When they came around a bend and spied an inn ahead of them, therefore, they were unworried by the fact that it looked weather-beaten and almost ramshackle. It was a refuge.

The horses were stabled but the carts had to stand out in the rain. Though she was distressed to see that Otto left his wife's coffin under the tarpaulin, Abigail did not feel that it was her place to protest in any way. The man had been kind and avuncular to them. As the natural leader of the travellers, it was he who discussed the sleeping arrangements with the landlord and haggled over the cost. He seemed to be arguing with the man on behalf of Abigail and Emily, pointing to them and raising his voice in a demand. A sly, shifty little man with straggly grey hair and a beak of a nose, the landlord tapped his walking stick angrily on the floor.

When Otto came over to them, he was very apologetic. Because the accommodation was so limited, the travellers would have to share beds. What he had managed to do was to secure a private room for Abigail and a place in the attic for Emily. Neither of them liked the idea of being split up but they soon found that Abigail's room was more like a large broom cupboard than a bedchamber. Emily saw that she would have to sleep in the attic but, before she left her mistress's room, she took the trouble to sweep away some of the cobwebs and check that the bed was habitable.

Over a hot meal and plenty of ale, the travellers had a jolly time and the Germans soon burst into song. Abigail thanked them for the way she and her maid had been welcomed the group and she had a special word of gratitude for Otto. As the ale flowed more freely and the songs grew more raucous, the Englishwomen made their excuses and retired early to bed. Emily was soon asleep in her dingy attic room but Abigail stayed awake to write in her diary by the light of a candle. The jollity was still continuing down below when she finally blew out the flame and lay back to think about Daniel Rawson.

An hour later, Abigail drifted quietly off. It was as well that she was a light sleeper because it was not long before the latch was lifted on her door and a heavy footstep made a floorboard creak. Coming awake with a start, she sat bolt upright and peered into the gloom.

'Who's there?' she asked. 'Is that you, Emily?'

Before she could say another word, a hand was clasped over her mouth and she was pushed back down on to the bed. A man's body pressed down on top of her and she could smell the ale on his breath. Struggle as she did, Abigail could not move him.

'Like her, you are,' said Otto, laughing softly in the dark. 'Just like my Marthe. To me, be good. Tonight, *you* are my Marthe.'

Abigail was distraught. He was too heavy to be moved and too strong to fight off. Worst of all, his free hand was starting do take the most alarming liberties, stroking her hair, squeezing her breast then trying to pull up her nightgown. A refined young lady who longed to surrender herself to Daniel Rawson was about to have her virginity snatched cruelly away by a drunken German widower. Abigail Piper's run of luck had come to a grinding halt.

When he moved his hand from her mouth, she

dared to hope that he had relented but all he wanted to do was to take a long, hard, bruising kiss from her. The taste was disgusting. Her stomach lurched, her blood ran cold and she began to tremble all over. As his tongue became more invasive and his hands more predatory, Abigail thought that she was about to be sick. Desperation made her do the only thing she could think of. Twisting her head slightly to the left, she bit deep into his lower lip and felt his blood spurt across her face.

Otto bellowed in pain and rolled off her, hitting the ground with a thud. The noise brought two people running to see what had happened. First through the door was the landlord, his candle lending a dull glow to the sordid scene. Realising what had happened, he began to wave a walking stick at Otto and abuse him in high-pitched German. The second person to arrive was Emily Greene and she did not waste any words. When she saw her mistress, hunched up in bed, shielding herself with a pillow, she grabbed the stick from the landlord and used it to belabour the midnight lover, hitting him with such force that he begged for mercy and crawled out of the room on his hands and knees. The landlord went after Otto to remonstrate with him. Annoyed that she had not been there to protect her mistress from the assault, Emily shut the door and put her back against it.

'Fetch our things,' said Abigail, still shaking. 'We're leaving.'

Emily was practical. 'It's the middle of the night, Miss Abigail.'

'Do as I tell you – *please*.'

Daniel Rawson finally got a taste of the action he wanted. When they reached Coblenz, a sizeable force was sent off in the direction of the Moselle valley but only as a means of distracting Marshal Villeroi and his men. Daniel remained with the main army as it moved south and crossed the Rhine where their ranks were swelled by the addition of 5000 Hanoverians and Prussians. To the French observers who were tracking them, it looked as if they were heading for Mainz and were prepared to go much deeper into Germany than they had ever done before. Daniel finally got a clearer idea of what was in the Duke of Marlborough's mind.

As usual, their commander rode on ahead with the cavalry squadrons, leaving the infantry, artillery and supply wagons to follow at a more sedate pace. Mounted on his horse, Daniel was near the front of a multi-coloured column of soldiers that stretched back into the distance. Having marched through open country at a steady pace, they now entered woodland. The farther they went, the darker it got as over-hanging branches blocked out the light or filtered it through their leaves to throw dazzling patterns on the ground. Birds sang in the trees, undisturbed by the tramp of many feet and rumble of supply wagons. There was no sense of danger.

When it came, therefore, it took them completely by surprise. As the leading regiments reached a large clearing, they stepped into the sunlight and became open targets. A volley of musket fire rang out, scattering the birds in a squawking cacophony, and hitting a number of men in Daniel's regiment. He reacted swiftly and ordered those under his command to fan out and take cover before the next hail of lead was discharged. Dismounting from his horse, he led it quickly into the trees for safety. From the sound of the attack, he guessed that somewhere between two and three dozen weapons had been fired. A couple of his men had been killed outright, many more had been injured.

Since there was no second volley, Daniel knew that the French snipers must have fled and he signalled his men to move forward in pursuit of them. Mounting his horse again, he drew his sword and kicked it into a canter. Other officers followed his example but he was way ahead of them, furious that they had been caught off guard and lusting for revenge. He soon caught the sound of many horses, pounding their way through the undergrowth until they came out of the woodland. Daniel emerged from the trees to see the familiar French uniforms strung out in front of him as they galloped away. His estimate had been fairly accurate. He counted thirty of them.

Spurring his horse on, he slowly began to gain on the stragglers. Two of them were dropping behind the other riders and they veered off to the left in an attempt to shake off the pursuit. Daniel left it to others to chase the main body of snipers and followed the pair who had become detached from it. His horse was fleet of foot and he was soon within thirty yards of the two men. Glancing over his shoulder, one of them was alarmed to see how close Daniel was but reassured by the fact that he was completely isolated from his fellows.

The musket slung around the Frenchman's shoulders had been discharged but he was also carrying a loaded pistol. Pulling it out, he waited until Daniel got closer then raised it to fire. Even at a short distance, accuracy was impossible from the saddle of a galloping horse and the ball went harmlessly past Daniel's ear. The next moment, Daniel drew level with him and slashed at the man's outstretched hand, slicing it off at the wrist and sending it tumbling to the ground with the pistol still in its grasp. The man gave a howl of pain and held the bleeding stump under his other arm in a vain attempt to stem the flow.

The other Frenchman had seen enough. He put his own safety before that of his comrade, abandoning him without a second thought as he rode away. Daniel was therefore able to sheath his sword, grab the reins of the wounded man's horse and bring it round in a circle as he slowed it to a halt. He promptly dismounted. Swearing at his attacker, the Frenchmen tried to kick at him but Daniel hauled him unceremoniously from the saddle and pushed him to the ground. When he tried to examine the wound, however, a gob of spit hit him full in the face. Daniel wiped it away then punched the man hard on the chin to subdue him before he pulled off his coat, easing the blood-soaked sleeve gently over the wounded wrist. He had seen too many hideous injuries on the battlefield to be distressed by the sight of blood. It was an emergency. Daniel turned army surgeon.

'You need a tourniquet, my friend,' he said affably, pulling at the man's shirt and tearing it into strips. 'We have to keep you alive so that you're able to talk to His Grace, the Duke of Marlborough. I'm sure you have a lot of interesting things to tell him.'

When the Allied armies crossed the River Main, it became certain to the enemy that the march on the Moselle valley had been a cunning ploy to mislead them. They set up camp and Daniel handed over his prisoner for interrogation. The ambush in the woods had inflicted serious injuries on some of his men, one of whom had been blinded while another had had to suffer amputation as a result. After checking on their condition and trying to cheer them up, he went back to his tent. Daniel was about to enter it when he saw Henry Welbeck in conversation with a tall, slim man in the uniform of a private. The sergeant was pointing at Daniel. His companion nodded. After studying Daniel for a moment, the man gave a nod of thanks to Welbeck and walked away. The sergeant strolled over to his friend.

'Who was that?' asked Daniel.

'A new recruit,' replied Welbeck. 'He joined us yesterday. The bugger has too many airs and graces for me but he was keen to serve in the ranks and he looks fit enough.'

'What's his name?'

'Will Curtis.'

'Why did he choose this regiment?'

'He says that his father served in it when it was first raised in 1689 by Colonel Sir Edward Dering. Curtis's father was killed in action against the French.'

'What was his name?'

'You'll have to ask him, Dan,' said Welbeck. 'All I see is another stupid Englishman willing to throw his life away in this pointless war. Besides, I've got more important things to worry about than Private Will Curtis. He's simply target practice for the enemy.'

'Why were you pointing me out?' wondered Daniel.

'He'd heard about this hare-brained officer who went charging off alone after those Frenchies and brought back a prisoner single-handed.' He bared his few remaining teeth in a grin. 'It seems the poor man lost his other hand somehow.'

'I hacked it off, Henry.'

'That was the rumour Curtis heard. He wondered who this intrepid Captain Rawson really was. Now he knows. He also knows how crafty these Frenchies can be,' he went on. 'That ambush killed two men, blinded a third, took a leg off a fourth and left another ten unfit for action. It cost me fourteen soldiers, Dan.'

'The French just wanted to let us know they are here.'

'I thought they'd all be waiting for us in the Moselle valley.'

'Marshal Villeroi might be,' said Daniel, 'so he's behind us now. Somewhere in front of us are Marshal Marsin and the Bavarians. We'll have them to contend with before the summer is over.'

'Will we have enough men to take them on?'

'When we cross the River Neckar, the hope is that we'll be joined by 14,000 Danes and Prussians. That's what I've been told.'

'The River Neckar!' echoed Welbeck. 'Are we going that far south? What's Corporal John playing at, Dan? Does he mean to march us all the way to Italy?'

'No, Henry,' said Daniel. 'He means to win a pitched battle against the French that will leave them in tatters. Where it will be, I can't tell you but there'll be a huge butcher's bill to pay.'

'There always is. We only lost a handful of men today. Thousands more will be killed or maimed before we're done.'

'That's why you should be grateful when people like Will Curtis volunteer to join us. We need every last soldier that we can get.'

Private Will Curtis, meanwhile, had found himself a quiet spot under a tree where he could draw a diagram of part of the camp with a pencil. Each tent was a tiny square that he numbered carefully so that no mistake would be made. Beside one tent, he put a large cross. Slipping the diagram into his pocket, he went to the corner of the camp that he had just sketched and paced out the distance from the first tent he had drawn and the one with the cross. He made a mental note of the number of paces. Charles Catto was content. He could find his way there in the dark.

As a result of the ambush, additional pickets were posted around the camp but the evening passed without incident. Knowing that they would be up again at dawn, most of the men took to their beds early but Daniel Rawson stayed up late to give Richard Hopwood a chance of retrieving some money at backgammon. They played in Daniel's tent by the light of two candles. Hopwood was a fresh-face young man who had recently bought a commission in the regiment and who – in spite of his enthusiasm – had almost no experience of battle. While Daniel liked him immensely, it did not stop him from making an assault on the lieutenant's purse.

That night, however, it was Daniel's turn to lose. Though he was by far the more skilful player, his mind was filled with the image of Abigail Piper, struggling to reach him. Wondering what had happened to her, and feeling guilty that he had unwittingly prompted her to follow him, he had several lapses of concentration. Hopwood was quick to seize the advantage, earning back some of the money he had lost in previous games. No matter how hard Daniel tried to oust Abigail from his thoughts, she kept coming back to trouble him. He knew that he would never forgive himself if any harm came to her.

'Another game?' asked Hopwood, winning yet again.

'It's late, Richard.'

'One more – your luck may change this time.'

'Very well,' agreed Daniel, 'but you'll have to excuse me for a minute while I answer the call of nature.'

Daniel stood up, the sudden movement creating a draught that made both of the flames dance crazily. He went out of the tent and made his way to the latrines that had been dug some distance away. A fire was burning to give him some guidance. When he had relieved himself, he chatted for a few moments to some of the guards who were patrolling the camp, then he returned to his tent. As he pulled back the flap, he was surprised to see that both candles had been blown out, leaving a haunting smell of smoke.

Assuming that Hopwood had decided against playing again and had instead gone back to his own tent, Daniel moved forward in the dark. Before he could stop himself, he tripped over something and fell to the ground. He got up quickly, groped his way to a candle and managed to light it after a few attempts. The sight that it illumined made him gape in horror. Richard Hopwood had not only been killed.

Someone had removed his head.

CHAPTER SEVEN

The alarm was raised at once. Captain Daniel Rawson gathered his men together and formed them into search parties to scour the camp. With flaming torches to guide them, they went off quickly in different directions. Sergeant Henry Welbeck added a few barked expletives to help them on their way.

'What exactly happened, Dan?' he asked, turning to his friend.

'I wish I knew,' replied Daniel, heaving a sigh. 'Richard Hopwood and I were playing backgammon. I went off to the latrines. By the time I got back, he was dead.'

'How was he killed?'

'Stabbed then decapitated.'

'Jesus!'

'The head has disappeared. What kind of monster wants that as a trophy? And why pick on someone as harmless as Richard?'

'Can I see him?'

'Yes, of course – come in, Henry.'

Daniel pulled back the flap of the tent and went inside. Welbeck followed him. The second candle had been lit now and the combined light of two flames showed the body of Richard Hopwood, lying on his back with a pool of blood where his head had once been. The rear of the tent had been slit open from top to bottom. Welbeck was aghast. He was accustomed to gruesome sights in battle but not in the safety of the British camp. Such a brutal murder was unprecedented.

'Poor devil!' he murmured.

'I think that the killer came in through the front,' said Daniel, trying to reconstruct the crime. 'Richard was at the table with his back to the flap. Thinking it was me, he wouldn't have turned round when he heard someone entering the tent. If he saw someone cutting his way in through the canvas, however, he would certainly have defended himself. The noise alone would have alerted him. He'd have been on his feet in a flash. Instead of which,' he went on, indicating a stool, 'he sat there without the slightest fear of danger.'

'So he was stabbed from behind then his head was cut off.'

'That's the way it looks, Henry. The stool was on the floor as if it had been knocked over. Once he'd got what he wanted, the killer made his escape through that slit in the canvas.'

'How long were you away, Dan?'

'Too long, I'm afraid.'

'It's so unfair,' said Welbeck lugubriously. 'Lieutenant Hopwood had only been in the army five minutes. Until that ambush today, he'd never seen action. I pity him.'

'I feel sorry for the Duke as well,' said Daniel. 'He'll have to explain to Richard's family what happened. It won't be an easy letter to write. The Duke hates losing men in combat even though that's inevitable. To lose an officer *this* way will really upset him.'

'It's upset me as well, Dan.'

'We'll find the bastard who did this.'

'Who on earth can it be?'

'There are only two possibilities in my view, Henry. It's either one of our own, someone from inside this camp, or it's someone from outside who was helped by a British soldier.'

'I find that hard to believe.'

'Look at the facts,' reasoned Daniel. 'The killer had to know the precise location of this tent. No outsider would have that information. Nor would he know where the pickets were posted. And there's another thing,' he went on, crossing to open the slit in the canvas. 'This escape route was planned. There are no tents behind this one but hundreds in front of it. Anyone leaving here could be in the trees within seconds.' He looked at his friend. 'We have a traitor in our midst, Henry.'

'Give him to me,' said Welbeck. 'I'll cut off more than his head.'

'We have to find him first.'

'I'll soon sniff the bugger out, Dan.'

'You may be too late to do that, I fear,' said Daniel, looking down sorrowfully at the corpse. 'After a murder like this, the villain would never risk staying in camp. I think the bird will have flown.'

Charles Catto had made all the necessary preparations. Having taken the trouble to inspect the camp thoroughly, he knew exactly where he could smuggle Frédéric Seurel in past the sentries and how to conduct him to Daniel Rawson's tent without being seen. When the murder had been committed, Seurel followed his orders and slit open the back of the tent, darting through the gap with a severed head in the small sack he had brought with him. Catto was waiting to lead him out of the camp. The hue and cry was raised faster than he had expected but Catto had allowed for that contingency. Having taken Seurel to a secure hiding place within the perimeter of the camp, he joined in the search, making sure that nobody went anywhere near his accomplice.

It was over an hour before the commotion finally died down. Catto was at last able to slip away, liberate Seurel from his refuge and escape from the camp with him. Their horses had been hidden over a mile away. When they had reclaimed them, they rode off until they were a

134

long way clear of the army encampment. It was only then that they were able to congratulate each on the way that their plan had worked. They stopped near an abandoned cottage and dismounted. Seurel was grinning at his triumph.

'It was so easy,' he boasted, holding up the blood-soaked sack. 'I took him from behind. I put an arm round his neck and stabbed him through the heart.' He mimed the action. 'His head was soon off.'

'You did well, Frédéric,' said Catto.

'Does that mean I get more money?'

'You get what we agreed.'

'I should have equal payment,' argued Seurel, tapping his chest. 'I killed him, after all.'

'Yes,' countered Catto, 'but who got inside the camp to make it possible? You could never have done that. Besides, it wasn't you that General Salignac chose for this assignment. He picked me and told me to choose my own accomplice and pay him what I thought fit. That's how you come to be here, Frédéric. You agreed to my terms.'

'That was before I knew what I had to do.'

'There's no going back on our arrangement now.'

'I think I deserve some reward,' said Seurel.

'I'll mention that to the General,' said Catto. 'You'll certainly get no more from me than we decided at the outset. But let's not haggle over money at a time like this,' he went on, adopting a more amiable tone. 'Our work is done. All we have to do is to present this little gift to General Salignac then we can go off to spend our money.' He nudged his friend. 'Take him out – I want to

135

see Captain Rawson.'

Their eyes had become accustomed to the dark by now so they were both able to get a reasonable idea of what the face looked like as the head was hauled out of the sack by Seurel.

'Well,' he said, expecting lavish praise, 'what do you think?'

Catto peered at the face. 'I think you must be even more stupid than I feared,' he said harshly. 'That's not Daniel Rawson.'

'Yes, it is!'

'I've seen the man and he looks very different.'

'But he was in his tent. You took me there.'

'I expected him to be alone at that time of night.'

'And so he was – that's why I killed Captain Rawson.'

'No, you buffoon,' yelled Catto, 'you killed someone else. We went to all that trouble and we end up empty-handed. You're an idiot, Frédéric, a brainless, blundering imbecile.'

'I obeyed your orders, Charles, that's all.'

'My orders were for you to kill Daniel Rawson, not some nameless individual who's no use to us at all. This man probably held a different rank altogether. Didn't you look at his uniform to make sure that he was a captain?'

'He wasn't wearing a jacket,' recalled Seurel. 'He'd taken it off to play backgammon. The board was set out on the table.'

Catto snarled. 'Who cares about that?'

Seurel was hurt. Having been brave enough to enter an enemy camp, he had committed a murder under the very noses of the British troops and felt entitled to admiration. Instead, he was being reviled by his partner. There was no hope of an immediate return to the camp. Now that Catto had deserted, he would be shot on sight by any soldier who recognised him. After staring at the head once more, he dropped it back into its sack. Seurel's brow was corrugated by thought. A few moments later, he snapped his fingers.

'I have it, Charles!' he exclaimed.

'Don't you dare tell me that you intend to stroll back into the camp, ask for Captain Rawson then cut off his head,' said Catto with scorn. 'That's just the kind of lunatic idea you'd think of.'

'We don't need Captain Rawson. We already have him.'

'We have someone else, I tell you.'

'We know that,' said Seurel slyly, 'but the General doesn't. All we have to do is to give him the head and tell him that I cut it from the shoulders of Daniel Rawson.' He grinned inanely. 'Don't you think it's a clever ruse?' Catto turned away in disgust. 'It is, Charles. It solves our problem. General Salignac has never seen Rawson so he'll be none the wiser.'

'If I thought that,' said Catto, rounding on him, 'I'd chop off *your* useless head and swear that it belonged to Captain Rawson. The ruse would never work.'

Seurel was dejected. 'Why ever not?'

'Don't you realise what he'll do?'

'Give us a reward, I hope.'

'No, Frédéric. He'll want to taunt his wife. When he gets back to Paris, he'll wave the head of her lover in front of her. Madame Salignac will see at a glance that this is not Rawson.'

'Oh,' said Seurel, scratching his cheek. 'I never thought of that.'

'Evidently.'

'What are we going to do, Charles?'

'To begin with,' said Catto, grabbing the sack, 'we'll get rid of this fellow.' He hurled the sack and its grisly contents into the ruins of the cottage. 'Then we follow the army again and bide our time. If and when we *do* get a second chance, try not to make a mess of it again.'

'It wasn't my fault,' bleated Seurel.

'Of course, it was.'

'How was I to know what Rawson looked like?'

'I described him to you, Frédéric.'

'It was dark in that tent. There were only two candles and I blew those out as I left. I did what I was told to do, Charles.'

'Nobody told you to kill the wrong man.'

'That was an accident.'

'It was a ruinous mistake,' said Catto nastily. 'Let's make sure it's the last one you ever make. And this might be the time to warn you that General Salignac does not tolerate failure. If we don't give him what he wants, he'll have us skinned alive.'

A report of the incident reached the Duke of Marlborough immediately upon waking. He summoned Daniel Rawson in order to hear the full details. Amid the bustle of a camp preparing to move on, they stood outside the Duke's tent as it was being taken down. The first gesture of light was appearing in the sky.

'This is extremely distressing,' said Marlborough, stroking his chin. 'Lieutenant Hopwood was a promising young officer.'

'He was also very unlucky, Your Grace.'

'That goes without saying.'

'I didn't mean it in the obvious sense,' explained Daniel. 'The fact of the matter is that Richard Hopwood died as a result of mistaken identity.'

'What do you mean, Daniel?'

'The intended victim was *me*, Your Grace.'

Marlborough was shocked. 'Is there any evidence of that?'

'On reflection, I think there is. When the killer went into my tent, he expected me to be there. How would anyone know that I had a visitor inside with me? If someone had wanted to kill Richard Hopwood, they would have gone to *his* tent and not mine. It was sheer misfortune that the lieutenant was alone when the man struck.'

'This is far more worrying than I thought,' said Marlborough. 'The death of any officer is a sad loss. The murder of Daniel Rawson would have been a disaster. No disrespect to Hopwood – he had all the makings of a fine soldier – but he could never have matched your achievements. You're an outstanding asset to us, Daniel,' he went on, 'and that was why you were singled out.'

'I'm not sure about that, Your Grace,' said Daniel. 'In an army of such magnitude, the deeds of one man will hardly stand out unless his name is the Duke of Marlborough. I don't flatter myself that the enemy consider me that important. If they wanted to disable our cause, why did the assassin not strike at *you?*'

Marlborough nodded. 'I accept the logic of that argument.'

'There was personal animus behind this outrage.'

'Whom do you suspect?'

'I don't know who his paymaster is, Your Grace, but I've found out the name of his creature. He's called Will Curtis, though I have no doubt that that was a false name. Private Curtis joined the regiment recently, claiming that his father had once served it.'

'Why do you suspect him of the murder?'

'He's deserted in the night.'

'Are search parties out looking for him?'

'Yes,' said Daniel, 'but they've had no success. He's a cunning man and he planned the crime with meticulous care.'

'But he would need to have known which is your tent,' said Marlborough. 'How could he find it among so many?'

'Sergeant Welbeck has the answer to that. Private Curtis asked him to point me out and I was standing outside my quarters at the time. It would not be difficult to memorise the exact spot.'

'Was this villain operating alone, Daniel?'

'Who can say?' asked Daniel. 'If he had assistance, I fancy that there would only have been one accomplice, someone who did the foul deed while Curtis – or whatever his real name is – kept watch. It would have been difficult to sneak more than one man into the camp.'

'The accomplice might already have been here.'

'Then he, too, would have deserted by now, Your Grace.'

'I take your point,' said Marlborough pensively. 'In the wake of the murder, inquiries would be very searching. It would be tempting fate for anyone to remain within our ranks and court discovery.'

'My belief is that the killer probably came from outside the camp,' said Daniel, 'or he would not have confused me with Richard Hopwood. Private Curtis wouldn't have murdered the wrong man, which is why I feel that his hand was not on the dagger.'

'But he's an accessory.'

'Oh, he's more than that, Your Grace. He organised the whole thing. It could only be done by someone inside the camp who knew our routine and our picket arrangements.'

'He *must* be called to account,' said Marlborough sternly.

'He will be. At least I know what to expect next time.'

'Next time?'

'Yes, Your Grace,' said Daniel philosophically. 'A man who's gone to such lengths to kill me will not give up after one failure. And, by now, he'll have realised that there was a terrible mistake.'

'Keep men around you at all time,' Marlborough urged. 'We can't afford to lose you, Daniel, especially now that we're getting closer to a confrontation with the French.'

'I'll take sensible precautions from now on but I won't surround myself with an armed guard. I want this man – or these men – to come in search of me again. It's the only way to be sure of catching them, Your Grace.'

'What – by acting as bait on the hook?'

'By giving the *appearance* of doing so,' said Daniel with a grim smile. 'Richard Hopwood was a friend of mine and a keen soldier. His family deserves some consolation. They need to be told that we've caught and punished the villains responsible for his death.'

The Confederate army continued its march south. Crossing the River Neckar, a tributary of the Rhine, they were joined by the expected reinforcements from Denmark and Prussia, thereby adding 14,000 soldiers to the army and instilling fresh confidence in it as a result. French spies watched the army's progress and sent regular reports to the King in Versailles as well as to his two leading commanders, Marshal Camille d'Hostun, Comte de Tallard and Marshal François Villeroi, a royal favourite but an uninspiring soldier. Early fears that Marlborough intended to invade Alsace had proved groundless as had the anxiety over a potential attack on the French fortress of Landau. When these objectives were discounted, observers concluded that the armies of the Grand Alliance were doing something considered to be unthinkable. They were heading for the Danube.

It was not a forced march but neither was it leisurely. Marching early each morning, they went on for three or four days then rested for a day. They were travelling through the countries of allies who had been forewarned of their approach.

Commissaries had therefore been appointed to see to the needs of both men and horses. Whenever they reached the site of their next camp, everything was in readiness. All that the soldiers had to do was to pitch their tents, boil their kettles and sit down to rest. They were in good heart

Louis XIV received news of developments in a towering rage.

'Marlborough had this planned in advance,' he roared at the group of advisers gathered around him at Versailles. 'Why did we know nothing about it?'

'The Duke has been very guileful,' ventured one man, electing to speak on behalf of the others.

'That's no excuse. We have enough spies in his army. Surely, one of them could have found out what his true intentions were. How can we stop him if we do not know where he is going?'

'But we *do* know, Your Majesty. His destination is the Danube.'

'What does he propose to do on the way?' demanded the king.

'That remains to be seen.'

'I can't wait for it to be seen, man. I want it anticipated now. What's the point of military advisers if they haven't the intelligence or the foresight to give me good counsel? Not one of you guessed what Marlborough's strategy was,' he said, glaring accusingly around the group. 'Not one of you ever mentioned the possibility of a march to the Danube. French armies should dictate events as they've always done in the past, not be forced to respond to them as we're doing now.'

'Marlborough has finally shown his hand, Your

143

Majesty,' said the spokesman, an elderly man with a pock-marked face, 'and we can therefore take appropriate action.'

'What do you believe that should be?'

'Strengthen our army between them and their destination.'

'We can't just build a barrier against their approach,' said Louis. 'There's always the chance they can march around it. Just look how steadily they are moving – almost 250 miles in a bare five weeks. Each time they reach camp,' he added irritably, 'they find food, drink and all other necessaries awaiting them. In short, they are expected – by everyone except *us*, damn it!'

The advisers exchanged nervous glances. They were used to making decisions about a French army whose power and expertise had made it universally feared. Since they were not acquainted with major failures and setbacks, they did not instantly know how to deal with them. Their spokesman was tentative.

'What would you suggest, Your Majesty?' he asked.

'I'd suggest that I need some new advisers.' There was a flurry of protest from the others but he waved them into silence. 'My strategy is this. We must separate Marlborough from his ally, Prince Eugene of Savoy. To that end, I will send Marshal Villeroi, with 40 battalions and 70 squadrons to keep Eugene occupied.'

'A wise decision,' said the spokesmen amid a chorus of approval from the others. 'What of Marshal Tallard?'

'He'll take an army of 40 battalions and 50

squadrons through the Black Forest to join Marshal Marsin and the Elector of Bavaria.' He saw the reservation in the man's eyes. 'Do you have any objection to that?'

'Not in the least, Your Majesty.'

'Tell the truth, man. I sense reluctance.'

'It's consent tempered by a slight anxiety,' explained the man. 'The Black Forest is a mountainous area. Our army would have to march through hostile territory under the most difficult conditions.'

'It's the most direct route.'

'Then you must prepare for losses along the way.'

'Don't tell me about losses,' snapped Louis, smacking the arm of his chair. 'I've controlled my armies for decades now so I know all about the losses they are bound to sustain. Marshal Marsin and the Elector need reinforcements and that's what they will get.'

The man nodded obsequiously. 'Yes, Your Majesty.'

'Whatever happens, Marlborough must not be allowed to cross the Danube. That's an article of faith with me.'

'The best place to cross is Donauworth,' said another of the advisers, 'where the Wornitz river meets the Danube. I've been there, Your Majesty. It's guarded by a fortified hill called the Schellenberg and that's almost impossible to storm. Of one thing I believe we can be assured,' he continued, looking around his colleagues with a smug smile. 'The Allied armies will never be permitted to cross the Danube.'

'We must cross the Danube,' said Marlborough, poring over the map laid out on a table in his tent.

'It will not be easy, Your Grace,' warned Eugene. 'Marshal Marsin and the Elector have established a camp in Dillingen – right here.' His finger prodded the map. 'A smaller force is guarding Donauworth and the heights above it. Even as we speak, they will be improving fortifications on the Schellenberg.'

'We shall have to take the hill.'

'You'll have to pay a high price in blood to do so.'

'It will be worth it.'

'I agree,' said Eugene. 'It is bold, brave and unexpected. The French never dreamt you would come this far into Germany. You have kept them guessing at every point, Your Grace. That's the mark of a great commander.'

Prince Eugene of Savoy spoke with authority, having been a keen student of military history. He was a slim, pale, almost effeminate man of forty with protruding front teeth and a mis-shapen nose. Notwithstanding his ugliness and his unwillingness to wash as often as he should, he was a skilful general. The irony was that he had been brought up in the French court where his ambitions to be a soldier were ridiculed by King Louis who decreed that the puny youth of sixteen, as he had once been, should enter the church.

Forced to receive a tonsure and wear a cassock, Eugene sought succour in the work of Plutarch

146

and others who wrote about heroes of the Ancient World. He remained in France until he could endure the king's arrogance no more, seeking a military career elsewhere and vowing that he would only ever return at the head of an army. An unlikely soldier, he nevertheless turned out to have great skill in the field and his support was prized by Marlborough. Had he been allowed to join the French army, as he had once wished, Eugene would now be fighting against the Grand Alliance. In treating him with such disdain, Louis XIV had created a dangerous enemy with an army of 28,000 men at his back.

'What are my orders, Your Grace?' asked Eugene.

'Marshal Tallard is coming through the Black Forest,' said Marlborough, 'and he will meet up with Marshal Villeroi's army. We need you to guard the Lines at Stollhoffen against their advance.'

'Consider it done.'

'Thank you, my friend. I cannot tell you how delighted we are to have you as our ally. Your successes against the Turks have earned you many plaudits. Three years ago, you also had notable victories at Carpi and Chiari against superior French armies.'

'I lost the battle of Cremona,' confessed Eugene, 'but I fought the French to a draw at Luzzara. They are not as invincible as they like to believe.'

'I know,' said Marlborough, looking up. 'They are rightly proud of their military achievements but pride can lead to complacency. We must exploit their self-satisfaction.'

'How many men do you have at your disposal?'

'The best part of 80,000 – on the long march here, we lost only a thousand or more to sickness. That was a blessing.'

'The French will lose many men as they come through the Black Forest. The mountains always claim some victims.'

'Their horses are suffering as well,' Marlborough told him. 'The latest intelligence is that a virulent disease has spread among them. If many of their horses die, they will be slowed down.'

'We will be waiting for them at the Lines of Stollhoffen,' said Eugene, a broad grin revealing the rest of his teeth. He brushed back his unkempt fair hair. 'We'll test the French to the utmost.'

'May good fortune attend you,' said Marlborough, exchanging a warm handshake with him. 'The next time we meet, it will be near the Danube.' He studied Eugene quizzically. 'Do you have no qualms about fighting a country in which you spent so much time?'

Eugene became serious. 'None at all, Your Grace,' he said. 'King Louis treated my mother shabbily and mocked me with the name of *le petit abbé*. He will soon see that I am no little priest.' He rested a hand on his sword. 'I'll make him rue the day that he made me quit France to follow my true calling as a soldier.'

Daniel Rawson had always enjoyed being in a camp preparing itself for action. The sense of expectation was exciting. He found the sight of men being drilled, weapons being cleaned or sharpened, and artillery being made ready, thrilling even after all his years in the army. Additional soldiers were coming in every day. They had met the Margrave of Baden and the Austrian army at Launsheim and there was a steady trickle of recruits. After their unfortunate experience with the man calling himself Will Curtis, the British army questioned any newcomers very closely, especially if they were deserters from the French or Bavarian forces. Once accepted into the ranks, they were still watched in case they turned out to be enemy spies.

Characteristically forthright, Sergeant Henry Welbeck expressed misgivings about what awaited them. He and Daniel were watching a small detachment of Dutch soldiers arriving in camp.

'What are those moon-faced fools grinning at?' he asked with scorn. 'Don't they know they are on their way to their death?'

'Death or glory,' corrected Daniel.

'There's not much chance of glory, Dan. The rumour is that we're going to cross the Danube. If we try to do that, most of us will end up as corpses floating on the water.'

'Your job is to inspire your men. If you tell them we're facing defeat before battle even commences, you plant seeds of doubt in their minds. They *have* to believe victory is possible, Henry.'

'I'm not sure that *I* do.'

'You refused to believe that we'd get this far,' Daniel reminded him. 'Yet we've managed it without too many problems.'

'Then your memory is very different from mine,' said Welbeck tartly. 'What about the days when it rained so hard, we could hardly see a hand in front of our faces? What about those mountains we had to climb? And what about Lieutenant Hopwood being murdered in your tent – that's what I'd call a real problem.'

'I haven't forgotten that,' said Daniel soulfully. 'I still feel guilty. Richard Hopwood died in place of me.'

'Then his sacrifice was not in vain. We need you, Dan.'

'We needed the lieutenant as well. I know he was untried but he had some fire in his belly. He *wanted* to fight the French. When they see urgency and commitment in an officer, the men respect him all the more. Richard Hopwood will be mourned.'

'Do you think we'll ever find his killer?'

'We must,' replied Daniel. 'It's a sacred duty.'

'It will be like finding a pin's head in a cart-load of hay.'

'I have a feeling it will be a lot easier than that, Henry.'

'We'll never see Will Curtis again.'

'He'll be back one day. If he's clever enough to get inside our camp the way he did, he won't give up. Sooner or later, he'll make a second attempt at killing me.'

'Why?'

Daniel smiled. 'I'll remember to ask him before I shoot him.'

'Take care, Dan,' said Welbeck with gruff affection. 'If anything happened to you, I'd miss you a lot. You're an ugly bugger but I'd still prefer to see your head staying on your shoulders.'

'Thank you.'

'I must go. Bear in mind what I said.'

'Do the same for me,' said Daniel. 'Remember what I said about imparting confidence to the men. Glow with optimism, Henry. We could be on the verge of a tremendous victory.'

'Oh, I agree,' said Welbeck gloomily. 'But will either of us still be alive to celebrate it?'

Daniel watched him go, knowing full well that his friend would not pass on his private fears to his men. Soldiers drilled by Sergeant Henry Welbeck were among the best-disciplined in the British army. Daniel knew they would acquit themselves well in combat. How the Dutch, Danish, Prussians, Italians, Austrians and other nationalities in the allied force would behave in action was an open question. As he considered it, Daniel's eye fell on the new arrivals. Like the main army, they had made the long and arduous journey from Holland. They looked exhausted and bedraggled.

Two wagons rolled in at the rear of the column and came to a halt. Daniel could not understand why they had sought out the British section of the camp instead of that of their countrymen. The answer came in the shape of two female figures who were helped down from the second wagon. One of them spotted Daniel immediately.

'Captain Rawson!' she called, waving joyfully.

It was Abigail Piper.

CHAPTER EIGHT

When she came hurrying towards him, Daniel Rawson did not know whether to be pleased or disturbed by her arrival. He was relieved to see that she was alive and apparently uninjured but troubled that she would expect much more from him than he was able to give. Her face was shining with such exultation that he could not resist giving her a warm smile in return and offering both his hands. Instead of seizing them in a gesture of greeting, however, she flung herself against him and forced him into a full embrace. Watching soldiers made ribald comments and Daniel felt self-conscious.

'How nice to see you again, Abigail,' he said, gently detaching himself from her. 'I'd heard that you sailed for Holland but I never imagined that you'd catch up with us.'

'I can do anything when I set my mind to it.'

'So I see.'

'Especially when I have someone like Emily to help me,' she said, turning to indicate her maid who stood beside the wagon. 'Emily has been a saint. When I asked her to come with me, she was afraid that Father would punish her for it but she came nevertheless. I think Father will praise her for the way she's looked after me.'

'You've caused Sir Nicholas a lot of heartache.'

'That couldn't be helped.'

'He wrote to the Duke of Marlborough to tell him what you'd done. That was how I got to hear of your little adventure.'

'Oh dear!' she exclaimed. 'I was hoping to surprise you.'

'You've certainly done that, Abigail,' he said. 'When I saw those troops riding up, the last thing I expected was for you to jump out of one of their wagons. Where have you been since you left England?'

'I've so much to tell you, Daniel. It's been extraordinary. Is there somewhere we can talk in private?'

'Yes, of course – we'll go to my tent.'

'Come and meet Emily first,' she insisted. 'She deserves thanks for getting me here in one piece.'

Daniel walked back to the wagon with her and was introduced to the maid. He had glimpsed her on his visit to the Piper household in London but had spared her no more than a cursory glance. Emily looked flushed and weary. When she shot Daniel a look of intense admiration, he realised how much Abigail had been singing his praises. Behind her deference and her blind loyalty to her mistress, he sensed that Emily was a resourceful young woman, brave enough to endure the vicissitudes of travel through foreign countries and robust enough to stand guard over Abigail.

Calling a man over, Daniel instructed him to escort Emily to the area where the camp followers were accommodated. The women who trailed the army in the baggage wagons were no longer the prostitutes and slatterns of former days. Because they caused distraction and spread

153

disease, Marlborough had outlawed them from his army. In their place were the wives and women friends of the soldiers, willing to accompany their men into places of great danger and acting as washerwomen, cooks, seamstresses and, occasionally, as nurses on the way. Emily went off with the soldier, who carried what little luggage she and her mistress had brought.

As they walked together through the camp, Daniel collected many envious stares while Abigail harvested appreciative whistles and muttered words of wonder. He was grateful to take her into his tent and away from the public gaze. Abigail gazed lovingly up at him then she suddenly burst into tears.

'What's the matter?' he asked, enfolding her tenderly in his arms. 'You're safe now, Abigail. There's no need for you to cry.'

'I never thought we'd get here,' she said, biting her lip. 'Some terrible things happened to us on the way. It was dreadful. What frightened me most was that, even if we did manage to reach the army, you might not be here. Our journey would have been in vain.'

'Why not sit down and tell me all about it?'

'It's so wonderful to see you again, Daniel.'

'And it's wonderful to see you,' he said, guiding her to a stool and sitting beside her. 'Now dry your eyes and let me have a proper look at you.'

Abigail took a handkerchief from her pocket and dabbed at her tears. The exigencies of travel had left their signature on her. Some of her bloom had gone and her hair was matted and lacking its former sheen. Her cheeks had hollowed slightly, making her beauty a little ravaged. As he appraised her, Daniel could see all the things that had attracted him to her but he no longer regarded her through the eyes of a potential lover. What she now aroused were his paternal instincts. Instead of wanting her in his bed, he felt impelled to protect her by taking on the role of a father.

'It was your fault,' she said quietly. 'You were responsible for my decision to come here.'

'I gave you no encouragement to do such a thing, Abigail.'

'Yes, you did. It was when we met over dinner that night. Lord Godolphin asked you about some of your escapades and you said – I remember it clearly – that there were times when you had to act on impulse and follow your inner promptings.'

'I was talking about the heat of a battle,' he recalled, 'about decisions made in a time of crisis.'

'That was exactly my position,' she said earnestly. 'When I heard that you were leaving me, I was faced with a crisis. So I did what you advised, Daniel, and acted on impulse. I let my heart rule my actions.'

'But think of the consequences.'

'I reached you at long last and that's everything to me.'

'Didn't you consider how hurt and anxious your parents would be? They must be sick with worry – and so must your sister. The wonder is that Dorothy made no mention of your flight in her letter.'

Abigail was stung. 'Dorothy *wrote* to you?'

'Her letter caught up with me in the Netherlands.'

'But she told me that it would be wrong to write to you. In fact, she dissuaded me from doing so, saying that it would make you think less of me if I put pen to paper. Yet all the time,' she went on, anger reddening her cheeks, 'my sister planned to send you a letter herself. That was vile treachery. What did she say?'

'She simply wrote to wish me good luck,' said Daniel, hiding the truth from her. 'I can only assume that her letter was sent before you decided to sail after me.'

'Has she written to you again?'

'No, Abigail.'

'Are you sure?'

'I had one short letter and that was that.'

'Have you kept it?'

'No,' said Daniel, 'and even if I had, I'd not have shown it to you. It's private correspondence, Abigail. It has no relevance to you.'

'It has great relevance,' she said, still enraged. 'It proves what a lying and deceitful sister I have. Dorothy is not content with having her own admirers, she's trying to steal you as well.'

'That won't happen,' he assured her.

'Do you give me your promise?'

'Yes, Abigail.'

'What Dorothy did was unpardonable.'

'On balance,' he said, 'I think that it might have been better for all concerned if your sister had not written to me and if you had not pursued me halfway across Europe.'

Her face crumpled. 'Aren't you pleased to see me, Daniel?'

'I'm always pleased to see you,' he replied

gallantly, 'but I'd rather do so in the safety of an English house than in a theatre of war. You've seen the size of our army, Abigail. The French and Bavarians will throw just as many men into the field. It's simply not a place for a young lady like you to be.'

'I thought you'd be touched by my devotion.'

'I am – very touched. You've shown amazing courage.'

'Yet you wish I hadn't bothered to come.'

'I wish it for *your* sake,' said Daniel, squeezing her hand. 'If you stay with us, you'll witness the most appalling things. A lot of those soldiers we saw as we walked past just now will give their lives in battle before long. War is a cruel and repulsive business, Abigail. I want to shield you from all that.'

'But I feel perfectly safe now I'm with you.'

'We can't stay together for long. I have duties.'

'I understand that, Daniel. Knowing that we're in the same camp is enough for me.' Her eyes moistened again. 'That's all I want. Surely, it's not too much to ask.'

He was moved by her plea. Though he wanted to send her back home, he felt it would be too unkind to tell her so at that moment. Abigail deserved time to recover from her travails and a chance to enjoy some leisure, albeit briefly, with the man she adored. She would soon see how hard and unremitting life in an army camp could be for a woman. Harsh experience of the realities of warfare would be more persuasive than anything he could tell her.

'No,' he said softly, 'it's not too much to ask,

Abigail. It was a treat to see your face when you recognised me.'

She brightened at once. 'I'd recognise you anywhere, Daniel.'

'You said that terrible things happened to you on the way here.'

'Did I?'

'Tell me all about them.'

'I just want to enjoy being alone with you, Daniel.'

'You can do both at the same time,' he said. 'If you had trouble or met with hindrance, I want to know about it and so will the Duke. Everything you've done in the last six or seven weeks is important to me, Abigail. Tell me the full story.'

Bad news was a fact of life during a campaign and the Duke of Marlborough had long ago learnt to accept that. Outbreaks of disease among the troops, the late arrival of reinforcements, adverse weather conditions and a whole series of unforeseen hazards could throw the best-laid plans into disarray. Marlborough never fretted over bad tidings. He responded by taking prompt action.

'Word has come from Prince Eugene,' he said, waving the despatch. 'He doubts if he can hold the line against the French and that Marshal Tallard will out-manoeuvre him.'

'It was asking a lot of the Prince,' opined Adam Cardonnel.

'The task I set him was too formidable. Even with the Danish infantry to support him, he had insufficient men. He can pursue Tallard but lacks

158

the troops to intercept his progress.'

Marlborough was in his quarters with his secretary and his brother, Charles Churchill, General of Foot and a very experienced soldier. A handsome man in his late forties, Churchill resembled his brother in appearance and manner. He was concerned by the news.

'Tallard will be here earlier than we anticipated,' he said.

'Yes,' agreed Marlborough. 'Even though he lost so many horses on the way, he's coming through the Black Forest at a steady pace. We can only hope he'll be delayed by bad weather in the mountains and by angry foresters who have no love for the French.'

'Prince Eugene will hound Tallard but be unable to stop him.'

'It means that we have to press on hard and establish supply depots at Donauworth. Once we cross the Danube and go deep into Bavaria, our depots at Nordlingen will be too far away.'

'And it would be possible for the enemy to cut us off from our supply line,' observed Cardonnel. 'That would be fatal.'

'Where are Marshal Marsin and the Elector?' asked Churchill.

'Snug and well-defended in Dillingen,' relied Marlborough. 'They realise that Donauworth is our most likely target. The latest reports say that the town and the Schellenberg above it are being fortified by Count d'Arco.'

'Do we know what resources D'Arco has at his disposal?'

'Yes, Charles – he has veteran French and

159

Bavarian infantry at his command, together with dismounted dragoons and two batteries of guns. Bavarian militia and a French battalion have garrisoned the town.' Marlborough consulted another despatch. 'The latest estimate we have puts the force on the Schellenberg at over 12,000.'

'That's a substantial number,' remarked Cardonnel.

'The hill must nevertheless be stormed,' said Marlborough. 'If we take Donauworth, as we must, we can proceed with the next stage of our plan. I won't even entertain the notion of failure.'

'What role will the Margrave of Baden have?' said Churchill.

'We'll need him to give us close support, Charles. I had hoped that he could act independently of us but that would leave us with a shortage of troops.'

'There may be some benefit there.'

'In what way?'

'We can keep an eye on him, John.'

Marlborough gave an understanding nod. Prince Louis-William, the Margrave of Baden, was a fine soldier. He had been appointed commander-in-chief of the Imperial army in Hungary in 1689 when he was still in his mid-thirties. Victory against Ottoman forces with a two to one advantage over him had earned him the nickname of 'Turken-Louis'. He went on to take command of the Imperial armies on the Rhine. He was a valued ally, not least because of the success he had achieved against the French in the previous year. A question mark, however, remained over his loyalty. According to intelligence reports received by Marlborough, the Margrave of Baden was maintaining friendly correspondence with the Elector of Bavaria even though they were on opposite sides.

'Nobody can doubt his bravery and skill,' said Cardonnel.

'But can we trust him?' said Churchill. 'That's the point.'

'I believe that we can.'

'We have no choice,' said Marlborough, pursing his lips. 'If he's prepared to fight alongside us, it doesn't matter if he's sending *billets-doux* to Louis XIV. As long as he's not making secret deals with the enemy to betray us, we must rely on him.'

'The Emperor clearly does,' said Cardonnel.

'Yes, Adam, and he's a shrewd judge of character.'

'I still think he needs to be watched,' advised Churchill.

'He will be,' said Marlborough. 'Well,' he added, striking his thigh with a hand. 'I think we know our course of action. We'll have an early night, rise at three and press on hard towards Donauworth. With luck, we'll reach the Schellenberg before they've had time to complete the fortifications. Battle will be joined at last, gentlemen.' He smiled at the prospect. 'It can't come soon enough for me.'

Daniel Rawson was patient. As he listened to her long narrative, he did not interrupt Abigail Piper once. Her account was detailed and, from time to time, she referred to her diary so that she could give the correct sequence of events. She told him about the terrifying voyage, about her journey through the Netherlands and how she and Emily had been cast adrift at one stage. They had been caught in heavy rain, chased by outlaws and forced to sleep in a barn more than once. They were on German soil when they were rescued by the detachment of Dutch soldiers who had eventually delivered them to the camp.

'I *knew* that we'd get here in the end,' she said, beaming at him.

'How could you be so sure?'

'I'm lucky by nature, Daniel. That's how I came to meet you in the first place.'

'I certainly had good fortune when I met you,' he said fondly. 'My stay in London was brightened by our acquaintance.'

'It's more than an acquaintance, surely?'

'Yes, Abigail, it is. I look upon you as a dear friend.' She almost swooned with pleasure. 'But that doesn't stop me from being cross with you for putting your life at risk. I get paid to do that. You do not.'

She smiled dreamily. 'I simply had to come.'

'I accept that,' he said, speaking quickly before she could make a declaration that he felt would be embarrassing. 'However, the truth of it is that you and your maid acted in a way that could have proved suicidal.' He leant in closer. 'Have you told me everything, Abigail?'

'Yes, of course.'

'Are you certain about that?'

'I'd never lie to you, Daniel.'

He was not accusing her of lying but of suppressing some facts. Though she appeared to be telling him the full story of her travels, he had the impression that something was missing, some unpleasant detail that she had either pushed out of her mind or simply held back from him. Abigail Piper had been changed by the long trek. She looked at once younger and older than before, an innocent, defenceless girl with no knowledge of the darker aspects of human behaviour and a mature young woman who had entered adulthood somewhere between The Hague and the Rhine valley. Daniel was bound to wonder what she was hiding but he decided that it was not the moment to press her on the subject of painful memories.

'You must speak to the Duke,' he said.

'I'd prefer to stay here with you, Daniel.'

'He'll wish to see with his own eyes that you are safe and sound so that he can send word to your father to that effect.'

'There's no need for Father to worry about me.'

'I'd say there was every need. You left without warning.'

'I had to, Daniel,' she said. 'If I'd told my parents what I had in mind, they would have forbidden me to leave the house. Dorothy would have done everything in her power to stop me as well.'

'In some senses, they'd have been right to do so.'

'My parents might have been,' she conceded, 'but not my sister. Dorothy would have held me back out of sheer spite.'

'I'm sure that she cares for you, Abigail.'

'She does – when it suits her.'

'Well, I don't want to come between you and your sister. But she would need to have a very cold heart not to worry about you and pray for your safe return.' He crossed to the tent flap and opened it. 'Follow me. It's not far.'

'Shall I see you later on?'

'To be honest, I think it unlikely.'

'Just for a few minutes,' she pleaded.

'We'll see, Abigail,' he said, careful not to commit himself. 'Let me take you to the Duke's quarters. He'll be as thankful as I am that you came to no harm.'

She gave a strained smile and went out after him. On their way through the camp, Daniel exchanged a few niceties with her, ignoring the curious stares they attracted on the way. After introducing her to Marlborough, he left the two of them together and walked briskly towards the area where the baggage wagons had been parked. He soon found Abigail's maid, standing beside a tent as she sorted out items of clothing that needed to be washed.

'May I speak to you for a moment, Emily?' said Daniel.

'Yes, sir,' she replied, flustered by his sudden appearance.

'Your mistress is with His Grace, the Duke of Marlborough. She's been telling me about the adventures you had along the way.'

'Miss Abigail was very brave.'

'I fancy that you showed just as much bravery, Emily.'

'I did what I had to do, Captain Rawson.'

Emily Greene had lost weight during the many

164

weeks they had been in transit. She still had the same homely appearance but her flabby cheeks and plump body had shrunk slightly. The maid had aged visibly as well. Abigail Piper had had a vision of her beloved to beckon her on. Emily had been driven by loyalty to her mistress. It was a loyalty that Daniel took into account. The woman would never volunteer information about Abigail that she felt was confidential. Daniel had to be tactful.

'What was the most enjoyable part of your journey?' he asked.

'Getting here alive, sir,' she replied.

'Yes, you had one or two uncomfortable moments, I hear.'

'They're all in the past now – thanks be to God.'

'Miss Abigail was telling me about an inn you left in the middle of the night. You must have been desperate to do that.'

'We could not stay there, sir.'

'So I gather,' said Daniel, who had not been told the real reason for their abrupt departure and felt it was one of the things that Abigail had deliberately kept from him. 'Miss Abigail told me all about it.'

'She talked about it for days afterwards.'

'That's understandable. It must have been a shock to her.'

'It was more than that, Captain Rawson,' said Emily, believing that he already knew the full details. 'The man had been so nice to us when he let us ride in his wagon. The last thing Miss Abigail expected was that he would come to her

165

room at night and force himself upon her. I got to her just in time.'

'She's eternally grateful, Emily.'

'I couldn't believe what had happened.'

'Is this the man who was travelling with the body of his wife?'

'That's right, sir,' said Emily. 'His name was Otto but I called him a lot of other names that night – God forgive me! Miss Abigail is young and unused to the ways of the world. It frightened her that such people could exist. She said that she'd be too ashamed to tell her parents that she'd been molested like that.'

'I can imagine.'

'She's a devout Christian – and so am I. We know what the Good Book tells us, sir. Only one person ever has the right to such favours.' She smiled shyly. 'Miss Abigail is saving herself for her husband.'

Daniel swallowed hard. As a serving soldier, his duties took him all over Europe and he had never considered marriage because he would be away from a wife for long periods. Marriage would also inhibit his private life and he was not yet ready to sacrifice that at the altar. Abigail, however, after meeting him only three times, had already chosen him as her future husband, revealing the depth of her feeling by embarking on a pursuit of him. Guilt welled up inside him. Always pleased to arouse admiration in a beautiful young woman, he was wounded by the knowledge that, in Abigail's case, infatuation with him had almost led to rape by a drunken stranger.

Striding back to his tent, Daniel had much food

for thought.

They followed the Confederate army as it moved south, keeping a few miles to the rear of it. The chances of Charles Catto being spotted by someone he met during his fleeting enlistment in a British regiment were remote but he nevertheless took pains to alter his appearance. Having discarded his uniform, he wore nondescript attire and grew a beard that changed the whole shape of his face. Frédéric Seurel was the same surly and unprepossessing individual as before. Travelling over muddy roads and being soaked by rain day after day had not improved his temper. As they searched for shelter that afternoon, he was gloomier than ever.

'How ever will we get to him again, Charles?' he asked.

'There has to be a way.'

'I think we should forget the whole thing.'

'Then you had better make your will,' said Catto, 'because General Salignac will have you hunted down and killed for failing to obey his orders.'

'I had no orders from him. You were given the assignment.'

'I told him that you would assist me. He wanted to know your name and be assured that you could do as you were told and keep your mouth shut. There's no escape from this, Frédéric.'

'But we've been trailing Captain Rawson for two months.'

'Yes,' said Catto with a reproachful glance, 'and we had the perfect opportunity to kill him until

167

you bungled it.'

Seurel felt unjustly accused. 'How was I to know that someone else would be in that tent? Anyway,' he went on, 'I did show you how quickly I could kill a man and take off his head. When I get close enough to Captain Rawson, I'll have him dead within seconds.'

'Make sure it's him next time.'

They rode on through a copse and came out the other side to see a wayside inn ahead of them. Catto stretched his arm to point.

'That's where we'll spend the night,' he said. 'It's a pity we can't lure the captain there. If we could separate him from the army, we'd have a much better chance of killing him.'

'Why don't we send him an invitation?' asked Seurel, grinning.

'We might just do that – though not in the way you think.'

'You mean we set a trap?'

'I mean exactly that,' Catto told him. 'And there's one advantage to our long journey. I know we've spent many weeks in the saddle but we're getting closer to General Salignac all the time. His orders were to leave Paris and lead his men to Bavaria where he was to join up with the Elector. In other words, he's not all that far in front of us.'

'Are you going to make contact with him?'

'Not until our job is done, Frédéric.'

'We could use more money.'

'We won't get a single franc from the general unless we can prove that Captain Daniel Rawson is dead. And we must make sure that we're the ones who kill him.'

'Must we?' said Seurel.

'Yes – if the captain is shot dead in battle, we will have failed. That's why we must get to him first, Frédéric,' he said. 'So keep that dagger of yours as sharp as a razor.'

The Duke of Marlborough opened a satchel and took out the letter before handing it to Abigail Piper. They were in his quarters.

'What's this, Your Grace?' she asked.

'It's a letter from your father,' he explained. 'It was enclosed with the last missive he sent to me. Should you ever reach us, he implored me to give it to you and to make sure that you read it.'

Abigail looked uneasy. She could imagine what her father had written and did not want to face any recriminations. There had been several moments during her travels when she had thought wistfully of the comforts of home and she had suffered pangs of remorse about the way she had fled from London without informing her parents where and why she was going. It had not taken Sir Nicholas Piper long to find out that she and Emily had boarded a ship for Holland. From that discovery, it was clear what her motives were.

Marlborough watched her closely. Though he had given her a cordial welcome and treated her with unfailing kindness, he was not pleased to see her in the camp. With a battle in the offing, he did not want to be distracted by the problems of the Piper family. At the same time, he had a duty of care to the daughter of an old friend. Abigail was

169

hesitant. Marlborough provided some encouragement.

'It's your father,' he said gently. 'Read what he has to say.'

'I'll look at it later,' she decided.

'I only have your word for that, Abigail. When I write back to him, I want to be able to assure him that I actually saw you open his letter. Go on – what are you afraid of?'

'I don't know, Your Grace.'

'You can't disown your own father, Abigail.'

Mastering her reluctance, she opened the letter and read the looping hand of Sir Nicholas Piper. Her father began by telling her how much he loved her and begged her to return as soon as possible. There was no word of condemnation or even of mild criticism. Instead, he had made a conscious effort to understand what she had done. He did not, however, hide the pain inflicted on the family. Abigail quailed as she learnt that her mother had been so shocked that she had required treatment from her physician. By the end of the letter, Abigail was so affected that she was even prepared to believe her father's assurance that her sister, Dorothy, had sent her love and her best wishes.

'There,' she said, lower lip quivering with emotion, 'you may tell Father that you bore witness to my reading it.'

'And what is your response, Abigail?'

'I will need to study it again in private, Your Grace.'

'As you wish,' said Marlborough, 'though I think I can guess the plea that it contains. In making this astonishing journey, you have more than proved your love and your courage but this is as far as you can go. You must see that.'

'Please don't force me to leave!' she cried.

'I'm not forcing you, Abigail, I'm simply inviting you to travel back to The Hague with more speed and less danger than you met on your way here. I send despatches every day to the States-General. Why don't you and your maid accompany the next messengers?'

'We've only just got here.'

'Then you achieved your objective,' he pointed out. 'You caught up with Captain Rawson and left him in no doubt about your feelings for him. He will have been mightily impressed. When he returns to England, as he will in due course, I'm sure that he will call on you at the earliest possible opportunity.'

'But that could be several months away.'

'The time will pass very quickly.'

'Each day will seem like a week,' she said plaintively. 'You must understand my position, Your Grace. I didn't travel halfway across Europe to be packed off home immediately.'

'You've arrived at an inopportune moment.'

'Emily and I will not be in the way, I swear it.'

'That's not the point at issue, Abigail.'

'Then what is, may I ask?'

Marlborough chose his words carefully. 'We're on the eve of battle,' he explained, 'and that means we shall enter the realm of the unknown. Nobody can predict what will happen. The one certainty is that a large number of our men will lose their lives or receive hideous wounds. No woman should have to look on such sights.'

'That's exactly what Daniel – Captain Rawson – told me but I am more robust than I look. I won't faint at the sight of blood, Your Grace. In any case, the baggage wagons will be well away from any action, surely. We'll be completely safe.'

'It's not your safety that concerns me, Abigail.'

'What else is there?'

'Your pain,' he said, speaking as softly as he could, 'your grief, your sense of being cheated by Fate. To speak more plainly, I think you should leave the camp before we close with the enemy in order to spare yourself what might – and I put it no higher than that – be a tragedy for you. I feel it would be far better for you to receive news of it at home where you'd have family and friends to comfort you.'

'Why should I need comfort?' said Abigail in bewilderment. 'I came here simply to be close to Captain Rawson. That fact gives me all the comfort I require.'

Marlborough was moved by the love in her eyes and the pride in her voice but he did not feel it right to conceal the truth from her. If she was determined to stay, she had to be prepared for disaster.

'Do you know what a Forlorn Hope is?' he said.

'Yes, of course, Your Grace.'

'Then you know how dangerous it is.'

'Captain Rawson told us about a Forlorn Hope that he once led. It was very successful and it earned him a commendation from you. It may have cost lives but it achieved what it set out to do.'

'Unhappily, that is not always the case.'

'It is whenever Captain Rawson is involved,' she asserted. 'I've never met anyone as daring as him.'

'He's a remarkable soldier, I have to agree. But he is a realist, Abigail. He knows that anyone who takes part in a Forlorn Hope is going to look into the very jaws of death.'

She became anxious. 'Why are you telling me this?'

'We will shortly be attempting to storm a fortified hill near Donauworth,' he said seriously. 'We believe that there may be as many as 13,000 French and Bavarian soldiers defending it. Heavy casualties are therefore expected. The assault will be led by a Forlorn Hope.' He paused for a moment then broke the news to her. 'Captain Rawson has volunteered to be part of it.'

Abigail was rocked by the news. At the very moment when she had finally been reunited with her beloved, he was about to take the most enormous risk on the battlefield. Having journeyed from England with thoughts of marriage to Daniel Rawson, she now feared that she might instead soon be attending his funeral.

CHAPTER NINE

When they reached the inn, a small but well-kept establishment beside the only road in the area, Charles Catto went in alone to make sure that no Confederate soldiers were there. He had a good

173

command of German and learnt from the landlord that the huge army had marched past that
morning. It was therefore safe to take a room
there. Catto and Frédéric Seurel ate a tasty meal
at the inn before setting out to do some recon-
naissance. The camp was some distance away and
they got within half a mile of it before they dismounted and concealed their horses behind some
bushes. They approached on foot. Both having
served as soldiers, and often taken part in surprise
attacks, they knew how to move with stealth.

Since Catto had already been inside the camp
at the earlier site, he was aware of its likely
deployment and of the position of its pickets. The
landscape favoured them. Though the camp was
set on a plain beside a stream, it was surrounded
by undulating ground that was generously
sprinkled with trees and shrubs. There was thus
plenty of cover. Leading the way, Catto chose to
stay on the opposite bank of the stream from the
camp. In case they were spotted, he decided, it
was wise to have the fast-running waters hamper-
ing any pursuit. As they crept furtively on, they
eventually found a vantage point.

'What can you see?' asked Seurel.

'Be quiet!'

'Let me have a look, Charles.'

'Wait your turn,' said Catto, lying full length as
he trained his telescope on the camp. 'This is no
use to us at all,' he soon added. 'We'll have to
move so much farther on.'

'Why is that?'

'All I can see are Dutch uniforms, as dull as the
people who wear them. The British contingent

must be somewhere ahead.'

'How will we pick out Captain Rawson's regiment?'

'It will have pitched its tents close to its colonel – the Duke of Marlborough. If we're lucky, we may get a sighting of his coach. That will tell us that Rawson is not far away.'

'I never travelled in a coach when I was a soldier,' grumbled Seurel, 'or even on horseback. I had to walk every foot of the way.'

'You were never a commander, Frédéric.'

'I never wanted to be.'

'Neither did I,' said Catto. 'I work best in the shadows. Instead of moving battalions about like pieces on a chessboard, I'd rather do my killing alone on the fringes of a battle.'

'I always liked a bayonet charge,' said Seurel nostalgically. 'I loved that look of despair in a man's eyes when I stabbed him in the stomach and spilt his guts on the ground.'

'There'll be no bayonet charge this time, Frédéric. All we will need is a thrust of a knife or a shot from a pistol. We simply have to contrive a way to get Rawson within range of one or the other.'

'I'll strangle him with my bare hands, if you wish.'

'We have to find him first.'

'See if you can pick out his regiment.'

'I will,' said Catto, moving off. 'Stay low and follow me.'

Daniel Rawson could not deny her. Though he had wanted to discuss with his fellow-officers the battle that loomed ahead, he could not ignore Abigail Piper. In response to her entreaty, he agreed to spend some time with her, feeling that it would be better to do so away from the prying eyes and waspish tongues of the soldiers. After conducting Abigail to the edge of the camp, he walked along the bank of the stream with her. The sky was overcast and the grass still damp from an earlier shower but the place seemed idyllic to her. She was alone with the man she idolised, a military hero resplendent in his uniform.

'What did His Grace, the Duke, say to you?' he asked.

'He was very considerate and very charming.'

'He always is, Abigail. He has impeccable manners.'

'I felt so nervous,' she confided, 'being with the captain-general of so large an army. I was flattered that he could even spare a few moments to see me.'

'He and your father have been in correspondence,' said Daniel, 'so he takes an almost parental interest in you. I daresay that he passed on a message from Sir Nicholas.'

'He did more than that, Daniel. Father had enclosed a letter for me, beseeching me to return home as soon as I could. The Duke offered me an escort back to The Hague.'

'In your position, I'd accept that offer gratefully.'

'And I may do so in time,' she said. 'But I'm not going to leave almost as soon as we've met. I'd feel as if I were deserting you.'

'That's a ridiculous idea!'

'I want to be *near* you, Daniel.'

'I appreciate that,' he said, 'but you must realise how impossible that ambition is. French and Bavarian soldiers are ahead of us, ready to prevent us from seizing a town that controls a crossing over the Danube. Marshal Tallard is following with a sizeable army, trying to catch up and attack us. All my thoughts must be concentrated on war, Abigail. Much as I relish your company, you are a diversion.'

'An agreeable diversion, I hope.'

'That's what makes it worse – you're a temptation.'

'I promise to stay out of your way,' she said, 'as long as you remember that I'm here, thinking about you and wishing you well.'

'Thank you.'

'Don't send me away, Daniel.'

'I've no power to do so.'

'And tell me – just once – that you are glad to see me.'

'I am very glad,' he said with a smile, 'not least because I was concerned for your safety. There's only one problem.'

'What is that?'

'I must forego the pleasure of your company, Abigail.'

'For the time being,' she added hopefully.

Daniel touched her arm. 'For the time being,' he said.

They walked on in silence, listening to the birds and watching the water ripple and surge. The sun made an effort to peep through the clouds but it was thwarted. Abigail savoured every moment of it. There had been times during their gruelling journey when she feared she might never see Daniel Rawson again. To enjoy a leisurely stroll in the country with him – even though it was on the eve of a battle – was the fulfilment of a dream.

Frédéric Seurel was restive. They had spent an hour or more hiding behind trees and crawling through bushes. It had all been in vain. Even with the aid of his telescope, Charles Catto had been unable to identify the Duke of Marlborough's regiment. Seurel was a man of limited patience. He soon began to protest.

'This is hopeless, Charles,' he said, swatting away an insect that landed on his face. 'The longer we stay, the more chance there is that we'll be seen by some of the pickets.'

'If we keep well-hidden, we're safe.'

'I'm fed up with lying on the ground.'

'How else can we keep the camp under surveillance?'

'I think we should get ahead of them tomorrow and watch out for Captain Rawson as they march past.'

'And then what?' asked Catto irritably. 'We can hardly ambush an entire army. You do make the most stupid suggestions, Frédéric.'

'I hate trailing after them for week after week. If we overtake them, there's a faint chance that we may find Rawson off guard at some point. We can try to separate him from his regiment.'

'We need to do that now, while he's in camp.'

'You keep saying that.'

'I've had more experience of stalking than you,'

said Catto, sitting up to stretch himself. 'I know how to wait, watch then strike when the right moment finally comes.'

'In this case, it may never come.'

'It already has come once, Frédéric.'

'Stop harping on that,' said Seurel testily.

'We had him at our mercy and you let him go.'

'It wasn't deliberate.'

'That doesn't make it any the less annoying.'

'I've never let you down in the past, Charles.'

'No,' conceded the other, 'that's true. It's the reason I chose you. I needed someone who thought and acted like a soldier, someone who could kill quickly and ruthlessly.'

'I've done that enough times, believe me.'

'Captain Rawson has to die to satisfy General Salignac's desire for revenge. The more painful the death, the happier the general will be. He wants his wife and her lover to *suffer*.'

'The best way to do that is to capture him and leave him alone with me for an hour,' said Seurel with a glint. 'I know all the refinements of torture. When I was in the army, I could always get prisoners to talk.'

'We're not here to have a conversation with Rawson,' said Catto, 'and we don't have the luxury of time. All that the general wants is unmistakable proof that the captain will never be able to share a bed with his wife again.'

'What about General Salignac – will *he* share a bed with her?'

'Not until his temper cools, Frédéric. He was still throbbing with fury when we spoke. Madame Salignac had been packed off to their mansion in the country where the servants have been ordered to watch her night and day.'

'She'll have no chance to find another lover then.'

'The general has clipped her wings.'

'I need a woman,' said Seurel restlessly. 'It's been weeks now. The last one I had was that tavern wench in Coblenz.'

'Save yourself until we've finished our task,' said Catto. 'When we get paid by the general, you'll be able to afford a different woman every night of the week.' He crouched down and applied his eye to the telescope once again. 'All we need is a slice of luck.'

'We'll never get it, Charles. This chase is doomed.'

'Chance sometimes contrives better than we ourselves.'

'Yes – it contrived to put the wrong man in that tent.'

'We have to forget that and try harder.'

'You are the one who keeps reminding me of it,' said Seurel resentfully. 'You won't let me forget it.'

'I'm sorry, Frédéric. I was partly to blame. I should have come in that tent with you so that I could see if we had the right man.'

'He was a British soldier and I'm always happy to kill those.'

'You can't behead a whole regiment until you finally come to Captain Rawson,' said Catto, then his body stiffened with interest. 'Then again, you may not need to do that.'

'What have you seen?'

'Manna from heaven – I can't be sure until he gets closer but someone who looks very much like the captain is walking along the river bank towards us. Here,' he said, passing the telescope to Seurel. 'See for yourself. I told you it was only a question of waiting.'

The sky was slowly darkening as they ambled along side by side. Abigail Piper's disposition, however, was sunny. She felt restored, refreshed and cheerful. It was a moment worthy of record.

'I shall put this in my diary,' she decided.

'What?'

'This wonderful time we've snatched together.'

'It must soon come to an end,' he warned her. 'We'll have to turn back before too long. But it's been a delightful break and you're right to make a note of it.'

'I wrote something in my diary every day.'

'That must have been difficult sometimes.'

'Why?'

'You had some unpleasant experiences, Abigail. You would hardly rush to put those down on paper.'

'I felt that I had to do so. No matter how late it was – or how horrid our accommodation – I always managed to scribble a few lines at the end of the day. When we slept in a barn,' she recalled, 'Emily lit a candle and held it for me so that I could write.'

'Are you going to show your diary to your sister?'

'No,' she replied. 'Dorothy won't see a single word of it.'

'She's bound to be curious.'

'I don't care. She betrayed me by writing a letter to you after she'd talked me out of doing so. That was mean and deceitful. What right did she have to get in touch with you?' Abigail went on. 'Dorothy only met you on that one occasion.'

'I was surprised to get a letter from her, I must confess.'

'If she sends another, tear it up without reading it.'

'The only letter you should worry about is the one that your father sent. He wants you back in England, Abigail. The whole family has missed you dreadfully and you must have missed them.'

'Yes, I have,' she admitted. 'I've missed them very much.'

'Then put an end to their misery,' he advised. 'Write to tell them that you are on your way back home.'

Abigail stopped and turned to face him. Her happiness suddenly gave way to a deep fear. She grabbed Daniel by both the arms.

'If I agree to go back,' she said with a note of supplication, 'will you do something in return for me?'

'That depends what it is, Abigail.'

'Please don't take part in a Forlorn Hope.'

Daniel was mystified. 'Why on earth do you ask that?'

'His Grace, the Duke, told me that you'd volunteered to join a Forlorn Hope when you reach Donauworth.'

'It would be a privilege to do so.'

'But it's so dangerous. Doesn't that concern you?'

'I'm more concerned about your change of mind,' he said. 'At our first meeting, you were entranced when I told you about a Forlorn Hope I'd once led. You praised me for my bravery. Yet now you are asking me to do something that's quite out of character.'

'I don't want anything to happen to you, Daniel.'

'I'm a soldier, Abigail. This is where I belong. Begging me to withdraw from a Forlorn Hope is like my asking you to stop being beautiful. It's a defiance of Nature.'

'I don't want to lose you,' she said, face clouding.

'The French have been trying to kill me for years,' he said blithely, 'and they've never managed to do it so far. Why should it be any different at the Schellenberg? Don't alarm yourself unnecessarily.' He grinned at her. 'I've had a lot of practice at dodging musket balls.'

'It's not something to be laughed at, Daniel.'

'I know.'

'What happens if you're *killed* in the Forlorn Hope?'

'Then at least I'll have died with honour,' he said proudly.

Abigail's heart began to pound and her eyelids fluttered uncontrollably. Her breath came in increasingly short bursts. The thought that her happiness might be snatched away from her on the battlefield was too much to bear. Violent images flashed through her brain. Tremors coursed through her body. After letting out a low moan, she suddenly collapsed in a faint. Daniel caught her just in time. At the very moment when he bent over to grab her, a pistol shot rang out and the ball passed just above his head. It was strange. Fearing that he might lose his life in combat, Abigail Piper had just unwittingly saved it.

They moved fast. Even though he limped, Frédéric Seurel could cover the ground at speed when necessary. Charles Catto led the way, using the trees as cover and zigzagging to confuse any pursuit. They heard raised voices behind them and kept running until they were out of earshot. The only time they had to hide was when horsemen came galloping in search of them. Concealed in the bushes, they watched the soldiers ride past and took the opportunity to catch their breath.

'Have you gone mad!' exclaimed Catto, hitting his companion. 'Why ever did you fire your pistol like that?'

'I couldn't resist it,' said Seurel. 'He escaped me in that tent and I wasn't going to let him get away from me again.'

'But that's exactly what he did. You not only missed him, you roused the camp and turned us into fugitives.'

'I'm sorry, Charles.'

'You gave the game away, you fool.'

'We've spent months on his tail without even a sighting of him then he walks within range of my pistol. I *had* to take a shot at him.'

'I should never have let you bring the weapon.'

'The general wants him dead, doesn't he?'

184

argued Seurel. 'That's what we were sent to do – kill Daniel Rawson.'

'And obtain *proof* of his death,' said Catto, punching him hard once again. 'How could we do that when we were running for our lives? It's not enough to tell General Salignac that we shot him dead. He'll insist on proof that Rawson died at *our* hands and not in battle.'

'I acted on instinct.'

'Then your instincts, as usual, were wrong.'

'It was too good a chance to miss, Charles. He was there, right in front of us, unguarded, completely unaware of us.'

'He's certainly aware of it now,' said Catto ruefully. 'When your shot alerted the sentries, it alerted Captain Rawson as well. He *knows* that someone is after him now. We'll never get near him again.'

'That's why I had to seize the opportunity.'

'Seize it and *waste* it, Frédéric – for the second time.'

'I would have killed him if he hadn't bent over like that. How was I to know that that woman would faint in his arms? She's the person to blame for this, not me.'

'On the contrary,' said Catto thoughtfully, 'we may yet live to thank her. In collapsing like that at a critical moment, she may have saved Rawson but she may also have saved our skins. Don't you understand?' he went on as Seurel looked puzzled. 'If we'd gone to the general and told him that you shot Rawson but we have no evidence to prove it, he'd have thought we were trying to cheat him.'

'Wouldn't he take your word for it, Charles?'

'No, he needs proof that he can dangle it in front of his wife. He wants to torment her with the thought that she was responsible for the death of her lover. If he tells her that Rawson was shot by a hired assassin, Madame Salignac may think he's inventing the story in order to make her writhe with guilt. Evidence is crucial.'

'Then we've failed,' said Seurel miserably. 'I was too eager.'

'All may not yet be lost.'

'I'll do *anything* to make up for it.'

'There could be a way to trap him,' said Catto, 'and it will be much safer than trying to kill him in the camp. Rawson's luck can't last forever. We know his weak spot now.'

'Do we, Charles?'

'You saw her as clearly as I did. She was a pretty little thing and she means a lot to him if he takes time off from his duties to stroll along the edge of the camp with her. That's the way to get him,' he concluded. 'We have to look to the lady.'

When the shot rang out, Daniel Rawson had lowered Abigail Piper gently to the ground and lain flat beside her. His eyes searched the bushes on the other side of the stream but he could see nothing. What he could hear was the sound of feet making a hasty departure. After a few moments, sentries came running to investigate. Daniel told them what had happened and sent two of them wading across the stream. He instructed one of the remaining men to dispatch riders in search of the interlopers. Muskets at the ready, the last few sentries guarded his back as he carried Abigail to safety. When he set her down beside a tent, he dismissed the men and attended to her.

His immediate impulse had been to pursue whoever had been hiding in the bushes but he could not leave Abigail in that state. She was slowly regaining full consciousness. Her head moved and one eye opened. She became aware that she was on the ground.

'What happened?' she asked in alarm.

'You fainted, Abigail.'

'Did I?'

'Yes,' he told her, 'it's probably a result of fatigue. You've been under the most immense strain for several weeks.'

'Help me up, please.'

'Sit up first, until you feel well enough to stand.'

'How long was I lying there?' she said, as he eased her up into a sitting position. 'I do apologise, Daniel. What must you think of me?'

'I think that you need to rest.'

'I can't remember a thing.'

'Don't even try to,' he advised. 'Just get your strength back.'

He was relieved that she had not heard the pistol shot and had no intention of telling her about it. She was already frightened at the thought of his taking part in a Forlorn Hope. If she knew that he was the target for an unseen assassin as well, she would be horror-stricken. What the attack proved to Daniel was that he had been right about the murder of Lieutenant Richard Hopwood. The designated target had, in fact, been Daniel himself and the killer had returned to make a second attempt on his life. He chided himself for walking so freely in the open and for exposing Abigail to unnecessary danger as well. The bullet that missed him could easily have hit her instead.

'I'm feeling much better now,' she said, embarrassed by what had occurred. 'I do apologise, Daniel. I've never done that before.'

'Let me help you up.' Holding her under the arms, he lifted her to her feet and kept a restraining hand on her. 'How is that?'

'I'm fine now, thank you.'

'Good,' he said, releasing her but standing close in case she fainted again. 'I'm afraid that your lovely dress has some stains on it.'

'Emily will soon get rid of those.'

'I'll escort you back to her and explain what–'

'No, no,' she said, interrupting him. 'There's no need for Emily to know about this. I'd rather it was kept private.'

'Very well,' he agreed. 'Does that mean there'll be no mention of this in your diary? I thought you recorded everything.'

'We'll see, Daniel.'

'Are you able to walk now?'

'Of course.'

'Then I'll escort you back.'

Abigail was a little unsteady at first but he did not have to support her as they walked through the camp. As her mind cleared, she began to recall a few details.

'I thought we were standing by a stream,' she said.

'We were, Abigail.'

'Then how did I come to be lying beside that tent?'

'I carried you there,' he said.

'Oh, I've been such a terrible nuisance to you.'

'Not at all – I was glad to be of assistance. But I do think you need a long rest. We won't be able to meet for a while, I'm afraid. That's why these moments alone with you have been so memorable.'

'They'd be memorable to *me*, if only I could remember them.'

They shared a friendly laugh. Daniel chatted with her all the way back but his mind was elsewhere. His memory was not impaired. What he remembered most vividly was the failed attempt at killing him. As he had predicted, the assassin had come back.

The Confederate army set out at 3 a.m. on July 2, 1704. After a long, tiring, demanding march over muddy roads, they arrived to find that Marshal Marsin and the Elector of Bavaria had, as earlier reports had indicated, occupied the fortified town of Dillingen with the major part of their army. Though a smaller force of over 13,000 soldiers guarded the Schellenberg, it was still a forbidding sight on its elevated position. Frantic efforts to strengthen the dilapidated defences of the hill were in progress and, more worrying to Marlborough, was the fact that an encampment for a large army had been laid out on the south bank of the Danube. Once that was filled with French and Bavarian soldiers, supplemented by the reinforcements on their way, any crossing of the river would be virtually impossible.

Count Jean d'Arco, commanding the force on the Schellenberg, was a Piedmontese soldier with a reputation for brilliance in the field. Though he was surprised by the sudden appearance of the enemy, he was relieved to see quartermasters marking out formal lines for a camp with a series of stakes. The army needed rest. Exhausted from their march, he reasoned, they would have neither the strength nor will to launch an attack until the following day. D'Arco and his senior officers therefore went off to dinner in the town without the slightest qualms. Confident that they would not require their weapons that evening, no fewer than ten battalions of Bavarians had crossed the pontoon bridge from the south bank of the Danube without their muskets.

They had all been tricked by Marlborough. He had quickly assessed the situation. To attack on the following day would be to give the enemy more time to fortify the hill, making it more difficult to storm and increasing the likely number of casualties in Confederate ranks. Marlborough therefore elected to attack at once, a decision that was strongly opposed by the Margrave of Baden who feared that a frontal assault would result in heavy losses. He was overruled by Marlborough who was ready to bear such losses if he could achieve his aim of securing a crossing on the Danube.

The Duke's Wing – with Captain Daniel Rawson part of it – had been leading the march and so was closer to the town than anyone else. They supplied the troops for the main assault. It

190

was led by 5,750 stormers, drawn from the grenadier companies and volunteers from every battalion in the Allied army. Since artillery would be vital, Colonel Holcroft Blood set up a battery between the outlying village of Berg and the foot of the Schellenberg. They were supported by an Imperial battery, sent forward by Baden. The Kaiback stream made the ground boggy and it took time to manoeuvre all the pieces into position. Marlborough had had to leave his heaviest artillery back in Flanders but still felt that he had enough to carry the day.

The attack began at six o'clock in the evening with only two hours of daylight left. It was preceded by a Forlorn Hope. Commanded by Lord John Mordaunt and drawn from the 1st English Foot Guards, it consisted of eighty courageous soldiers ready to defy death as they drew the enemy fire so that their generals could determine where the defences were strongest. Daniel Rawson had joined the Forlorn Hope, undeterred by the fears of Abigail Piper and feeling the familiar buzz of excitement as they went forward at a brisk pace. When he glanced at Lord Mordaunt beside him, he was amused to recall that the man had once nursed vain ambitions of becoming Marlborough's son-in-law.

The stray thought flew out of Daniel's mind as quickly as it had entered it. All his attention was needed for the fight. Like his comrades, Daniel was carrying a fascine, a bundle of tightly packed branches cut from the trees of the Boschberg by the dragoons. They were to be cast into the ditches in front of the breastworks so that they would be easier to cross. As they charged on, shouting and cheering at the top of their voices, many of the men hurled their fascines into the sunken lane at the bottom of the hill where they would be of little use. Daniel and a few others kept theirs until they reached an entrenchment farther up the hill.

The enemy had been outwitted. D'Arco and his officers came running back to take command of their men while the Bavarian battalions scrambled back across the pontoon bridge to retrieve their weapons from the camp. Even before the first shot was fired, the noise was deafening as the attackers yelled 'God save the Queen!' and, on a signal from their officers, broke ranks to charge at full speed. The Forlorn Hope was a mere eighty paces away when the Bavarian Electoral Guards and the Grenadiers Rouges unleashed a fierce volley that killed or wounded dozens of the attackers. Daniel was knocked helplessly to the ground as the soldier next to him was hit by three simultaneous musket balls and thrown sideways by the force of the impact.

The Schellenberg was a bell-shaped hill with a flattened top on which the French troops were ranged. The first artillery bombardment from Colonel Blood and his men wreaked havoc on the summit but went harmlessly over the heads of the Bavarians on the lower slopes. It left them free to repulse the first attack with raking fire that had British and Dutch soldiers crashing down on all sides. Daniel was dismayed to see General Goor, leading the Dutch troops, cut down by the enemy. Resounding volleys of musket fire were supported by fearsome canister shot from the battery on the hill. When they saw the attackers retiring, the Bavarian guards charged down the hill to harry them with the bayonets at the ready. Daniel had to slash away with his sword to keep them at bay.

He killed one man with a thrust then hacked two more to the ground before falling back with the others towards a sunken road, fifty yards from the ramparts, that gave them moderate cover. Only steady and disciplined fire from the English Guards and from Orkney's Regiment stopped the Bavarians continuing their charge. The hail of bullets beat them back behind the fortifications. After re-forming in the sunken road, the Confederate army stormed back to renew their assault, only to be met by another burst of deadly fire from muskets and another pounding from artillery. Corpses lay in heaps everywhere. Daniel had to climb over fallen soldiers to go forward then use some of the human mounds as shields when the volleys rang out.

Marlborough already had some idea of the troop disposition of the enemy from a corporal who had deserted from the Schellenberg. The early stages of the battle confirmed what the captain-general had been told. Defences were stout at the point of attack but there had to be weaknesses elsewhere. Marlborough sent an officer to survey the defences that linked the fort with the town of Donauworth. The report that was brought back was encouraging. The line of gabions – wicker baskets filled with stones – was completely unoccupied. The Regiment de Nettancourt, the French troops guarding that particular area, had been assigned elsewhere, leaving D'Arco's position exposed on the left.

It was time to bring the Margrave of Baden and his Imperial Grenadiers into the battle. Baden hurried his men along the bank of the Kaiback stream, out of range of any musket fire from Donauworth. There followed a steep climb up grassy slopes made treacherous by the light rain that was falling. When they reached the abandoned gabions, they attacked the French in their flank so that D'Arco and his men were put under fire from two directions. The Regiment de Nettancourt bore the brunt of the attack and, along with the French dragoons who came to their aid, resisted bravely but they were unable to withstand it for long. They were soon overwhelmed.

Seeing that their comrades were in difficulties, the four battalions defending the town fired ineffectually at Baden's men yet made no attempt to come out and fight them. The Electoral Guards and Grenadiers Rouges had fought gallantly against the initial onslaughts but they could not cope with an attack on their flank as well. As the remorseless advance continued in front of them and to their side, they lost their nerve and ran for their lives. Daniel Rawson joined the murderous chase. Having seen so many friends of his mercilessly cut down by enemy fire, he would give no quarter.

So many French and Bavarian soldiers hurtled madly across one of the pontoon bridges that it broke under the combined weight and tossed everyone into the water. Scores of them who could not swim were drowned in the Danube and many of those who did strike out for the south bank were picked off by Confederate musketry. It was a scene of absolute carnage. To complete the rout, Marlborough let loose his cavalry, and his remounted dragoons, in hot pursuit of the fleeing enemy and the fugitives were systematically hacked to death by flailing blades.

The Schellenberg had been successfully stormed but the Allied army had paid a high price for the victory. Over a quarter of the strong assault force – 1500 soldiers at least – had lost their lives. To set against such losses were important gains. Some 9000 of the garrison had been killed or taken prisoner. Also captured were 15 pieces of cannon, 13 colours and a large quantity of ammunition, weaponry, tents, baggage and camp utensils. In his haste to escape, Count d'Arco had left behind his plate and other rich booty. It was distributed among the victorious soldiers.

It was not until the fighting was over that Daniel realised how bruised and bloodied he was. One musket ball had grazed his cheek and others had ripped through his sleeve. While parrying one bayonet thrust, he had received a glancing blow from another that split open the back of his coat and left him with a gash that oozed blood. His whole body was now aching with fatigue and he felt as if he had been trampled in a cavalry charge. Covered in mud and in the gore of his fellows, he was nevertheless buoyed up by the sheer exhilaration of victory. The first stage of Marlborough's plan had been accomplished. They had attained their objective.

Only now, when it was all over, could he think about Abigail Piper once more. He recalled the plea she had made on the bank of the stream. She had been right to express fear about his involvement in the Forlorn Hope. It had been a communal act of sacrifice.

Of the eighty men in that first doomed charge, only ten British soldiers had survived. Daniel Rawson was one of them.

CHAPTER TEN

There was still plenty of work left for the Confederate army. They had captured the fort on the Schellenberg but the town of Donauworth remained intact and well-defended. It had to be taken because it would block the road to Vienna and stop Marlborough's forces moving deep into the rich countryside of Bavaria, threatening its towns and villages on the way. When the fleeing garrison from the hill had been hunted down by the cavalry, the remnants of the assault force regrouped to count the cost of their victory and to tend the wounded. Captain Daniel Rawson returned to take charge of his battalion. His orders were to join the attack on the town.

It had been a disastrous engagement for Count d'Arco. His corps had been utterly destroyed and many of his finest officers had been killed. When he saw that his cause was hopeless, he had fled to the town and had some difficulty persuading the garrison commander to let him in. The report that he gave to the Elector of Bavaria was laced with sorrow and apology. Though his men had withstood the early assaults with characteristic valour, they had succumbed in the end to superior numbers and a flanking movement by Baden's men.

The Elector was shocked. In the fierce engagement, his army had lost some of its best soldiers and been significantly weakened. The Elector himself was now in danger. In the interest of personal safety, he and Marshal Marsin were forced to retreat ignominiously to a fortified camp at Augsburg in order to wait for Marshal Tallard.

The Duke of Marlborough was deeply saddened by the severe losses he had sustained but accepted that they were an unfortunate necessity. Having seized the initiative, he was quick to press home his advantage. He knew that, before quitting the town, the enemy would try to lay waste to Donauworth so that its usefulness as a base for the Confederate army would be drastically reduced. His artillery was therefore repositioned and his battalions redeployed. Throughout the evening and into the night, there was a constant exchange of fire as Marlborough's men slowly tightened their grip on Donauworth.

It fell to Colonel du Bordet to destroy the town and he ordered his men to put straw into the houses so that they could be burnt to the ground. Time, however, was against him. When reports came in that the Allied army had breached the defences and was fighting its way through the suburbs, the French colonel feared that their retreat would be cut off. An immediate evacuation ensued. Fire raged through some houses but the rest were abandoned before they could even be torched. The first thing that the incoming troops did was to help the beleaguered townspeople put out the flames. By four o'clock in the morning, Donauworth was in the hands of the Confederate army.

Daniel Rawson had been one of the first officers to lead his men into the town. Having helped to douse the fires and chase the last few French soldiers out of Donauworth, he was able to take stock of what they had actually gained by the seizure of the town apart from a strategic position on the Danube. Back in the camp, he passed on full details to his commander in the latter's quarters. Daniel still bore the scars of battle and his long red coat was scuffed and torn.

'It was an excellent haul, Your Grace,' he said cheerfully. 'We've secured three cannon, muskets, ammunition, utensils, 3000 sacks of flour and oats and everything you'd expect to find in an army camp. Most of the officers left their baggage behind as well. As for the river, we now have a dozen pontoon bridges at our disposal. The last French regiment in the town fled across one of them like frightened rabbits.'

'This is all very heartening,' said Marlborough, taking the inventory from him so that he could inspect it. 'I've waited a long time to put a French army to flight.'

'I fancy that the Bavarians can run even faster.'

'Those who escaped will be back, Daniel. When they've licked their wounds, they'll join up with Marshal Tallard and seek revenge. Talking of wounds,' he added, peering closely at Daniel's bloodstained face, 'you look as if you've picked up a few of them yourself.'

'My injuries can wait for attention, Your Grace. I was not going to leave the fray until we'd taken both the hill and the town. Besides,' he went on, gritting his teeth, 'the surgeons have enough on their hands at the moment. Some of our men have crippling injuries.'

Marlborough nodded gravely. 'The worst cases will be taken back to our hospital at Nordlingen though many may not survive the journey. I don't relish passing on details of casualties to Parliament and to the States-General in Holland,' he confided. 'Public opinion in both countries will be outraged by the size of our losses.'

'Given the situation, they were unavoidable.'

'Politicians never understand a military situation, Daniel. They view everything in terms of numbers lost and costs incurred. I'll come in for sharp criticism, especially in Holland.'

'That may be so,' said Daniel, 'but the Emperor will have the sense to appreciate the importance of this victory. The Imperial capital is now protected from French and Bavarian advance.'

'That was a major objective of the enterprise. Emperor Leopold will also be pleased to hear how well Louis of Baden and his men conducted themselves. In scaling the hill and attacking the left flank, they did us good service.'

'Your strategy was sound, Your Grace. You

struck when they least expected it. Had you postponed the assault by a day, the outcome might have been very different.'

'Either way, I would have been left with a lot of letters to write.'

'Of course,' said Daniel, taking the hint. 'I'll hold you up no longer but I felt that you might wish to include some of the details of that inventory in any correspondence.'

'I most certainly will. Before you go,' said Marlborough as his visitor was about to leave, 'I meant to ask you about Abigail Piper. Is she still resolved to stay?'

'I'm afraid that she is.'

'I did my best to persuade her to return home.'

'So did I, Your Grace, but she's an obstinate young lady.'

'Love can instil the most extraordinary tenacity.'

'True,' said Daniel, 'but even her tenacity might wilt if Abigail knew that I came very close to dying right beside her. It seems that I'm fighting a war on two fronts.'

He told Marlborough about his stroll along the bank of a stream with Abigail and how she had saved him from being shot by fainting in his arms at the critical moment. Marlborough was aghast.

'Why didn't you tell me this before?' he asked.

'You were preoccupied with other matters, Your Grace. I'm not vain enough to think that my personal problems take precedence over the storming of the Schellenberg and the capture of the town. When you are concerned with the deployment in battle of thousands of men, the troubles of one are immaterial. In any case,' he continued with a grin, 'I've long believed that I have a staunch friend in heaven. If I can survive that Forlorn Hope with only a few scratches, I have no worries about a lone assassin.'

'You should do, Daniel – he may strike again.'

'I hope that he will.'

'Have men about you at all times.'

'From now on, I'll have eyes in the back of my head.'

'Whoever he is, this man is clearly determined to kill you.'

'I'm equally determined to take his life first.'

'And you say that Abigail is not aware of this attack on you?'

'No, Your Grace,' said Daniel. 'And there's no reason why she should be. She's had to face enough shock and upset already. The ugly truth must be kept from her.'

Abigail Piper turned pale when she heard the news. She made Emily Greene repeat the details again. Abigail was dazed.

'Where did you learn all this?' she asked.

'I spoke to a woman whose husband was on sentry duty at the time,' said Emily. 'He heard the shot and ran to see who had fired it. He saw you lying on the grass beside Captain Rawson.'

'I fainted. It seems that Captain Rawson caught me.'

'At first, the sentries thought that you'd been shot,' said Emily, 'but the captain explained what had happened. He sent two men across the stream and ordered a search party on horseback.'

'Did they find anyone?'

'No, Miss Abigail.'

'Who could have done such a terrible thing?'

'They have no idea.'

'I could have been *killed*,' said Abigail, shuddering at the idea.

'I don't think the shot was aimed at you, Miss Abigail. The target was Captain Rawson. With respect, you would be no loss to the army but the captain would. According to the woman, her husband was certain that the attacker was trying to kill a British officer.'

Abigail gasped. 'That's even worse!' she cried. 'I'd rather have died myself than live without him. This is appalling, Emily. I knew nothing about any of this.'

'Perhaps the captain felt that it was better that way.'

'He should have *told* me.'

'He didn't wish to alarm you, Miss Abigail.'

The suggestion did not reassure Abigail. If anything, it made her feel even more distressed. She believed that Daniel Rawson had kept the facts from her because he perceived her as too weak and fragile to cope with such grim tidings. Instead of sharing his worries with her, he had kept them to himself. Abigail had been deliberately kept in the dark and that hurt her. Daniel was under threat. Her pleasant stroll with him now took on a more sinister and disturbing aspect.

It was the morning after the battle and the two women were standing outside the tent in which they had spent the night. Most of the camp followers slept in the back of wagons or rigged up some rudimentary cover. Abigail and her maid were more fortunate because Marlborough had arranged for them to have a small tent. Though they were miles away from the battle, the women had heard all too clearly the booming of the cannon, the popping of musketry and the constant roll of drums. News of victory had been brought back but it was offset by reports of heavy losses. Abigail had lain awake all night, praying that Daniel Rawson was not among the fallen.

Already tired and distraught, she was close to despair when she was told about the attempt on Daniel's life. While she had been imploring him to withdraw from the Forlorn Hope, he had almost been killed by a sniper in the bushes. Clutching her hands tightly together, she walked up and down as she tried to absorb what she had been told. Emily took a more practical view.

'We shouldn't be here, Miss Abigail,' she said firmly.

'We *have* to be here, Emily.'

'If that's your wish, then I'll obey you as I've always done. But I've been talking to the others. They *belong* here. They know what to expect and are hardened by experience.'

'We, too, have shown endurance.'

'It's not the same,' said Emily. 'We're outsiders.'

'The other ladies have been very kind to us.'

'That's because they all pull together in adversity. They're used to supporting each other. I've been talking to some of them, Miss Abigail. Their stories are heart-breaking.'

'I know that army life can be testing.'

'It's an ordeal. You deserve better.'

'I still prefer to stay, Emily.'

'Then I'll stay with you,' said the other with resignation. There was some commotion off to their right and they traded an anxious glance. 'What's that noise?'

'Let's go and find out,' decided Abigail.

Picking their way through the tents, they came to an avenue down which a long column of wagons rumbled. Blood-curdling moans were coming from wounded soldiers brought back from the battlefield and the sound was swelled by wailing women who had just discovered that their husbands had lost limbs or had their faces shot off. Abigail and Emily were transfixed by the gruesome sight. Medical provisions were primitive and the most that surgeons had been able to do was to amputate arms and legs before gangrene set in, or to bandage hideous wounds without being able to stem the bleeding.

It was a scene of undiluted horror. Gallant soldiers who had marched off proudly into battle were now little more than bundles of bones in ragged uniforms, crying out pitifully for someone to relieve their agony. There were so many of them. The column stretched back out of sight. Abigail stood there and gaped as an endless stream of human misery went past. She blenched when she saw a man waving a bandaged stump of an arm at her and was sickened when she observed another who had lost both legs at the knees. Wherever she looked, there was some new assault on her sensibilities. It was like viewing an endless parade of corpses.

Yet she could not tear herself away. Afraid that Daniel Rawson might be part of the mournful traffic to Nordlingen, she forced herself to look into every wagon, revolted by the sight of so much blood and shocked by the fact that some of the men had already expired from their injuries. The cloying stench of death and the stink of putrifying wounds invaded her nostrils and made her retch with nausea. As she checked yet another cargo of mutilated soldiers, a skinny hand shot out and grabbed her by the wrist.

'Give me a kiss, darling!' begged a desperate man whose head and body were swathed in blood-soaked bandages. 'I need something to keep out this terrible pain.'

But even as he spoke, his strength waned visibly and he lost his grip on Abigail. His fingers fell away, leaving a bloody imprint on the sleeve of her dress. She jumped back in alarm. Emily had already seen more than enough.

'Come away, Miss Abigail,' she said. 'You shouldn't look.'

Abigail was trembling. 'I hadn't realised it would be like this.'

'Turn your back on it.'

'I have to see if Captain Rawson has been wounded.'

'If he has, you'll be told soon enough. He'd not want you to see him in the state these poor men are in. Most of them are nearer to death than life. Could you stand to see the captain like that?'

'No,' said Abigail, closing her eyes. 'It would be intolerable.'

'Then let me take you away,' suggested Emily,

205

holding her by the arm and leading her off. 'You may not think it to look at them but those are the lucky ones.'

'Lucky!'

'They survived the battle.'

'But what kind of lives do they face with injuries like that?' asked Abigail as she envisaged their bleak futures. 'And what kind of burden will they be on their wives and children?'

'Women who marry soldiers know where it may all end. If they don't have to watch their man being buried, they may well have to care for an invalid. That's their lot and they put up with it because they have no other expectation. I told you before,' said Emily, 'they belong here and we don't. I think we should go home.'

Sergeant Henry Welbeck had fought with his usual blend of skill and ferocity when they stormed the hill. Now that the battle was over, it was time for recriminations. Alone with Daniel Rawson, he felt able to express his complaints in language he would never dare to use to any other officer. Daniel's tent gave him the freedom of privacy.

'It was bloody madness, Dan!' he bellowed. 'Sending us up that hill was the worst fucking thing that Corporal John has done.'

'The end justifies the means, Henry.'

'He always used to *care* for his men.'

'He still does,' said Daniel, 'but there was no way that he could protect them yesterday. They had to be ordered into battle.'

'But why did it have to be British bloody soldiers who died? Aren't there enough Dutch and

Danish and Austrian troops to send off to their deaths? Why did we have to provide the Forlorn Hope?' he went on. 'More to the point, why did you take leave of your bloody senses and volunteer to join it?'

'I wanted to be in the thick of the action.'

'Well, you came very close to being in an early grave. I had to organise the burial details. Do you know how many of my men I saw being dropped into the ground – what was left of them, that is. Going up that hill was nothing short of suicide.'

'What else could we have done, Henry?'

'We could've had a good night's rest, for a start.'

Daniel laughed. 'Have you ever rested on eve of a battle?'

'You know what I mean, Dan. We'd marched all day. We were in no condition to give of our best. Yet that's what His Grace, the Duke of Bloody Marlborough, expected us to do.'

'I saw nobody shirking on the battlefield.'

'It was needless fucking slaughter.'

'They had far more casualties,' said Daniel.

Welbeck glowered. 'Is that supposed to make me feel better?'

'We won, Henry. That's all that matters.'

'Thank you for telling me,' said the other sarcastically.

Daniel was sitting on a camp stool but his friend was striding restlessly to and fro. Both of them had picked up their share of grazes and bruises during the battle. Welbeck had been stabbed in the arm by an enemy bayonet and the wound was heavily bandaged. He had also acquired a black eye. Daniel's face had been washed but his scars and bruises remained and his lower lip was swollen. The gash on his back had been cleaned and dressed. Now that the thrill of battle had gone, he could feel every bruise and abrasion but, in view of their victory, it was an almost satisfying pain.

'At least, you were there,' said Welbeck, stopping beside him. 'I heard that someone tried to kill you.'

'Thousands of French and Bavarians tried to kill me, Henry.'

'I'm talking about what happened in this camp.'

'Ah, yes – that.'

Welbeck was scornful. 'Listen to the man!' he said. 'Someone fires a shot at him and all he can say is "Ah, yes – that." If it had been me, I'd be furious.'

'You always are, Henry.'

'What exactly happened?'

Daniel gave him a brief account of the walk beside the stream. When he was told that Abigail Piper had fainted in Daniel's arms, the sergeant emitted a howl of contempt.

'Bloody women!' he exclaimed. 'She distracted you, Dan.'

'I should have been more careful, I agree.'

'From the way you tell it, I could almost believe she led you to that particular spot so that an accomplice could take a shot at you.'

'That's arrant nonsense,' said Daniel hotly. 'Abigail loves me. She'd rather take a bullet herself than see me killed. No, Henry, it was pure coincidence that we were on the edge of the camp like that.'

'It was no coincidence that the man who fired the pistol was there. He was lying in wait, Dan. And although you didn't see so much as a glimpse of his arse as he ran away, I reckon I could put a name to the bastard.'

'Can you?'

'Of course – it was Will Curtis, as he used to call himself.'

'You could be right,' said Daniel, mulling it over. 'He crossed my mind as well. He or his accomplice failed to kill me in this very tent so he had a second attempt.'

'He would have known how we pitched our camp and where to find the British contingent. It has to be Will Curtis.'

'But why single out *me*, Henry?'

'Haven't you worked that out yet?'

'I'm not that important to the army.'

'This is nothing to do with army matters,' said Welbeck, hands on his hips. 'You've been sowing wild oats in someone else's field, Dan Rawson. That's my guess, anyway. This is the work of some bloody woman – or of her husband, anyway. You've upset him by tupping his wife. He's after your balls.'

It was a sobering thought and it brought Daniel to his feet. Until now, he had forgotten all about Bérénice Salignac and their time together in Paris. She suddenly came rushing back into his mind, accompanied by the spectre of her husband.

It was a risk that could pay handsome dividends.

Having grown a beard, Charles Catto completed his disguise by winding a bandage around his head so that it half-covered an eye. He had kept the uniform in which he had fled the camp and put it on once more. If he were caught, he expected no mercy but then he would get none from General Salignac if he failed. Trapped between menacing alternatives, he chose the one that was at hand.

'How do I look, Frédéric?' he asked.

'Like someone I ought to kill,' replied Seurel, studying him through narrowed lids. 'What happens if someone recognises you?'

'Then he'll have excellent eyesight.'

'You're taking a big chance, Charles.'

'There's a big reward if I succeed,' said Catto. 'I'll keep well away from the men I met when I enlisted, especially that crusty Sergeant Welbeck. He's the one person who might pick me out.'

'What do I do?'

'Wait until I return.'

'And if you don't get back?'

'Then you'll know I was caught. That's highly unlikely, however,' said Catto. 'You know what armies are like after a battle. All they want to do is to rest, nurse their wounds, mourn their dead comrades and boast about what they did to secure the victory. None of them will even remember their brief acquaintance with Private Will Curtis.'

'How will you get into the camp?'

'Leave that to me, Frédéric.'

'As long as you don't kill Captain Rawson,' said Seurel with a warning growl. 'He's all mine.'

'I don't expect to get anywhere near the captain this time.'

'Then why are you going to the British camp?'

'For the best possible reason,' said Catto suavely, adjusting the bandage over his eyebrow before putting on his tricorn hat. 'I'm going to meet a beautiful young lady.'

Abigail Piper had been shaken to the core by what she had seen. To be so close to so many grotesque injuries had been a revelation to her. Tales of military heroism heard at the dinner table were always exciting but they never dwelt on the savagery and anguish of a battle. They never mentioned the consequences. Abigail felt the need to be alone. Emily Greene was happy to go off and talk to some of the other women, leaving her mistress in their tent. There was one consolation for Abigail. A scribbled note from Daniel Rawson had assured her that he was alive and well. She had gone dizzy with relief.

Perched on a stool in her tent, she now began for the first time to question her actions in sailing after the army. Daniel had given her no encouragement to do so and had seemed faintly embarrassed by her arrival. They were meeting in the wrong place at the wrong time. As long as he was engaged in the campaign, she now understood, there would never be a right time. Abigail was in the way. It was a painful truth but it had to be acknowledged. With disarming politeness, the Duke of Marlborough had made the same point to her.

She was still locked in thought when a voice

interrupted her.

'Abigail,' said Daniel from outside the tent. 'Are you there?'

'Yes, yes,' she answered, leaping up and opening the flap to let him in. 'I've been hoping against hope that you would come, Daniel.'

Expecting an embrace, she was instead checked by his battered appearance. The cuts, grazes, and swollen lip disfigured his face. A dark bruise coloured his forehead. She stepped back in dismay.

'I'm sorry that I don't look my best,' he apologised.

'I thought that you'd be unharmed.'

'It's asking too much to avoid any injury in a battle. The wonder is that I'm still standing. The Forlorn Hope was indeed forlorn. Most of my comrades were killed outright.'

'I pleaded with you not to join them.'

'I'm always going to chase glory, Abigail, and I love the sensation of leading an attack on the enemy. It sets the blood racing in a way that nothing else could.'

'I'm so glad that you came safely through the battle,' she said. 'I know that hundreds of our men died and I saw how badly wounded some of the survivors were. Had you been among them, I'd have been inconsolable.' She searched his eyes for a full minute before continuing. 'Why didn't you tell me, Daniel?'

'Tell you what?'

'About what happened when we went for that walk together.'

'I did tell you,' he said. 'You fainted and I

carried you away.'

'That isn't true. Emily spoke to one of the women here. Her husband was on picket duty and heard a shot being fired. When he ran to find out what was going on, he saw you on the ground beside me as if you were taking cover from something. The reason you picked me up,' she said, 'was that you wanted to carry me to safety.'

'Yes,' he confessed. 'That was exactly the reason.'

'So why did you mention none of this to me?'

'I didn't want to frighten you, Abigail.'

'If someone is set on killing you, I want to know why.'

'It's usually because they belong to an opposing army,' he said with a carefree smile, 'and I don't blame them for that. It's what they're trained to do. A red coat is a tempting target.'

'But when we stopped beside that stream,' she argued, 'there were other soldiers in red coats not far away. Why was the shot fired at you and not at one of them?'

'I can't answer that.'

'In other words, you won't tell me.'

'The truth of it is, I don't know.'

'You must have some suspicion.'

'Oh, I do,' he said, 'but suspicion is nothing without proof.'

'Tell me what you suspect.'

'This is not your concern, Abigail.'

'Any danger you face is my concern,' she countered, 'and since I was there at the time, I think I deserve to be told why someone fired a shot at you?'

'All that I can do is to hazard a guess.'

'Go on.'

'It's pure speculation, Abigail.'

'I'd still like to hear it.'

He collected his thoughts. 'I was in Paris a few months ago to gather intelligence,' he explained. 'That meant winning the confidence of people who would have been very angry when they learnt that I was, in fact, a spy. It's possible – only possible – that someone felt the urge to kill me because I'd betrayed them.'

'Is this the first time there's been an attempt like this?'

'No,' he admitted. 'There was an incident some while ago.'

'What happened?'

'I escaped the attacker,' he said evasively. 'And I did the same again when we took that walk. If there's a third attempt, I'll catch the man behind it. I'm on guard now.'

'This is dreadful!' she said. 'Someone is lying in wait for you.'

'There's nowhere safer to be than in the middle of thousands of armed soldiers,' he claimed, hiding from her the fact that the would-be assassin had actually contrived to get inside the camp on the first occasion. 'I have no fears for myself. My concern was for you, Abigail. What I heard was a pistol shot. It's difficult to be accurate over that distance with such a weapon. The bullet intended for me might easily have hit you instead.'

'I was so scared when I realised that.'

'There was no need for you ever to know.'

'But there was,' she retorted. 'I hate being

214

treated like a child who's too young and frail to be told the truth. Knowing the facts may hurt me but I'd much rather that than be kept ignorant of them.'

'Everything is now in the open,' he said.

'And you swear that you'll take extra care from now on?'

'I'll take every precaution.'

'Thank you, Daniel.'

Abigail was disappointed. Having fretted so long over the possibility that he had been killed or wounded in battle, she had hoped that any reunion between them would have more urgency and passion. Daniel had been profoundly altered by combat. It was not merely his physical appearance that had changed but his manner. He was still storming the Schellenberg and fighting his way over the walls of Donauworth. He was still mourning the dead. Since his arrival, Daniel had been never less than affable but never more than courteous. Even though he stood only a foot away from him, Abigail could not reach him in the way she desired. It all served to reinforce the decision that she had made.

'I've finally accepted the truth,' she said with a wan smile.

'What truth?'

'This is no place for me, Daniel. We can't be together here.'

'I could have told you that before you set out from England.'

'I had to come and I don't regret that I did so. It's taught me a great deal about you and about army life. Most important of all, I think, it's taught me a lot about myself.'

'You should be proud of what you did,' he said encouragingly. 'It took immense willpower – and a touch of folly.'

'All I can see at the moment is the folly.'

'You have nothing to be ashamed of, Abigail. I admire the spirit you've shown and I'm grateful that you had such a reliable helpmeet in Emily. I do hope that Sir Nicholas can find it in his heart to forgive her for joining you on your wild adventure.'

'He made a point of saying so in his letter,' she said. 'I've read it several times now and it always brings me to tears. Father is so kind and understanding. He knows that Emily did not lead me astray. In a sense, she's the victim of my recklessness. When we get back home, her position will be safe.'

'I'm pleased to hear it.'

'And you'll be pleased to see me go as well, won't you?'

'Pleased and displeased,' he said frankly. 'I'm happy that you are leaving a theatre of war where even fiercer fighting may soon take place but I'm sorry to see you go, Abigail. I'll miss you.'

'I'd stay if you asked me to, Daniel,' she offered gamely.

'No, no, I certainly won't do that. You've made a wise decision and I applaud it. His Grace will do likewise and supply you with an escort all the way back to Holland.'

'After the setbacks on the way here, that will be a blessing.'

'When will you go?'

'Tomorrow or the day after,' she said, 'all being well.'

'We're in enemy territory but we've scattered their army far and wide so you should encounter no real obstacles.'

'That's reassuring to hear.'

'I'll make His Grace aware of your intentions.'

'I'll hope to see him before I go,' she said. 'I know that he's very busy at the moment but I'd like the opportunity to apologise to him for popping up the way that I did. In retrospect, I can see that it was highly inconvenient for him. Also, of course, I wish to bid him a proper farewell.' Uncertainty crept into her voice. 'Will there be any chance my doing the same for you?'

Daniel was torn between desire and relief, wanting to embrace her yet glad that she was returning home. Their friendship could only ever develop in England where Abigail was in her own environment and where he had the leisure for a dalliance. On a military campaign, she was an incongruity and her presence in the camp was bound to hamper Daniel. As long as she was there, his guilt would continue to trouble him and he would feel responsible for her. Abigail was gazing up at him with large, adoring, questioning eyes.

Daniel wanted to leave her on a note of promise. Instead of taking her in his arms, he settled for leaning over and placing a gentle kiss on her forehead.

'Yes, Abigail,' he said. 'When the time comes, we'll exchange proper farewells. I'll insist upon it.' She laughed gratefully. 'Until then, get plenty of rest while you can, happy in the knowledge that you have thousands of soldiers to guard you.'

Darkness was falling as he dismounted from his horse and handed the reins to Frédéric Seurel who remained in the saddle of his own mount. The two men were in a copse that shielded them from the pickets on the fringe of the camp. Charles Catto took his bearings before turning back to his companion to issue an order.

'Meet me here at the same time tomorrow.'

Seurel was worried. 'What if you don't come back?'

'Oh, I'll come back,' said Catto with supreme confidence. 'Have no qualms on that score, Frédéric. I'll come back and I won't be alone.'

CHAPTER ELEVEN

The Duke of Marlborough was not a man to rest on his laurels. Victory had been achieved but there was no time for celebration. While the burial teams were still busy tipping corpses into mass graves, and while the army surgeons were struggling to save the lives of badly wounded soldiers, Marlborough was thinking about his next move. He had been joined in his quarters by his brother, Charles Churchill, and by his secretary, Adam Cardonnel. Evening shadows enveloped the camp. Over a glass of brandy, they conversed by candlelight.

'What news of Prince Eugene?' asked Churchill.

'There's none to speak of,' replied Marlborough. 'He's gone ominously quiet. We can only assume that he continues to bark at the heels of Marshal Tallard and his army.'

'Where is Tallard?'

'The latest despatch we have puts him at least three weeks' march away, probably more. That gives us time to establish ourselves firmly in the Bavarian heartland.'

'The Elector will be mightily upset at that,' noted Cardonnel.

'I intend to upset and harass him as much as I can, Adam,' said Marlborough. 'If we press him hard enough before Tallard arrives to support him, the Elector might realise that he would be far better off if he joined us and fought the French. I hinted as much in the letter I sent him about an exchange of prisoners.'

'Have you had any reply?' said Churchill.

'Not yet, Charles, and I don't expect an immediate one. The Elector is a slippery character. He'll want to consider all his options before he commits his thoughts to paper and even then they'll be wreathed in ambiguity. At least, we've shown him what we can do on a battlefield and it's a lesson he can't ignore.'

'It was a signal victory, Your Grace,' said Cardonnel, 'and you are to be congratulated.'

'Thank you, Adam,' said Marlborough, 'though I don't expect any congratulation from the Dutch. Opprobrium is more likely. They seem to think that wars ought to be fought without a drop of blood being spilt.'

'We'll have carping critics in England as well,' warned Churchill. 'When Parliament learns the scale of our casualties, there'll be the most unholy rumpus. Have you written to the Queen yet, John?'

'Her Majesty's letter was among the first batch sent. I simply informed her of our success and told her that Secretary Harley would lay full details of the battle before her. I sent Robert Harley a long account of the action.'

'I hope that you did the same for Emperor Leopold.'

'Of course,' said Cardonnel. 'The despatch has been on its way for hours. Word will reach Vienna before it gets anywhere near London. The whole city will rejoice at the news.'

'So they should. We've saved it from a possible invasion.'

'Emperor Leopold will be the first to recognise that, my Lord.'

'Yes,' said Marlborough. 'I look for no reproach from him. He has some insight into the nature of warfare. In order for some people to live in peace, others have to die on a battlefield.'

'What about the Margrave of Baden?' asked Churchill. 'Did you tell the Emperor how well his commander-in-chief fought?'

'I heaped praise upon him, John.'

'That may turn out to have been unnecessary.'

'What do you mean?' said Marlborough.

'It seems that Baden has taken it upon himself to sing his own praises. According to whispers I've heard,' said Churchill darkly, 'he's been claiming that, but for his intervention, the battle would have been lost. He's trying to steal all the credit.'

'That's dishonest!' protested Cardonnel.

Marlborough was hurt. 'Can this be true, Charles?' he said, blenching slightly. 'When the fighting was over, Baden was gracious enough to compliment me. I recall his very words – "I am delighted your proposal has proved such a success." And it *was* my decision to attack when we did. I discussed it with him beforehand and Baden opposed the idea vehemently.'

'I was there, Your Grace,' said Cardonnel. 'I'm your witness.'

'Why is he making such a monstrous claim?'

'We knew from the start that he was untrustworthy.'

'This is tantamount to bare-faced deceit, Adam.'

'I'd use a stronger term than that,' said Churchill, roused on his brother's behalf. 'Baden and his troops only joined the battle after we had borne the full force of the enemy resistance. You held command throughout, John,' he said. 'It was your calmness, prudence, presence of mind and readiness to strike promptly that won the day for us.'

'Baden obviously thinks otherwise.'

'Then someone should acquaint him with the plain truth.'

Marlborough smiled. 'It's we who have been forced to make an acquaintance with it,' he said wryly. 'The plain truth is that we have to be wary of all our allies. Prince Eugene will be extremely annoyed that he was not here to take part in the storming of Schellenberg and will no doubt blame me for sending him off to intercept Tallard.'

'Which he has failed to do,' remarked Cardonnel.

'The commander who *was* there – Baden – is now trying to take all the glory. That pains me more than I can say. One of the wisest pieces of advice,' Marlborough went on, 'is to know your enemies. In view of what's happened, I think it just as important to know your friends.'

Emily Greene had been delighted to hear that they would be returning to England before long. The effort of looking after her mistress for so many weeks and of sharing endless tribulations had taxed her. Being in the camp had cheered her at first because it seemed like a haven of peace. Now that she had had her first glimpse of war, however, she found the place unsettling. All that she could think about was escape.

'When will we be leaving, Miss Abigail?' she asked.

'Very soon, I hope.'

'Have we been given no date?'

'Not yet,' said Abigail. 'Captain Rawson spoke to His Grace, the Duke of Marlborough, and everything is in hand. We'll leave when there's a wagon available and an escort to take us.'

Emily brightened. 'We're to travel in a wagon, then?' she said. 'I was afraid that I'd have to ride a horse again.'

'You managed pretty well on the way here.'

'It was agony.'

'One gets used to the discomfort.'

'I'd never get used to it, Miss Abigail.'

'It's only a question of practice, Emily.'

The maid lowered her head and Abigail realised that her comment was misplaced. When they got back home, Emily would never get anywhere near a horse. Riding was a privilege from which her station in life excluded her. During their time together, the two women had grown so close that Abigail sometimes forgot that Emily was simply a domestic servant. They were in the tent where they would spend another night together. Such familiarity would be unthinkable in London. Abigail would have the luxury of a large and well-appointed bedchamber there while Emily occupied a small, bare room with two other servants.

It was a moment for Abigail to show her gratitude and affection.

'I could never have done any of this without you, Emily,' she said. 'It was the certainty that you'd come with me that made me decide to leave England in the first place.'

'I have to be honest,' said Emily. 'I'd rather have stayed home.'

'There were times when I never thought to see home again.'

'The voyage was the worst bit for me, Miss Abigail.'

'We'll have to endure it again, I'm afraid, but perhaps the sea won't be quite so rough next time. What I really want to say,' she went on, touching Emily's arm, 'is how indebted I am to you. I'll never forget the way you've helped me and kept my spirits up. When all this is over, I'll be able to reward you properly.'

'I fear that Sir Nicholas will do that,' said Emily glumly. 'Your father will reward me by throwing me out.'

'That's not the case at all.'

'I ran away with you, Miss Abigail.'

'That was my doing. I was headstrong. I've told you before that Father won't hold you responsible. He said so in his letter. He wants you to stay in our employment.'

'I wonder if he's just saying that to persuade you to go back. I'm not complaining,' Emily continued. 'I did what I did and I'm ready to suffer for it. My first duty was to you and not to Sir Nicholas.'

'Thank you,' said Abigail, kissing her on the cheek.

'It's always been a pleasure to serve you.'

'There hasn't been much pleasure so far, alas.'

'I'd do anything for you, Miss.'

'Would you?' teased Abigail. 'In that case, I'll travel in the wagon and you can ride behind.'

'No!' protested Emily. 'That would be cruel!'

'I was only joking. There may be days when *I* prefer to ride.'

'Then I'll enjoy watching you.' They began to undress by the light of the candles. Emily was curious. Before she could stop it, a question popped out. 'Are you happy, Miss Abigail?'

'Happy?'

'That we came, I mean – that we finally caught up with the army and that you met Captain Rawson again.'

'I'm very happy, Emily. Why do you ask?'

'I've no right to talk to you like this,' apologised the other with a deferential smile. 'Forget that I ever said anything.'

'I want to hear what prompted your question.'

'I was being nosey.'

'There's something behind your interest. What is it?'

Emily licked her lips before speaking. 'It's just that you've been a little strange today, Miss Abigail.'

'Have I – in what way?'

'Your mind seems to wander off somewhere. I've spoken to you a couple of times and you never even heard me.'

'That's because I was thinking about those wounded soldiers we saw. They keep coming back at me. I can see all that blood and smell that revolting stench again.'

'We should have turned our backs on it all.'

'No,' said Abigail. 'I was meant to see it.'

'No woman should ever look at things like that.'

'Many of them have no choice,' Abigail reminded her. 'Think of the wives whose husbands have been maimed or blinded in battle. Those women will have to gaze at those war wounds for the rest of their lives. I feel for them.'

'They're so brave and loving.'

Emily wanted to ask something else but she felt it would be too intrusive. Since they were both in their night attire now, it was time to turn in. Abigail got into her camp bed but Emily had to sleep on a blanket laid out on the ground. When they had both pulled their respective sheets over them, Abigail blew out the candles and plunged the tent into darkness. She then said her prayers and offered up a whole series of heartfelt supplications. When she opened her eyes again, she could sense Emily's unspoken question hanging in the air.

'Yes,' she said quietly. 'It did affect me, Emily. It affected me very deeply. Seeing all those terrible injuries and understanding what happens on a battlefield has made me look at Captain Rawson in a very different way.' There was a long pause. 'Good night, Emily.'

'God bless you, Miss Abigail.'

Years of service in the army had habituated Daniel Rawson to an early start. Though the next day was set aside for rest, he was awake before dawn and dressed before most of the camp had even stirred. Since his face was still tender, he delayed shaving until later. The weather was fine for a change and he was encouraged to take a stroll in the morning air. Mindful of what had happened when he strayed to the edge of the camp at a previous site, he contented himself with walking in the area designated for his battalion.

Tents were conjured out of the half-dark and the occasional soldier could be seen, putting a kettle of water on the fire or slipping off to the latrines. Birds were heralding dawn with full-throated song. Daniel did not begrudge his men their additional sleep. It had been well-earned. Even those who had escaped injury during the storming of the hill and the capture of the town had been exhausted by their efforts. In Daniel's opinion, soldiers who had collected minor wounds deserved an even longer rest. When they had recovered, every one of them would be needed.

He had always liked the atmosphere of an army camp. It was his natural habitat. He relished the idea of a large body of men gathered together for a common purpose that was based on a compound of bravery, patriotism and sheer physical endeavour. While the troops were at rest, there was nevertheless a sense of latent power in the camp, weapons laid aside but within easy reach of the sleeping soldiers. He could hear banter from inside a few of the tents and a lone voice was actually singing a welcome to the new day. But, in general, there was a tranquil air to the camp.

It soon changed. Daniel went around the angle of a tent to be met by unexpected danger. A figure jumped out to accost him. Arms spread wide, the man was in a menacing crouch, ready to spring. Daniel reacted with lightning speed, grappling with him as his attacker lunged forward then flinging him violently to the ground. It was only then that he realised the man was a friend of his.

'That's enough,' said Henry Welbeck, hands up high in mock surrender. 'I give in, Dan. Help me up, you big bully.'

'What were you doing?' asked Daniel, hauling him to his feet. 'I thought you'd try to kill me.'

'I've got more sense than to try that. No, all I wanted to do was to make sure you were on guard. You've had two attempts on your life already. I proved that you're ready for a third one.'

'You're getting slow, Henry. There was a time when you'd have thrown *me* to the ground.'

'I was only pretending to attack you.'

'Well, it felt real enough at the time.'

'It was meant to, Dan,' said Welbeck, dusting off his coat. 'I'm glad that nobody else is about or I could be reported for striking an officer. Mind you, one or two of the buggers *need* striking.'

Daniel chuckled. 'I can't disagree with that.'

'What are you doing up at this hour, anyway?'

'I might ask the same of you, Henry.'

'I always like to get up well before the men. It breeds respect.'

'My excuse is simple – I fancied a stroll.'

'Remember what happened the last time you did that?'

'I had no company with me on this occasion,' said Daniel.

Welbeck smirked. 'Has the lass turned you down, then?'

'If you must know, Miss Piper is going back to England.'

'Good news at last!'

'I think she found army life a little too raw for her taste.'

'Women are poison,' said Welbeck roundly, 'and the worst of it is that the poison comes in such appealing little bottles. No wonder men are led off the straight and narrow path.' He held Daniel's gaze. 'How do you feel about the lady going?'

'I'm relieved, Henry. If I'm honest, I'm delighted that she's made this decision. Miss Piper and her maid will have safe conduct all the way home. As long as she was here, I'd be worrying about her.'

'Lusting after her, more like!'

228

'That's one way of looking at it,' said Daniel with a laugh.

'It's the only way. Save your strength for fighting the Frenchies.'

'I will, Henry.'

'And those bloody Bavarians.'

'There was a time when we hoped they'd be on our side.'

'Well, they weren't on our side at the Schellenberg!' Daniel rolled his eyes. 'I noticed that.'

'So – what do we do next?'

'We await orders.'

'What kind of orders, Dan?'

'Your guess is as good as mine.'

'You're on speaking terms with Corporal John,' said Welbeck. 'You must have some inkling of what the old fox has in mind.'

'We'll cross the Danube, that's all I know. Having fought so hard to secure the crossing, I'm sure we'll make full use of it.' They walked on together. Daniel nudged him with an elbow. 'And don't you dare jump out of me like that again,' he warned with a companionable grin, 'or you'll get a lot more than you bargained for, Sergeant Welbeck.'

He had talked his way past the pickets with ease. Deliberately choosing to enter the camp through its Dutch section, Charles Catto had made his way towards the area where the British battalions had set up their tents. There was still just enough light for him to discern the different colours of the uniforms. The standard uniform was the one that he was wearing – a long red coat turned back at the lapels and cuffs to show the facings of the regimental hue. They were dark blue for the guards and royal regiments. Others were distinguished by yellow, green, white or buff. Having fought against – and occasionally served with – British regiments, Catto recognised their facings at once. He also knew that the Royal Horse Guards wore blue uniforms, as did the artillery units. It paid to know the colour of an enemy.

On that first evening, he had contented himself with finding his way around the camp and looking for the safest way to leave it. Making sure that he never went near the regiment he had joined earlier, he had slept in a large tent that was stocked with supplies captured from the enemy after the battle. Catto had risen early to eat the food he had brought with him. Daylight brought the whole place alive and there was a continuous hubbub. He walked towards the area reserved for the baggage wagons and camp followers, taking a clearer look at the disposition of the army as he did so. If he was able to pass on accurate details of the enemy to General Salignac, he would be praised and rewarded. His mission took on an extra dimension.

The hostilities had left the women with much to do. Uniforms had been torn, tricorn hats had been bent out of shape and shirts had been muddied or stained with blood. Mending and washing were going on everywhere. Catto singled out a stout woman of middle years who was sitting alone beside a wagon and smoking a clay pipe. He lifted his hat to her as he approached.

'Good day to you, ma'am,' he said politely.

'And to you, sir,' she replied.

'I wondered if I might ask a favour.'

Her jaw tightened. 'What sort of favour did you have in mind?'

'Not that kind,' he said, charming her with a smile. 'I just need someone to repair my sleeve. It got torn while we were storming the Schellenberg and my fingers are hopeless with a needle.' He stuck out his arm to display the long tear that he had made earlier. 'That and this head wound are my souvenirs of the battle.'

'My only souvenir is lying six feet under the ground,' she said morosely. 'I knew my husband would get himself killed sooner or later. They told me he fell in the first charge. Ah, well,' she sighed, 'since I've nobody else to sew for, you might as well take off that coat and give it to me.'

'Thank you – I'm happy to pay.'

'Then I'll be happy to take the money.'

While Catto slipped off his coat, she got up and reached into the back of the wagon. She returned with a little wicker sewing box and searched in it for some red yarn. Resuming her seat on the stool, she took his coat and laid it across her legs. There were plenty of people milling around. Other women were repairing uniforms or washing linen in tubs and hanging it up to dry on lines they had strung between wagons. Several men were also there, chatting with their wives or displaying their injuries to anyone inquisitive enough to want to see them.

Catto studied the scene with interest. Though he kept up a conversation with the woman beside him, his gaze wandered everywhere. People came and went but he was looking for a particular face. He had only seen it from across a stream but it had a luminous beauty that had stayed in his mind.

'I'm sorry to hear about your husband,' he said to the woman.

She puffed on her pipe. 'I'm only one of many who lost her man.'

'How long had he served in the army?'

'Nigh on twenty years,' she said, plying her needle, 'though it seemed longer. He had a taste for fighting, my husband did. That's how he come to be in the army. He was always getting drunk and hitting people, though he never laid a finger on me. The magistrate got fed up with fining him or locking him up. "If you like a fight," he told him, "you might as well serve King and Country at the same time." It's Queen and Country now, of course,' she explained, 'but it makes no difference. Fighting is fighting. His time had come.'

'I admire your stoicism.'

She looked up. 'What does that mean?'

'Nothing,' he said. 'You have my deepest sympathy.'

The woman went off into a series of maudlin reminiscences about her late husband but Catto was only half-listening. He kept his eye on every new person who drifted into sight. His vigilance was eventually rewarded. There was no possibility of mistaking her. When the young woman walked into view, she had fine clothing that set her immediately apart from all the others and a loveliness that almost gleamed. He tapped his seamstress on the shoulder.

'Who's that?' he enquired, pointing a finger.

'Oh,' said the woman, glancing up, 'she's not one of us. She only joined the camp a few days ago. We have to sleep where we can,' she went on bitterly, 'but not her and her maid. They had a tent from the Duke himself. They had everything done for them.'

'Why?'

'They say it's because the Duke knows her father. He certainly never knew mine,' she said with a throaty cackle. 'My father was hanged for stealing sheep – God rest his soul!'

'Do you happen to know her name?'

'Yes, we all know that.'

'Why?'

'We've talked to her maid, Emily. I liked her.'

'What's her mistress's name?

'It's Miss Piper,' said the woman. 'Miss Abigail Piper.'

'Thank you,' he said, thrusting some coins into her hand.

She examined the money. 'This is far too much.'

'You've earned it,' said Catto, watching Abigail bow her head as she went into her tent. 'Believe me, you've earned every penny.'

The aftermath of a battle was always depressing. Once the thrill of victory had finally ebbed away, there were practicalities that needed attention. Most of the wounded had been taken away but those with near-fatal injuries were left to die where they lay. Graves were dug by teams that worked in shifts throughout the day and into the night. Their priority was to give a decent burial to British casualties and regimental chaplains were on duty to conduct services for the fallen. It was grim, monotonous, disheartening work but it had to be done.

Enemy soldiers who had been killed had to wait their turn and infect the air while they did so. The Confederate army had already relieved them of weapons, ammunition and valuables. Scavengers from the town had come out under cover of darkness to strip them of anything that could be worn or sold. As Daniel Rawson gazed across the battlefield that afternoon, there were still hundreds of half-naked Frenchmen and Bavarians littering the ground. Burial details made up of prisoners captured in the battle were holding their breath as they laboured amid the piles of decaying flesh.

Mounted on his horse and viewing it all from a distance, Daniel could smell the pervasive reek of death. It was something to which he could never become accustomed. After offering up a silent prayer for the souls of his comrades, he kicked his heels and rode back towards the camp. A few hundred yards away were two figures on horseback. Daniel identified them instantly. The Duke of Marlborough was using his telescope to survey the battlefield. Adam Cardonnel waited beside him. When Daniel cantered over to him and reined in his horse, Marlborough lowered his telescope.

'I was watching you,' said Marlborough. 'You stayed a long time.'

'I was paying my respects, Your Grace.'

'It's only right that we should do so.'

'I lost some good friends on that hill,' said Daniel. 'I wanted to make sure they'd had a Christian burial. Birds of prey and wild animals have been at some of the bodies. I didn't want that to happen to anyone from my battalion.'

'They fought with distinction, Captain Rawson,' said Cardonnel.

'They always did, sir.'

'You set them a fine example.'

'Not everyone believes that,' admitted Daniel. 'Some of my senior officers thought it rash of me to volunteer for the Forlorn Hope. They felt that I should have been leading my battalion instead of taking part in that initial charge.'

'You did what was required,' said Marlborough gratefully. 'You helped to draw the enemy's fire and allowed me to see where their defences were strongest. My one regret is that most of the Forlorn Hope threw their fascines into the wrong ditch.'

'I yelled at them to hold on until we reached the trench farther on but my voice was drowned out by the din.'

'Mistakes are always made in battle.'

'Fortunately, they made more mistakes than we did, Your Grace,' said Daniel. 'In leaving their left flank unprotected, they gave us our opportunity. The Austrians came to our rescue.'

'They may never let us forget it,' said Cardonnel.

'Why is that, sir?'

'It seems that they were solely responsible for winning the battle. At least, that is the story that the Margrave of Baden is putting about and I, for one, find it downright insulting.'

'It's downright false!' said Daniel with feeling. 'We had already weakened the enemy considerably before the Austrians even joined the fray. Our cannon had spread chaos among the French on top of the hill and we'd accounted for dozens of the Bavarians behind the lower ramparts. Let's give credit where it's due.'

'Let's give credit where it's due,' repeated Marlborough with emphasis. 'You're our linguist, Daniel. We'll have to get you to translate that into German so that Adam can write it down and offer it to our ally, the Margrave of Baden, as a motto.' His smile was replaced by a frown. 'This battle is in the past now and we must look to the future. Towns ahead of us will already have been told that we are on the way and will be working hard to improve their defences. There will be sieges ahead.'

'Then we need heavier cannon, Your Grace,' said Daniel. 'We'll face stronger fortifications than the Schellenberg offered us. The guns we captured are no bigger than our own. What we require is a proper siege train.'

'It would have been too onerous to drag it all this way.'

'And it would have slowed us right down,' said Cardonnel.

'Besides which,' added Marlborough, 'we had assurances from Emperor Leopold that *he* would provide us with heavy artillery.'

'Does he still intend to do so, Your Grace?' asked Daniel.

'I sincerely hope so.'

'We've saved his capital for him. The French had every intention of marching on Vienna and driving him out. The least that the Emperor can do is to supply us with what we need.'

'I've made that point explicitly in all my despatches to him.'

Cardonnel was waspish. 'Let us hope that he puts more trust in *your* despatches, Your Grace, than in those from his commander-in-chief. You may be fortunate to get a mention in the latter.'

'History will judge me more fairly than Baden has done.'

'The miracle is that he agreed to attack,' said Daniel. 'Look at his military record, Your Grace. He's a master of defence. That's how he built his reputation – by sitting behind trenches and ramparts while the enemy fell to his musket fire. Mounting an attack is a new experience for him and the novelty of it has gone to his head.'

'I think you're being too kind to him,' said Cardonnel.

'Those who fought in the battle know who won it, sir.'

'That's all that matters to me,' said Marlborough. 'But let's turn to a less contentious topic, shall we?' he continued. 'I thought you'd like to know that I've made arrangements for Abigail Piper's return.'

'Thank you, Your Grace,' said Daniel. 'It's very kind of you to find time for something so trivial when you have far weightier matters on your mind.'

'I'd never regard a daughter of Sir Nicholas

Piper as trivial.'

'The word was perhaps ill-chosen.'

'Given the effect you appear to have had on the family, it would not have been surprising if both sisters had been impelled to follow you across the North Sea.'

'One is more than enough, Your Grace,' said Daniel, grimacing.

'Two would have been a case of gilding the lily.'

'That's not quite how I would have put it.'

Marlborough laughed. 'No, I'm sure.'

'When will Abigail leave?'

'Tomorrow.'

'That was quick, Your Grace.'

'I'm sending a small detachment back to Holland. Abigail and her maid can travel with them. We need have no qualms about safety.'

'I shall make a point of seeing her before she goes.'

'And so will I,' said Marlborough cheerfully. 'She's a delightful young lady who would decorate any assembly but she is hopelessly out of place on a military campaign. I'd not wish this experience on any daughter of mine, I know that. Yes,' he decided, 'I fancy that Abigail will be very happy to depart.'

Emily Greene burst out laughing and clapped her hands in gratitude.

'We really are leaving tomorrow?' she said.

'I had it from the Duke himself.'

'That's wonderful news!'

'There'll be some packing to do,' said Abigail.

'Everything is already packed. I've been hoping

for this moment.'

'Has it been such a trial for you, Emily?'

'Yes,' said the other, 'but I've tried not to show it. I feel like a fish out of water, Miss Abigail. It's been awful.' She gave a hollow laugh. 'I've learnt one thing – I could never marry a soldier.'

'You prefer to save yourself for a sailor,' taunted Abigail.

'That would be even worse!'

They were still laughing when a man's voice interrupted them.

'Miss Piper?' he called from outside the tent. 'Is that you?'

'Who is it?' she asked.

'I have a message from Captain Rawson for you.'

'Then let's hear it.'

Abigail ducked out of the tent to be met by Charles Catto with an innocuous smile. Noting the bandage around his head, she felt immediate sympathy.

'Were you wounded in the battle?'

'Yes, Miss Piper,' he replied, 'but I came off lightly. My name is Private Curtis and I have the supreme honour to serve in His Grace, Duke of Marlborough's regiment, the 24th Foot.'

'And you've brought a message from Captain Rawson?'

'He sends his compliments and asks if you would be kind enough to join him for a while.'

'I'd be glad to,' she said, a hand going to her hair as the breeze teased at it. 'Excuse me for a few moments.'

'Take as much time as you wish, Miss Piper.'

239

Abigail went back into the tent and reached for a mirror. Having heard the invitation, Emily wanted her to look at her best for the visit. She brushed Abigail's hair then burrowed in a satchel to find a bottle of her mistress's favourite perfume. Emily made several small adjustments to Abigail's dress before she was satisfied. It was minutes before preparations were complete. When she stepped out of the tent, Abigail found her escort waiting patiently.

'I'm sorry to be so long,' she said.

'There's no hurry, Miss Piper.'

'What exactly did Captain Rawson say?'

'That he was anxious to speak with you.' Catto extended an arm to indicate the way. 'Come with me, if you will.'

'Thank you.'

They walked on in silence. Abigail was so pleased at the invitation that she placed complete trust in the man who had brought it to her. It was a long walk but she was untroubled by that. It gave her time to rehearse what she was going to say to Daniel.

Eventually, they reached the tent where Catto had spent the night. He pulled back the flap and gestured for her to enter. Expecting to see Daniel Rawson, Emily went in with a broad smile of her face. It soon vanished. The only things there were piles of assorted supplies. Before she could say a word, she felt a hand covering her mouth to prevent her screaming. Charles Catto put the barrel of a pistol against her temple. His voice was low and caressing.

'I'm so glad to be alone with you at last, Miss

240

Piper,' he said, inhaling her perfume. 'Captain Rawson is delayed at the moment but I'm confident that he'll be joining us in due course.'

CHAPTER TWELVE

Abigail Piper was petrified. The pistol was only resting gently against her temple but it seemed to be burrowing into her skull. Her whole head felt as if it were on fire. Charles Catto removed his hand from her mouth but, even without the threat of death, she would have been unable to speak. Her mouth was dry, her heart racing and her brain numb. She had been taken in completely by the man's appearance and polite manner. The promise of a meeting with Daniel Rawson had been dangled in front of her and she had never questioned it for a second. She squirmed as she recalled how gullible she had been. In entering the tent so willingly with a stranger, she had stepped into a nightmare.

'Do exactly as I say,' he told her, 'or I'll have no compunction about pulling the trigger. Do you understand?'

'Yes,' she croaked.

'Good.'

Keeping the pistol levelled at her, he stepped back to appraise Abigail properly. He flashed a smile of approval that sent shivers right through her. Catto gestured at a large wooden box and she moved across to sit on it, perching uneasily

241

on the very edge. She eventually found the courage to ask a question.

'Who are you?'

'Someone who controls your destiny,' he said meaningfully.

'What do you have against me? I've done you no harm.'

'You're about to do me a great deal of good, Miss Piper.'

'Must you point that gun at me?' she said nervously.

'Not if we come to an amicable agreement,' he replied. 'If you swear to make no attempt to escape, or even to cry out, then I'll stop waving this pistol at you. Should you do either of those things,' he added coldly, 'you'll be dead within a second.' He lowered the weapon and rested it against his thigh. Abigail relaxed slightly but remained fearful. 'There now – does that feel better?'

'Yes.'

'Do I have your word that you'll keep your side of the bargain?'

'Yes, you do.'

'Thank you.' He sat down on a box between her and the tent flap, blocking any sudden dash she might make. 'Then we can make ourselves comfortable for a while and become more closely acquainted.'

'What are you going to do with me?'

'In the first instance, I shall take a stroll with you.'

'A stroll?' she echoed in surprise.

'Yes, Miss Piper. When a soldier and a young

lady are seen walking together in camp, the natural assumption is that they are husband and wife or, at the very least, betrothed to each other. In short, nobody will challenge us. It all depends on your doing exactly what you are told, of course,' he went on, holding up the pistol. 'Open your mouth to call for help and it's the last thing you'll ever do.'

Abigail was bewildered. 'Why do you wish to walk with me?'

'Any red-blooded man would wish to do that. You are positively delightful. As it happens, though, I have a very special reason for desiring your company. And I know that you enjoy an evening stroll,' he said with a smirk. 'It was not so long ago that I saw you and Captain Rawson sauntering along beside a stream.'

Abigail quailed. His comment hit her with the force of a blow and she was stunned. Words tried to form themselves on her lips but no sound came out. Catto read her thoughts.

'That's correct,' he admitted. 'I was hiding in the bushes on the other side of that stream. I watched you both for some time. But I did not fire the shot at Captain Rawson,' he emphasised. 'Had I done so, he would no longer be alive. I'm renowned for my accuracy with a flintlock pistol. Please bear that in mind.'

'Who did shoot at Daniel – at Captain Rawson?' she asked.

'It was a foolish mistake.'

'He might have been killed.'

'There was also the danger that *you* might have been hit, Miss Piper, and that would have been a dreadful loss. The person who did fire that shot has been sternly admonished, believe me.'

'Why did he shoot?'

'He acted on impulse.'

'But why aim the gun at Captain Rawson?'

'That's a private matter,' he said blandly, 'and I don't think, in any case, that you'd care to know the details. It might damage your high opinion of the captain.'

'I doubt that,' she said, showing a little spirit at last. 'Captain Rawson is an officer, a gentleman and a hero. You'll answer to him for this outrageous behaviour.'

Catto was amused. 'Indeed?'

'I demand that you release me at once.'

'You're not exactly in a position to make any demands,' he said, holding up the pistol. 'Instead of issuing orders, your job is simply to obey them.'

'Who *are* you?' she cried.

'Oh, I'm not a very interesting topic for conversation, Miss Piper. You, on the other hand, certainly are. Since we have some time on our hands before we leave, perhaps you'd tell me a little about yourself. Evidently you come from a good family,' he went on, eyes roving all over her, 'and I can hear the breeding in your voice. Tell me who you are and how you came to befriend Captain Daniel Rawson.' When she refused to answer, his tone was menacing. 'I won't ask you again.'

Though the Confederate army had stayed in their camp, they were not allowed a complete rest.

Soldiers in the British regiments were drilled on open ground. When he had fought alongside Marshal Turenne in the French army, the Duke of Marlborough had been struck by the superior discipline of the troops. It was not only by virtue of greater numbers, better equipment and more powerful artillery that they held sway over all other European armies. French soldiers had been trained and drilled to a degree that gave them a considerable advantage over their enemies and helped them to achieve a long series of successive victories. Marlborough had taken note. Among the improvements he had made to the British army was his insistence on thorough preparation.

It depended to some extent on the lungs of his drill sergeants and, as far as Henry Welbeck was concerned, his commander had no cause for complaint. Welbeck's voice rang out like a roll of thunder. Never daring to put a foot out of line, his troops kept to the drum-calls and went briskly through their routines. Daniel felt a pang of regret as he observed how many were now missing from the ranks. When they were dismissed, the soldiers drifted past him and he had a friendly word with several of them. Welbeck eventually came over to him.

'You certainly put them through their paces,' said Daniel. 'That was a most impressive display, Henry.'

'You have to drive them hard or they lose discipline in battle. We have to remember that most of these men didn't *want* to join the army, Dan. They did so under compulsion or because they had some stupid idea of being heroes. Ha!' he exclaimed. 'A lot of these so-called heroes come from the gutter or from prison. We have the dregs of London inside those red uniforms.'

'Not any more,' argued Daniel. 'You've turned them into good soldiers and responsible human beings. You converted them, Henry.'

'You make me sound like a bloody chaplain.'

'Have you never considered taking holy orders?'

'I'd sooner eat horse shit!'

'I could just see you in a pulpit.'

'Then I'd probably be setting fire to it,' said Welbeck. 'You know my feelings about religion. It's a trick played on the innocent fools.'

'I don't regard myself as either innocent or foolish.'

'And I don't you regard you as a true Christian. Oh, I know you read your Bible and attend church parades but, then, the Devil can cite Scripture for his purposes.'

Daniel grinned. 'Are you calling me a devil?'

'Well, you're certainly no angel.'

'None of us is, Henry – we have blood on our hands.'

'That's another thing,' said Welbeck. 'One of the Ten Commandments forbids you to kill. How many times have you broken that particular commandment, Dan?'

'I'm not getting into a theological argument with you,' said Daniel amiably. 'I just wanted to give you advance warning. When we've got our breath back, it seems as if we're going to cross the Danube and lay siege to Rain.'

'Why?'

'It's directly in our line of march.'

246

'That means I'll lose more of my men to the gravediggers.'

'Rain is not a big town, by all accounts. It shouldn't hold us up for long or cost us many lives. The other piece of news that might interest you is that Abigail Piper is leaving us tomorrow.'

'That calls for a celebration!' said Welbeck.

'You don't even know the young lady.'

'I know two things about her, Dan, and they both worry me. First, she's a woman. Second, she almost got you killed. Put it this way,' he went on as Daniel tried to protest, 'would you have gone walking alone outside the perimeter of the camp?'

'No, Henry.'

'Then she led you into danger.'

'Not deliberately,' said Daniel. 'Abigail was as much at risk as me so you could claim that I led her into danger.'

'You're as bad as each other. Good riddance to her, I say!'

'I'll take a rather fonder farewell than that.'

'Are you going to see her now?' Daniel nodded. 'Then I ought to come with you to stand guard. I know what fond farewells can do. I must have lost over a dozen men who went to wave off their sweethearts then never came back again.'

'There's no chance of my deserting, Henry. All that I intend to do is to wish her well on the journey. What harm is there in that?'

'Miss Piper is a woman and women are *made* of harm.'

'You malign the sex unjustly,' said Daniel, laughing at his friend's curt misogyny. 'But you

247

won't be able to grumble about Abigail for much longer. This time tomorrow, she'll be miles from here.' He set off. 'I'll see you later, Henry.'

'Make sure you come without *her*,' Welbeck called after him.

Daniel had long ago divined the source of Welbeck's hatred of women. The sergeant came from a family that consisted of a tyrannical mother and three older sisters, all of whom made his life a misery. Outnumbered and too small to fight back, he had endured the persecution until he was old enough to run off to the army. Behind his loathing of the opposite sex was a lurking fear of them. While he would readily confront any foe in battle, Welbeck was quietly terrified of being left alone with a woman. In that respect, he and Daniel were worlds apart. His friend might flee from intimacy and hide behind his alleged contempt for women but Daniel always welcomed closeness.

After striding through the camp, he reached Abigail's tent and called out her name. It was Emily Greene who emerged to give him a token curtsey.

'Good afternoon, Captain Rawson,' she said.

'Hello, Emily. I was hoping to see your mistress.'

'She went off to your tent over an hour ago, sir.'

'Did she?' said Daniel in surprise. 'Then she must have lost her way. I was there most of the afternoon and saw no sign of her.'

'A soldier brought a message from you.'

'What message?'

'It was an invitation to join you,' said Emily,

starting to worry. 'I helped Miss Abigail to get ready then the man took her off. He was a private from your regiment, Captain Rawson.'

'Well, I certainly never sent him.'

'Then who could he be?'

'That's exactly what I'm asking myself,' said Daniel, controlling his disquiet. 'It would have taken her no more than five minutes to reach my tent from here yet you say she's been gone for over an hour.'

'Yes, sir.'

'Did this man give a name?'

'No, Captain Rawson. He just passed on his message.'

'I'd never have sent a verbal invitation. I'd have done Miss Piper the courtesy of writing a short note to her. Let's go back to the start, Emily,' he advised. 'Describe this man as accurately as you can then tell me precisely what he said.'

Emily gulped. 'Do you think Miss Abigail is in trouble, sir?'

'I think we need to find her as quickly as possible,' said Daniel seriously. 'Now – what did this man look like?'

She could not believe it. Abigail Piper was surrounded by thousands of soldiers yet not one of them came to her aid. After being imprisoned in the tent for a while, she was forced to walk out on the arm of her captor. Before she did so, she let her handkerchief drop behind the box in the hope that it would be found and act as a clue to her disappearance. She prayed that the man beside her would make a mistake and arouse the suspicions of the sentries. It did not happen. Charles Catto had enough confidence to chat freely with the pickets as he and Abigail went past them. She could not understand why they did not recognise the distress she was in. Abigail was exuding fear and panic yet nobody seemed to notice. All that the men observed were her youthful beauty and her shapely figure.

Once outside the perimeter, they took a leisurely stroll in the direction of some trees. Abigail was on tenterhooks. The farther away they went from the safety of the camp, the more rattled she became. The fact that she had no idea who her companion was and what designs he might have upon her, made it even worse. The man had given nothing away. He had interrogated her about her friendship with Daniel Rawson, and was very pleased when she told him that she had left England solely in order to follow the captain. Encouraged by the man, she had found herself talking more candidly about her feelings than she had done to Daniel himself, admitting how those feelings had changed somewhat in the wake of the battle.

As long as she was in the camp, there had always been an outside chance that she would be missed then sought out. It was a thought that had sustained her throughout her incarceration in the tent with an armed man. In the event, nobody seemed aware that she had gone astray and she was now taken out of reach of any possible rescue. Approaching the copse, she suddenly stopped.

'Let me go,' she pleaded. 'I'm no use to you.'

'On the contrary,' said Catto, 'you are of great use.'

'If it's money you want, I have some that I can give you.'

'I need a lot more than money from you, Miss Piper.'

'Where are we going?'

'Keep walking.'

'We're not supposed to be outside the boundary of the camp.'

'Keep walking,' he ordered, tightening his grip on her arm so that he could pull her forward. 'You've behaved yourself this far, Miss Piper. If you become obstructive, I shall get very angry.'

'I just want to know what's happening!' she exclaimed.

'We are going for a pleasant walk, that's all.'

'Where are you taking me?'

'Stop asking questions.'

'I want to know what's going on.'

'Come now, Miss Piper,' he said. 'You're an intelligent young lady. You must have worked it out by now. You're being kidnapped.'

The search was systematic and wide-ranging. Organised by Daniel Rawson, teams of men scoured the camp in the fading light and looked into every tent and wagon. To his credit, Sergeant Henry Welbeck suppressed any comments he might have wished to make about the troublesome nature of women and joined in the hunt with enthusiasm. Having investigated every inch of the route between the tent where Abigail Piper had been staying and Daniel's quarters, they

251

broadened the search. When it failed to find any trace of the missing person, Daniel was baffled.

'*Somebody* must have seen her, Henry,' he said to Welbeck. 'She was the sort of young lady to turn heads.'

'More than heads, from what I gather,' murmured Welbeck.

'She simply has to be here.'

'Well, we can find neither hide nor hair of her, Dan. My guess is that she may no longer be in the camp.'

'Where else can she be?'

'I've been thinking about that description you gave me of the man who may have abducted her. The beard deceived me at the start until I realised that he might have grown it since we last saw him.'

'Who?'

'That skulking deserter,' said Welbeck. 'Private Will Curtis.'

Daniel started. 'Would he be bold enough to sneak back into the camp?' he asked, disturbed by the notion.

'He was bold enough to try to behead you, Dan, and – if my guess is right – he was daring enough to fire that shot at you. Curtis is as bold as brass. It was the first thing I noticed about the bugger.'

They were still speculating on what might have happened to Abigail when a corporal brought a man over to them who wore the uniform of the Dutch army.

'This is Private Berchem,' said the corporal. 'He's a blacksmith, sir. His English is poor but he thinks he can help us.'

'Can you?' asked Daniel, speaking to him in Dutch.

'I hope so, sir,' replied the man. 'I was shoeing a horse when they went past me. They were only yards away.'

'What did you see?'

'I saw a British soldier and a beautiful young lady. I wondered why they were so close to the Dutch camp. The last time I saw them, they went towards a large tent.'

'Did you see them go into it?' pressed Daniel.

'No, sir,' said the man. 'When you are hammering a horseshoe into place, you have to keep your eyes on what you are doing. But I fancy that they might have gone into the tent.'

'Could you take us there now?'

The Dutchman nodded. 'Yes, Captain.'

Welbeck was exasperated. 'What the hell is the fellow saying?'

'I'll tell you on the way,' said Daniel.

Understanding the urgency of the situation, the Dutchman set a good pace. Daniel and Welbeck walked beside him. After a few minutes, they came to the large tent being used as a store.

'My men have already looked in there,' said Welbeck. 'It's full of stuff we captured at the Schellenburg. There's nobody in there.'

'Let's take a second look,' said Daniel.

Opening the flap, he peeped into the tent but it was too dark for him to see anything properly. He borrowed Welbeck's lantern so that he could conduct a proper search. The sergeant, meanwhile, turned back the flaps of the tent. At first, Daniel found nothing of interest but he did not give up. Holding up the lantern, he looked behind boxes, baggage and piles of equipment. When he shed some light on a large wooden box, he saw something on the ground behind it. He reached down swiftly to retrieve a lady's handkerchief. As he sniffed it, he caught a faint whiff of the perfume that Abigail had worn on the occasions when they had met in London.

'This belonged to her,' he said. 'She was *here*.'

'Are you sure?' asked Welbeck.

'She must have left the handkerchief deliberately. At least, we know where she was brought when she left her quarters.'

'But where is she now, Dan?'

'Abigail must somehow have left the camp,' concluded Daniel, masking his anxiety. 'We must speak to the pickets. *Someone* must have seen them leave. Once we know the direction in which they went, we can continue the search on horseback. Hurry,' he added as he rushed out of the tent. 'Every minute may be crucial.'

There had been no time for introductions. Frédéric Seurel was waiting for them with the horses but he was only able to give Abigail Piper a brief glance before they set off. Charles Catto rode on one horse with Abigail sitting astride behind him. They cantered through the woods until they came out into the open. Light was slowly being squeezed out of the sky but they could still pick out the silhouette of a cottage that stood beside a fork in the road. Leading the way, Seurel veered off along the track to the left and rode on for miles before they came to a small village.

Candles gave off a faint glow in the windows but the street was in dark shadow. Reaching the inn on the far side of the village, they rode into the courtyard at the rear. Seurel had already reserved rooms for them. A servant came out to stable the horses while they entered the inn. Charles Catto took Abigail by the arm.

'Remember what I told you,' he said, as he guided her through the door. 'Behave yourself or you'll regret it.'

'Where is this place?' she asked.

'It's a long way from the good Captain Rawson.'

They came into the main room where a couple of local men were quaffing their ale at a table. Catto exchanged a greeting with the landlord before taking Abigail upstairs. Seurel followed and indicated their rooms. They went into the first of them, a small, untidy, low-ceilinged chamber with a musty smell and noticeable gaps between its oak floorboards. When Catto had lit some candles, Abigail saw that it was a dingy room filled with ugly furniture. Taken there against her will by two strangers, she looked at the little bed with trepidation. It took on the air of an instrument of torture.

Seurel was studying her for the first time, running lecherous eyes all over here and grinning as he did so. He spoke in French.

'She's very pretty, Charles,' he said, leering at her. 'We can take it in turns.'

'Keep your hands off her,' warned Catto. 'She's a hostage and nothing more. I didn't bring her here for your entertainment.'

'We can't waste a chance like this.'

'You'll do as I tell you.'

'I need a woman to warm my bed at night.'

'Then find yourself another one. Miss Piper is not for you.'

Seurel was resentful. An argument soon flared up and both men raised their voices. Conscious that they were talking about her, Abigail became increasingly frightened. She knew very little French and they were talking so rapidly that it was impossible to decipher more than a word or two. Nevertheless, she sensed what the dispute was about and she shuddered as she glanced across at the bed. At length and with ill grace, Seurel accepted that Catto's decision was final and withdrew into a sullen silence.

'Frédéric apologises for his display of bad temper,' said Catto.

'Why did you bring me here?' she asked.

'We needed somewhere to rest. You must get what sleep you can because we'll be leaving before dawn.'

'Where are we going?'

'We have to find another hiding place, Miss Piper. You will be missed and a search will take place. By the time the soldiers reach this inn, we must be miles away from here.'

'My maid will have realised by now that something must have happened to me,' she said, 'and she will have raised the alarm. Captain Rawson will have hundreds of soldiers at his command. There's no way that you can escape.'

'He won't find us in the dark, though I daresay

he'll try.'

'Those sentries saw us leaving the camp.'

'I know,' said Catto. 'They were consumed with jealousy. It's not everyone who has the chance to take a stroll with a lovely young lady. You were born to attract envy, Miss Piper. Look at Frédéric, for example. He's bubbling with envy at the way I'm talking to you now.'

Abigail turned to Seurel who was gazing at her with an intensity that worried her. Though she hated being the prisoner of anyone, she preferred to have Catto as her captor than his glowering companion. She felt it safer to keep one of them talking.

'You're in the French army, aren't you?' she said.

'We were,' replied Catto.

'Why does an Englishman fight for the French?'

'You'll have to ask the Duke of Marlborough that. He learnt his trade under a French flag and so did I.' He took off his hat and began to undo his coat. 'I can stop pretending that I'm a British soldier now.'

'Captain Rawson will catch you, whatever disguise you wear.'

'I look forward to meeting him.'

'He's probably leading a search party at this very moment.'

'I'm sure that he is, Miss Piper,' said Catto easily, 'but he'll not come here. Do you remember that cottage we passed near the fork in the road? Frédéric had the forethought to bribe the old man who lives there. If he gets that far this evening, Captain Rawson will be sent off in the wrong direction.'

Daniel Rawson took a dozen riders with him, experienced men who were armed with muskets. It had taken him some time to find sentries who had seen a British soldier and a young lady strolling along the edge of the camp. They described Abigail so accurately that it simply had to be her. Since she had monopolised their attention, the details they were able to give about her companion were decidedly sketchy. Daniel had heard enough to lead off his search party. Some of his men carried torches but they could only create small circles of light in the darkness that now enveloped the countryside.

At the fork in the road, they paused to knock on the door of the cottage. The old man was not pleased to see British soldiers. Daniel spoke to him in German and asked if he had seen anyone riding past that evening. Given the chance to mislead them, the old man nodded.

'There were three of them, sir,' he said.

'Was a woman among the three?' asked Daniel.

'Yes, sir – there was one woman and two men.'

'Which way did they go?'

The old man pointed and they did not even stop to thank him. Cantering along the road, they went on for over five miles but the search was in vain. They passed several tracks down which fugitives could have turned and rode through woods in which they could easily have hidden. In the end, Daniel accepted defeat.

'We'll never find them in the dark,' he said, ruing the failure of the search. 'We'll try again at first light.'

It was unnerving. Abigail was trapped in a small room at night with two men, one of whom would certainly have molested her had he not been prevented from doing so by the other. Her situation was hopeless. She was in a foreign country with no chance of immediate help. Having lost all appetite, she refused the offer of food but had to watch the burly Frenchman as he gobbled his way through a meal and swilled it down with tankards of ale. The man who had kidnapped her did at least have an acquaintance with table manners. When they had finished eating, they began to talk in French and she had to guess what they were saying by their expressions.

'You can sleep in the other room,' said Catto, putting his plate back on to the tray. 'I'll stay in here.'

'So that's your game is it? I sleep alone and you jump into bed with the girl. No,' said Seurel, gesticulating, 'you're not getting away with that. If you have her, then I have her as well.'

'Nobody is having her, Frédéric.'

'Then what use is she?'

'I told you before – we can trade her.'

'We can do a lot of other things with her as well,' said Seurel, running a hand across his wet mouth as he stared fixedly at Abigail. 'She's young and ripe and ready. Let me taste her. Let me teach you how a Frenchman pleasures a woman.'

'You're not touching this one,' said Catto, standing up to confront him. 'The only reason I'm staying is that someone has to guard her. I couldn't trust you to do that.'

'Why not?'

'Go to the other room.'

'This is not fair,' said Seurel, trying to sound reasonable. 'Both of us need sleep and you won't get any if you're watching her all night. Why not share the burden, Charles? You stand guard for a couple of hours then I'll take over.'

'We both know what would happen in that event.'

'I won't lay a finger on her, I swear it.'

'You can't help yourself, Frédéric.'

Seurel exploded. 'A man has his needs, for heaven's sake!'

'Miss Piper deserves to be treated with respect.'

'That's exactly what I'll do,' said Seurel, shooting her a glance. 'When I've had my sport with her, I'll be sure to thank her politely.'

Catto opened the door. 'Good night, Frédéric.'

'Just let me have ten minutes alone with her.'

'Good night!'

Abigail watched the silent battle of wills. After glaring his defiance, Seurel finally capitulated but he did not leave without one act of bravado. Before Catto could stop him, he suddenly grabbed Abigail and stole a kiss from her. He left the room laughing. Closing the door after him, Catto made a gesture of apology. Abigail did not even see it. She was still recoiling from the foul taste of Seurel's lips and the brutish feel of his hands. Catto resumed his seat.

'Try to get some sleep,' he suggested.

'I'm not tired,' she said, determined not to lie on the bed.

'You're safe with me, Miss Piper.'

She was scornful. 'Is this what you call being safe?'

'Would you rather share the room with Frédéric?' Abigail shrank back defensively. 'No, I thought not. I'm the lesser of two evils, I can assure you. Frédéric believes that women only exist for one thing but I know that they have much else to offer. Take your own case, for instance. You are a valuable asset. If I had abducted your maid, there would be nothing like the hue and cry that your disappearance will have provoked. You are a young lady of quality, Miss Piper.'

'Then treat me as such and let me go,' she begged.

'All in good time,' he told her. 'You'll certainly be released without harm – provided that Captain Rawson does what he is told, that is. In the circumstances, he will have no choice.'

Daniel was in the saddle again early next morning. Daylight helped him and his men to ride faster and see much better than on their previous outing. They split into two groups and went off in different directions so that they could search a wider area. The hunt was fruitless. When he returned to the camp that afternoon, Daniel was tired, apprehensive and jaded. As soon as Henry Welbeck saw him, he knew that the search had been futile.

'Send out more men, Dan,' he urged.

'I've already done that,' replied Daniel, having just despatched a fresh team of riders, 'but the man who sneaked Abigail out of the camp had too big a start on us. He could be forty or fifty miles away.'

'I still think this is Will Curtis's doing.'

'I don't care who's behind this. My only interest is in Abigail's safe return.' He turned to his friend. 'Thank you, Henry.'

'What have I done to deserve thanks?'

'It's what you *haven't* done. We all know your opinion of women yet, from the moment that Abigail disappeared, you've never once used the situation to traduce the whole sex. You've been helpful.'

'I hate to see any young lady in distress,' said Welbeck, 'and there are few things more upsetting than being snatched away like that. The poor woman must be shaking with fear.'

'That's why we must rescue her soon.'

'Did you find no sign of her at all?'

'No,' said Daniel worriedly. 'Abigail obviously didn't have any more handkerchiefs with her or she could have left us a trail to follow.' He shrugged an apology. 'I'm sorry, Henry – that was a bad joke. The truth is the only whisper of evidence we have is from an inn where two men and a young lady spent the night.'

'That means Will Curtis has an accomplice.'

'All three of them left before dawn but the landlord had no idea in which direction they were heading. We pressed on until the horses tired then decided to come back here.'

They were in Daniel's tent. As he was talking, he took a bottle of brandy from a leather chest and poured out two glasses. He handed one of them to Welbeck.

'Here's to her safe return!' said the sergeant, raising his glass.

'Yes,' agreed Daniel. 'Drink to her immediate and safe return!'

They both took a long sip of their brandy. Welbeck savoured the drink as it coursed down his throat. Brooding on Abigail's plight, Daniel hardly noticed the taste. He was reminded yet again that, but for him, Abigail would never have been anywhere near an army camp. Instead of being at home in the bosom of her family, she was in grave jeopardy and he was unable to help her. It was excruciating.

'Captain Rawson!' called a voice from outside the tent.

'Yes?' said Daniel, opening the flap to look out.

'This came for you, sir.'

The private gave him a letter then waited while Daniel handed his glass to Welbeck so that he could open the missive. He read the contents and looked up at the messenger.

'When was this delivered?' he asked.

'It was handed to one of the sentries, sir,' answered the other. 'A carter said that he was paid to deliver the letter here.'

'Did he say by whom he was paid?'

'No, sir – he simply handed it over and went on his way.'

'Very well,' said Daniel, dismissing him. 'Thank you.' He went back into the tent. 'He's made me an offer, Henry.'

'Who has?' asked Welbeck.

'Whoever wrote this letter.'

'Private Will Curtis!'

'He was careful not to sign his name.'

'What exactly does he say, Dan?'

'Read it for yourself,' said Daniel, passing the letter to him. 'At least, it sounds as if Abigail is still alive, though what state she's in is another matter altogether.'

'He wants to exchange Miss Piper for *you*,' said Welbeck with dismay as he read the letter. 'No disrespect to her but the army gets the worse part of that deal. We gain a terrified young woman and we lose the best captain in the British ranks. That's a rotten bargain.'

'It's one you might have to accept,' said Daniel. 'Abigail's safety is paramount. If this is the only way to get her released – so be it.'

CHAPTER THIRTEEN

The Duke of Marlborough read the letter with deep concern then passed it to Adam Cardonnel. His secretary scanned it with equal disquiet. They were in Marlborough's quarters. Daniel Rawson had brought the anonymous letter regarding the fate of Abigail Piper. The two men were as disturbed as he had been.

'This is intolerable!' said Marlborough angrily. 'I'll not have anyone dictating terms like this. Abigail Piper must be found at once. I'll send out a whole regiment, if need be.'

'That would be unwise, Your Grace,' said Daniel. 'We are ordered to call off the search. If her kidnapper sees a large body of men hunting for Abigail, he'll kill her instantly.'

'That could be a bluff.'

'It doesn't sound like one,' said Cardonnel, returning the letter to Daniel. 'From the tone of his demand, I take him to be a ruthless and decisive man. And since he inveigled his way into our camp, he's not lacking in guile or bravado either.'

'It could be the second time he tricked us,' said Daniel.

'What do you mean?'

'According to Sergeant Welbeck, this man volunteered to join us under the name of Will Curtis. Immediately after the death of Lieutenant Hopwood, our new recruit disappeared.'

'We must catch this devil!' said Marlborough.

'Our first task is to rescue Abigail Piper, Your Grace.'

'Quite so.'

'She has already been in this man's hands far too long.'

'What do you suggest, Captain Rawson?' asked Cardonnel.

'That I abide by the terms stipulated in the letter.'

'But that would expose you to certain danger.'

'I know how to cope with danger, sir,' said Daniel calmly. 'The young lady does not.'

Marlborough was thoughtful. 'There has to be a way to get her safely back without putting your life at risk, Daniel,' he said. 'Could you not appear to meet his demands yet have a detachment of men within easy reach? As soon as Abigail is handed over, reinforcements could come

265

out of hiding and ride to your assistance.'

'They would never get to me in time, Your Grace. A pistol shot takes less than a second. Lieutenant Hopwood was stabbed to death and beheaded within a couple of minutes.'

'Don't remind me.'

'I must acquiesce to the man's demands.'

'I can't see you walk off to your death like that.'

'Why not?' asked Daniel with a twinkle. 'After all this time, it must be a familiar sight to you. I've walked off to my death in more battles than I can remember. Fortunately, I've always walked back again.'

'This is different.'

'I don't see why, Your Grace.'

'If your supposition is correct,' said Marlborough, 'this man has already made two failed attempts on your life. He's gone to enormous lengths to get close to you. Taking a hostage is his last desperate throw of the dice. You'd be willingly handing yourself over to your executioner.'

'I'm inclined to agree with His Grace,' said Cardonnel.

Daniel was resolved. 'Abigail must be rescued at all costs,' he said earnestly. 'She is an innocent victim. By rights, she should not even be here. As a British soldier, I can hardly plead innocence. I've killed many men in combat and I've worked behind enemy lines to gather intelligence. It's hardly surprising that someone wants to see me dead.'

'That doesn't mean you have to sacrifice yourself, Daniel.'

'Adam is right,' said Marlborough. 'You're too

valuable to lose.'

'It's kind of you to say so, Your Grace,' said Daniel, 'but let me ask you this. Do you wish to write to Sir Nicholas Piper to explain that you could not rescue his younger daughter because you preferred to save the life of one of your captains?'

'No, I would not.'

'Then I must follow my instructions.'

After further consideration, Marlborough gave a reluctant nod. 'Whom will you take with you?'

'Sergeant Welbeck. We'll take a spare horse with us so that Abigail will be able to ride back here to the camp. I see that as a hopeful sign.'

'Well, I can't say that I do,' said Marlborough.

'If this man means to kill me,' he reasoned, 'he could do so on the spot and allow Abigail to return here on my horse. But his letter stressed that we bring a mount for her.'

'There is a glimmer of hope in that, I suppose,' said Cardonnel. 'What struck me about this man is that he has an educated hand. His letter is crisp, well-written and explicit.'

'Oh, there's no question about his intelligence, sir,' said Daniel. 'It was reading this letter that persuaded me that Henry – Sergeant Welbeck, that is – may be right. It must have come from the fellow who posed as Will Curtis. The sergeant told me he had too many airs and graces to serve as a private. We're up against a clever man.'

'He's clever and merciless.'

'He's also very calculating. He kidnapped someone whom he knew was a friend of mine. Look at the way he's planned to exchange us,' he continued, waving the letter. 'I have to ride across a plain so that he can see me from miles away and check if I obeyed his orders. That's why I can only take one man with me.'

'There's our answer,' said Marlborough. 'While you ride towards him, I send troops around to the rear.'

'We can't be certain where he is, Your Grace. At the far end of that plain is a series of hills. He could be hiding on any of them and, from an elevated position like that, he could pick out any flanking movement with a telescope.'

'Captain Rawson is correct,' said Cardonnel. 'This man has no intention of being surrounded. At the first sign of trickery on our part, he'll vanish altogether – and he'll probably cut Miss Piper's throat before he does so.'

'I have to go,' said Daniel.

'It's against my better judgement,' Marlborough told him.

'I'll speak to Sergeant Welbeck.'

'Is he willing to accompany you?'

'Yes, Your Grace – there's no better man for the task.'

'I hesitate to give the mission my blessing.'

'With or without it,' said Daniel, 'I still mean to go.'

'How do you know you can trust this fellow?' asked Cardonnel. 'There's the frightening possibility that Miss Piper is already dead. Her name is simply being used to lure you out of the camp.'

'Then that's an even better reason to go. If anyone has harmed her in any way,' said Daniel, thrusting out his jaw, 'I want to meet him. He'll answer to me.'

Concealed behind a boulder, Charles Catto surveyed the plain through his telescope. There was nobody in sight. Frédéric Seurel took the telescope from him and applied an eye to it. After a minute, he handed the instrument back.

'He's not coming,' he declared.

'He must come – there's too much at stake.'

'Why should he care about one silly little English girl when he can charm his way into the bed of a general's wife? Captain Rawson can pick and choose his women at will. He won't bother about losing one of them.'

'Yes, he will,' said Catto. 'Miss Piper is special to him.'

'She's special to me as well,' said Seurel, glancing over his shoulder at Abigail. 'Don't forget your promise, Charles. You told me that, if Captain Rawson fails to appear, I could have my way with her before I choked the life out of that lovely body of hers.'

'It won't come to that, Frédéric.'

'It *must*. It's agony being so close to such beauty yet forbidden to touch it or taste it. I only have to look at her to want her. Don't you have that same fire in your loins? Don't you have that urge to–'

'Be quiet,' snapped Catto, cutting him off. 'Miss Piper is not some tavern wench for you to tumble in the hay. She's a lady of quality and she'll bring in a far greater prize.'

'Captain Rawson won't bother about her.'

'I'll wager anything that he will.'

'How can you be so sure?'

269

'Because I exploited his weak spot – I appealed to his honour.'

Seurel was contemptuous. 'Honour!' he said with a sneer. 'What use is that? I never cared about honour when I was a soldier. The only thing I wanted to do was to make people suffer before I killed them.'

'Captain Rawson has higher ideals than you.'

'When it comes to women, he has the same ideals as me!'

Abigail Piper heard his crude laughter and quivered. She was sitting some yard behind them. To prevent her escape, they had bound her hand and foot and put a gag in her mouth. She had never felt so utterly powerless. One man had treated her with a modicum of respect but the other merely ogled her. Unable to understand Seurel's speech, she found his fervent glances all too comprehensible. There would be no Emily to rescue her from a man's clutches this time. With her hands tied behind her back and her mouth covered, she had absolutely no means of defence.

She was in a quandary. Desperate to be rescued, she did not want her freedom to be at the expense of Daniel Rawson's capture. If he fell into their hands, Abigail feared for his life. Even before her abduction, she had started to regret her decision to flee from home in the cause of true love. As a result of her impetuosity, she and her maid had undergone all sorts of pain and mortification and she had finally reached the British camp only to discover that Daniel did not requite her love in the way she had imagined.

Abigail had not only embarrassed him, she had

now put him in mortal danger. It made her writhe with guilt. At the same time, she was praying for release from her predicament and that could only be achieved by Daniel's arrival. Whatever happened, one of them was going to suffer dreadfully. The conviction that it was all her fault made Abigail quake with remorse. Tears dribbled freely down her face. She was stuck on the horns of a dilemma. Needing him to come to her aid, she wanted him to stay away for his own sake and the more she thought about it, the more she felt she deserved her fate. Closing her eyes, she prayed for strength to endure her ordeal.

Daniel Rawson came out of the trees and started to ride across the plain. Henry Welbeck was beside him, eager to support his friend and taking care to shed no blame on the woman who, in his opinion, had actually created the fraught situation. For most of their journey, the sergeant had held his peace. Daniel, too, had been lost in thought. It was Welbeck who first came out of his reverie.

'I wouldn't trust Will Curtis as far as I could throw him,' he said sourly. 'Watch him like a hawk, Dan.'

'He holds the advantage at the moment,' admitted Daniel.

'Not as long as I'm beside you.'

'Thank you, Henry. I appreciate what you're doing.'

'I want to see that young lass safe but I also want you to come out of this unharmed. Something tells me I can't have both.'

'Don't worry about me,' said Daniel. 'I can look after myself.'

'You can give Will Curtis a message from me. If anything nasty happens to you, I won't rest till I've caught up with the bastard and cut out his black heart. Will you remember to warn him?'

'I don't think he's a man who fears warnings, Henry.'

'He'll fear me when I catch up with him,' asserted Welbeck.

They rode on in silence until they got within a few hundred yards of a large hill. A voice rang out across the plain.

'Stop there!' ordered Catto. They reined in their horses. 'That's as far as you go, Sergeant Welbeck.'

'Is that you, Will Curtis, you yellow-bellied deserter?' shouted Welbeck, searching the hill with his eyes. 'Have the guts to show yourself, man!'

'Do as he says,' advised Daniel, trying to calm his friend. 'We don't want to antagonise him.'

'Speak for yourself – *I* bloody do!'

'Let me handle this, Henry.'

'Leave him there, Captain Rawson,' yelled Catto. 'Ride forward on your own. Do as I tell you or you'll never see Miss Piper alive again. Come on – leave the sergeant there.'

Daniel obeyed. Nudging his horse into a trot, he moved forward and let his gaze drift across the hill. He eventually saw something glinting in the sunshine and knew that it must be a telescope. It gave him a direction in which to guide his horse. When he was fifty yards or so away from the hill, he came to a halt.

'Keep riding forward!' demanded Catto.

'Let me see Miss Piper first,' retorted Daniel. 'You only get me if she is released without harm. Show her to me.'

There was a long pause then Abigail was pushed out from behind a large rock. She was still gagged and her hands were tied behind her back but Daniel could see that she was alive. Before he could address her, she was pulled back behind the rock. He eased his horse forward until he got close to the hill and well within range of any firearms that might be trained on him.

'Stop there and dismount!' ordered Catto. When Daniel obeyed, a second command followed. 'Remove your hat and coat and drop them on the ground.' Daniel complied once more. 'Now hold up your arms and turn round slowly so that I can see you're unarmed.' Aware of the man's scrutiny, Daniel followed the instructions. 'Good,' said Catto. 'Miss Piper will be released but, if you try any tricks, you'll both be shot down where you stand.'

There was a lengthy pause before Abigail came out from behind the rock again and began to scramble down the hill. Her gag and her bonds had been removed and she was able to cry out his name. Daniel strode forward to greet her. Weeping with relief, she flung herself into his arms. He patted her reassuringly.

'A very touching reunion,' noted Catto, 'but we no longer have any need of Miss Piper. Send her back to the sergeant. Go on – do as I say, Captain Rawson.'

'How many of them are there?' asked Daniel quietly.

'Two,' replied Abigail.

'Then leave them to me.' He stood back from her and pointed behind him. 'That's my good friend, Sergeant Welbeck. He'll take you safely back to the camp. Go on, Abigail – run!'

'What about you, Daniel?'

'I can't start worrying about myself until you're safe.'

After a final squeeze of his hands, Abigail turned and trotted towards Welbeck, looking back from time to time to see what Daniel was doing. He had already forgotten her. His mind was concentrated on his captors, both of whom had now appeared from their hiding places. Frédéric Seurel was pointing a musket at him. Holding a pistol on the prisoner, Charles Catto came down to take a closer look at him.

'Put your hands up!' he said.

'I've no weapons on me,' Daniel told him, raising his arms.

Catto patted him all over. Satisfied that Daniel was telling the truth, he made him put his hands behind his back so that he could tie them tightly together. He then led both the prisoner and his horse into the shelter of the rocks at the base of the hill.

Bounding forward, Seurel put the barrel of his musket against Daniel's forehead. 'Let me blow out his brains!' he cried.

'Wait a moment!' cried Catto, pushing the weapon away.

'You said that he was mine.'

'That was before I realised that we could capture him. He's worth more to us alive than dead.

If we take him back to the general he'll be delighted with us, Frédéric. He can have the pleasure of killing Rawson himself. You must recall General Salignac,' he said to Daniel. 'He'd like to talk to you about his beautiful wife.'

Abigail Piper was overcome with emotion. Having been rescued from being ravished by Seurel, she had seen Daniel surrendering himself on her behalf to the two men. Her feelings of guilt were more intense than ever. She wanted to go back to plead for Daniel's release but she knew that it would be pointless. The chances were that they had already killed him. Henry Welbeck was troubled by the same thought. He immediately began to contemplate revenge. When they had ridden across the plain and into the trees, he eventually spoke to her.

'Who were they, Miss Piper?' he asked.

'I don't know.'

'You must have heard them call each other by names.'

'One was called Charles,' she said, 'and he was English. The Frenchman was called Frédéric. He was a dreadful man.'

'What else can you tell me about them?'

'Not very much, I'm afraid. They spoke in French all the time.'

'Where did they take you?'

'We spent the night at an inn but I have no idea where it was. I was in a complete daze most of the time. I couldn't eat or drink anything and I didn't get a wink of sleep.'

'Did they bother you in any way?' asked

Welbeck tentatively.

'The Frenchman would have,' she said, tensing at the memory of Seurel's kiss, 'but the other man held him back. I'm so grateful to escape from them at last.'

'So am I, miss. It's the captain I'm worried about now.'

'They wouldn't tell me why they wanted to kill him. All that, the Englishman would say was that it was something to do with what happened in Paris. Do you know anything about that, Sergeant?'

'Nothing at all,' replied Welbeck discreetly.

'What could Captain Rawson have been doing in Paris?'

'I have no idea.'

'It must have been something very important.'

'Whatever it was, he'll be sorry about it now. Dan Rawson may have taken one chance too many.'

'I don't follow.'

'There's no reason why you should, Miss Piper,' he said quickly, unwilling to confide what he feared. 'You've obviously had a harrowing time. No food, no sleep and the anxiety of not knowing what was going to happen to you – the sooner we get you back to camp, the better.'

After riding for five miles or more, they stopped to make sure that they were not being followed. Daniel Rawson still had his hands tied behind his back and his horse was pulled along by its reins. It was an uncomfortable way to ride but he consoled himself with the fact that he was alive to do it. His red coat and tricorn hat still lay on the plain where he had been forced to discard them. He hoped that they would soon be retrieved by British soldiers.

They had paused on rising ground that enabled Charles Catto to have a good view of the terrain over which they had just travelled. He used his telescope to scan the landscape.

'Well?' said Seurel.

'There's nobody there, Frédéric.'

'Good.'

'They have more sense than to track us,' said Catto. 'They know that, at the first hint of pursuit, we'd kill their precious captain.'

Seurel chortled. 'Then leave him without his head.'

'Was that your doing?' asked Daniel, surprising Seurel with his command of French. 'Was it you who beheaded Lieutenant Hopwood?'

'It's a special talent I have,' boasted the other.

'Killing the wrong man does not require talent.'

'I've already pointed that out to him,' said Catto brusquely.

Seurel was petulant. 'What does it matter?' he claimed, waving a hand. 'We have the right man now.'

'No thanks to you, Frédéric. It's only by the grace of God that Captain Rawson was not killed by that shot you fired near the camp.'

'So that was his doing as well,' noted Daniel.

'He's inclined to be hot-headed at times,' said Catto. 'It's something you should remember if ever you're tempted to make an escape bid. Frédéric will be prompted to kill you.'

277

'I think I understand all about Frédéric just by looking at him. You clearly provide the intelligence that he signally lacks.' Seurel voiced his protest. 'I believe that you joined us as Private Will Curtis.'

'That's correct.'

'May I know your real name?'

'Charles Catto. I'm employed by General Armand Salignac.'

'In other words, you're a traitor.'

'Not at all,' said Catto smoothly. 'France is my spiritual home. I have stayed true to my principles. As for betrayal, you are hardly the right person to accuse another of a crime you've committed yourself.'

'I've never betrayed my country,' affirmed Daniel.

'No, but you did betray Madame Salignac.'

'That was a private matter.'

'It's become a political matter as well, Captain Rawson. The general may be a cuckold but he's not blind. He knows that you didn't seduce his wife out of pure and unbiased love. You took the lady to bed in order to squeeze her dry of every last detail she knew about the French army.'

'Madame Salignac and I were simply friends.'

'You are a spy.'

'I'm a soldier who's proud to serve his country.'

'Well, you'll not be serving it again, Captain Rawson.'

'Tell us about Madame Salignac,' asked Seurel with an oily grin. 'What was she like as a lover? What did she let you do to her?'

'Shut up, Frédéric!' said Catto.

'But I want to know the truth.'

'Then you'll have to seduce her yourself. And in case you're wondering,' he went on, turning to Daniel, 'it wasn't the lady herself who confessed your name. It was her maid, Célestine. The general soon broke her. He knows everything now.'

'Is that why he sent you after me?' said Daniel.

'The general has a vengeful streak. "How ever long it takes, how ever much it costs, I want Captain Rawson killed." Those were his very words. But, instead of simply taking your head as a trophy, we can deliver your whole miserable carcass.'

'How much is he paying you?'

'That's between us and General Salignac.'

'Whatever the amount,' said Daniel, trying to negotiate with him, 'His Grace, the Duke of Marlborough would readily double it to buy my freedom.'

Catto laughed derisively. 'Let him treble it, if he wishes,' he said, 'then double that same figure. Frédéric and I would still treat it with scorn. There's no way out of this, Captain Rawson.'

'None at all,' added Seurel forcefully. 'We are loyal to France.'

'And so is General Salignac. Before he kills you, I'm sure he'll want to hear everything you have to tell him about the Confederate army. He has a gift for making even the most reticent men talk. By the time the general has finished with you,' he said, kicking his horse into action and towing Daniel along behind him, 'you'll wish you never persuaded that lovely wife of his to spread her legs for you.'

The first thing that Abigail Piper did when she reached the camp was to change out of her dress and wash herself thoroughly. As she did so, she unburdened herself to Emily Greene. The maid was sympathetic.

'It must have been a torment, Miss Abigail.'

'I felt certain that they intended to kill me.'

'But they didn't – thank God!' said Emily. 'We've got you back at last. You must try to forget all the horrible things that happened.'

'How can I do that when Captain Rawson is in such jeopardy?' cried Abigail. 'He surrendered to those villainous men in order to set me free but it's not a freedom I can ever enjoy.'

'I can see that.'

'He saved my life, Emily, and I made him *lose* his!'

Overwhelmed by fear and remorse, Abigail burst into tears and collapsed into Emily's capacious arms. Soothing her as best she could, her maid let her cry her fill then found a clean handkerchief with which to stem her tears. Only when she had recovered something of her composure did Abigail feel able to report to Marlborough, taking Emily with her in case she lost her control once again.

Marlborough was alone in his quarters, leafing through some despatches. After giving Abigail an effusive welcome, he offered her his chair and perched solicitously beside her as she told her tale. Emily hovered in the background, interested to hear how many of the details she had been told were kept from Marlborough because her mis-

280

tress was too embarrassed to divulge them. Though her voice trembled, Abigail maintained her poise.

When it was all over, Marlborough told her his decision.

'You'll begin your journey home tomorrow,' he told her.

'Tomorrow?' she said in alarm. 'But I need to stay here in case Captain Rawson is released.'

'There's no question of your remaining with us, Abigail. I've already delayed your escort long enough. Reports have come in that Marshal Tallard and his army are on their way here. If you do not leave soon,' he pointed out, 'you may find the road north blocked by French soldiers. The decision has been taken.'

'What if Captain Rawson comes back and I'm not here?'

'He'll be relieved that you're safely out of harm's way.'

'But I have to see him – I have to apologise to him.'

'There'll be no time to listen to any apologies,' he said. 'If he does manage to return – and we all pray for that outcome – then he will immediately join us as we besiege Rain. He is here, like the rest of us, to fight a war. That will take all our energies.'

There was an authority in his voice that deterred her from further argument. Marlborough did not criticise her in any way but she knew that she was viewed as a distraction. The fact that she was leaving only served to exacerbate her feelings of guilt. While she would be riding off to safety,

Daniel Rawson was in peril of his life. It was as if she were deserting him and the thought sickened her.

'I'll see you before you go,' said Marlborough, rising to his feet to indicate that it was time for her to leave. 'I'm sorry that your stay with us has been so troublesome. An army on the march has little to offer in the way of comfort to a young lady such as yourself.'

'I care little for that, Your Grace,' she said, getting up. 'I was happy enough with the accommodation you kindly provided.'

'You'll be even happier when you reach home.'

Abigail stifled a reply. As long as she was unaware of Daniel's fate, she knew that she would never be happy. She glanced at Emily who was patently delighted that they would be returning to England again even though she was uncertain of the welcome they might receive from the family. Abigail had to concede defeat.

'You must think very badly of me, Your Grace,' she said.

He shook his head. 'I think very highly of you, Abigail.'

'I've been a nuisance to you and to Captain Rawson.'

'If that's the case,' he said courteously, 'then you've been a very charming nuisance. But I'm glad that I'm able to write to Sir Nicholas to tell him that his daughter is on her way home.'

He crossed to the tent flap and pulled it back for her. After a brief farewell, she went out with Emily at her heels. Walking back through the camp, Abigail tried to accustom herself to the notion that she would soon be leaving it. She remembered her last fleeting contact with the man who had offered his life in return for hers. Over and over again, she kept asking the same question.

'Where *are* you, Daniel?'

Daniel Rawson knew where they were going. Having crossed the Danube by means of a pontoon bridge held by the French, the three of them continued south. Their destination was Augsburg, the city to which the Elector of Bavaria and Marshal Marsin had fled after the Confederate victory at Donauworth. Among those who had been compelled to retreat with them was General Armand Salignac whose pride had been badly wounded by the experience. Daniel would therefore be handed over as a prisoner of war to a man who wanted him for personal as well as for military reasons. He was not looking forward to the encounter.

His companions were in a hurry. They had stalked him long enough and were now eager to collect their reward before returning to France. Charles Catto dictated the pace. They rode for a few hours, stopped to feed and water the horses, allowed themselves a rest then pushed on hard. Darkness slowed them but they continued on their way through the night, pausing at regular intervals to eat rations they had bought at an inn. Daniel was not offered food and the closest he came to a drink was when Frédéric Seurel poured water jokingly over his head. As it ran down his face, Daniel was grateful to catch some drops on his tongue.

They were not held up by French or Bavarian patrols. Catto had documents that guaranteed them safe passage. Augsburg was situated at the confluence of the Rivers Lech and Wertach, occupying a prime strategic position. When the city finally came into view, Daniel could see why the retreating army had chosen to stay there. Surrounded by a high wall, Augsburg had impressive outer ramparts and defensive ditches. During the Thirty Years War in the previous century, the city had been invaded by marauding Swedes and had lost half its entire population. To ensure that it was never stricken in such a way again, its citizens had strengthened its fortifications so that it was almost impregnable. The Confederate army lacked guns heavy enough even to attempt an assault.

Though the meeting with Salignac was at the forefront of his mind, Daniel did not ignore the opportunity to gather information about the enemy. On entering the city, he took note of the troops and their deployment, paying especial attention to the artillery mounted on the walls. French and Bavarian uniforms were everywhere. In spite of his humiliation at Donauworth, it was evident that the Elector had not yet been persuaded by Marlborough to change sides. Safe inside the solidity of Augsburg, the Elector was standing by his allies.

General Salignac's quarters were in an upstairs room in a large house. When the visitors arrived, he was involved in a discussion with some senior officers but, on learning that his wife's lover had been captured, he dismissed them summarily. Catto and Seurel held an arm apiece as they dragged Daniel into the room. Salignac's face had tightened and veins stood out like whipcord on his brow. Fire was dancing in his eyes as he glared at the prisoner.

Without warning, he raised a hand and slapped Daniel hard across both cheeks time after time. Held firmly by the others, all that Daniel could do was to take the punishment. His cheeks were stinging and his head reeling. The final slap was the hardest of all. Seurel tried to ingratiate himself. Standing behind Daniel, he put an arm around his throat and applied pressure.

'Would you like me to snap his neck?' he asked.

'No,' said Salignac. 'That would be too easy a death. Leave go.'

'Yes, sir.' Disappointed, Seurel released his hold.

'We thought he might be able to tell you what you need to know about the Confederate army,' explained Catto. 'That's why I decided to bring him alive. Captain Rawson has Marlborough's ear.'

'I'll send the Duke of Marlborough *both* of the captain's ears – along with other parts of his anatomy.' Salignac's threat made Seurel cackle. 'So what have you to say for yourself, Captain Rawson?'

'I can only observe that your wife was mistaken,' said Daniel.

Salignac grabbed him by the throat. 'Don't you dare talk to me about her!' he howled.

'Many others have made the same comment

285

about you,' Daniel continued, speaking with difficulty until Salignac relaxed his grip. 'You have a reputation for being a fine soldier, General Salignac – a fine soldier and a true gentleman.'

'That reputation has been well-earned.'

'Not by striking a defenceless man when his hands are tied.'

'No,' said the other, taking a couple of steps back, 'perhaps not.' He snapped his fingers and both Catto and Seurel stood away from their prisoner. 'Given the circumstances, there's a much more honourable way to settle this.'

'Would you like me to torture him first?' volunteered Seurel. 'To see what he can tell you about the Duke of Marlborough's plans.'

'We already know his plans,' said Salignac testily. 'He's on his way to lay siege to Rain at this very moment. We have reliable spies in his camp. They don't need to resort to Captain Rawson's methods.'

'We are at war, General Salignac,' argued Daniel. 'Any methods are deemed acceptable when it comes to securing intelligence.'

'They are not deemed acceptable by *me*.'

'Then we must agree to differ.'

'I agree to nothing!' snapped the other. 'Take him out!'

'Where are we going, General Salignac?' asked Catto.

'We'll find a place where we won't be interrupted. Since the captain taunts me about my lack of civilised behaviour, I intend to cut him to pieces in the most civilised way.' He reached for his sword. 'He and I will fight a duel.'

The courtyard was situated in a quiet corner near the edge of the city. Though soldiers occasionally marched past on the road nearby, it was a relatively peaceful spot. Daniel Rawson was in an awkward situation. Since his hands had been tied behind his back for so long, his wrists had been chafed and his arms subject to cramp. He was tired from the long ride. General Salignac was older and slower but those disadvantages were negated by Daniel's stiffness.

The real problem for Daniel lay in the choice of his adversary's seconds. Charles Catto and Frédéric Seurel were not merely there to act in an official capacity. If, by any chance, the general faltered, they would step in to kill Daniel in his place. The duel was a fight against three men. Other factors favoured Salignac. Having spent his career in a cavalry regiment, he was very proficient with a sword, whether using it to cut and slash in battle or indulging in the subtleties of fencing practice. While the general would use his own sword, Daniel would have to manage with a weapon borrowed from Catto. From the start, it seemed like an unequal contest.

Daniel was given no time to stretch his arms and flex his muscles. As soon as his bonds were cut, a sword was thrust into his hand and he was forced to defend himself. General Salignac dispensed with the formalities of a duel. Once Daniel was armed, his opponent rushed at him with his sword flailing. All that Daniel could do was to parry, duck and retreat. It went on for minutes. The clash of blades sent sparks into the air. Encouraged by the two bystanders, Salignac built on his early advantage, pressing Daniel back before going down on one knee for a vicious thrust that was only partially deflected. The point cut through Daniel's shirt and drew blood from his left arm.

'A hit, a hit!' yelled Seurel, relishing the injury.

'Take him whenever you wish, general,' urged Catto.

Salignac renewed his attack but it lacked the venom of his first assault. He was palpably tiring. In the heat of the noonday sun, he was also starting to sweat profusely. Daniel drew comfort at last. Instead of simply offering a defence, he was able to show off his swordsmanship a little, flicking his wrist to great advantage and using his superior balance to weave and feint. When his counter-thrust removed a button from the general's coat, he saw the man's face turn crimson with rage. Gathering all of his energy, Salignac fought so hard that Daniel was pushed back yet again. When his shoulders met a wall, he realised that he could go no further.

Pausing to get his breath back, Salignac kept him pinned against the brickwork. He was so confident that he could kill Daniel with a single thrust that he took time to choose his spot. When he was ready, he feinted twice to draw Daniel's blade out of the way then let out a cry of triumph as his arm went at full stretch in a bid to pierce the heart. Daniel was too quick for him. Twisting sideways, he moved his body out of the way so that the point of the general's sword met the wall with murderous force, jarring his arm so painfully that he dropped the weapon to the ground. It was Daniel's turn to abandon the niceties. Taking the general by the collar, he swung him round at speed and hurled him straight at Catto, knocking both men violently to the ground. Seurel had his dagger out at once and darted forward. Before he could be stabbed in the back, however, Daniel swung round in a flash and lifted his sword up, running it deep into the Frenchmen's stomach and leaving him impaled in agony.

Seizing his opportunity, Daniel took to his heels.

CHAPTER FOURTEEN

He had never run so fast in all his life. Darting out of the courtyard, Daniel Rawson sped along a lane before zigzagging his way through a series of narrow alleys. He knew that pursuit would be immediate and that he would have dozens of soldiers on his tail. When he came out into a wide road, therefore, he slowed to walking pace so that he could mingle with the crowd. Anyone hurtling wildly along the thoroughfare would be identified at once as a fugitive. His only hope lay in blending with the people who thronged the main streets. It was market day and he was carried along by the mass of bodies converging on an array of stalls, hand-carts and wagons covering an entire square.

Daniel knew that General Salignac would not

fight a duel with him for the second time. He would be baying for Daniel's blood and castigating himself for failing to kill the prisoner when he had the opportunity. The search would be thorough and the quarry would face certain death if caught. Daniel needed a hiding place. Escaping from Augsburg would be difficult in broad daylight so he had to lie low somewhere in the city until nightfall. The market offered all kinds of possibilities. When he heard the sounds of a chase somewhere behind him, he kept his head down and lengthened his stride until he was able to plunge in gratefully among the jostling hordes, buying, selling and haggling in the marketplace.

As soon as he could, he ducked under a wagon, crawled along the ground and came out behind a line of stalls. Piles of goods were stacked haphazardly and there was a multitude of empty wooden boxes, baskets and sacks left on the ground by vendors. Above the pandemonium of the market, Daniel could hear soldiers' voices rising in volume as they got nearer. The hunt was on in earnest. Since he was not allowed the luxury of time, he was forced to make an instant decision. Carpets were being sold on one of the stalls and, in case it was needed, an additional supply of them had been stacked upright at the rear. Daniel tucked himself in behind the carpets, unfurling the edge of one of them a little so that he was completely concealed. It was only a temporary refuge but it gave him chance to rest and to reflect on what had happened.

General Salignac had evidently discovered his

wife's adultery and he was so obsessed with revenge that he had hired assassins to track down and murder her lover. One of them, Frédéric Seurel, had now met his own death and it gave Daniel great satisfaction to know that he had killed the man who had so callously beheaded Lieutenant Hopwood. His satisfaction was marred by his fears for Bérénice Salignac. A brief acquaintance with her husband had been enough to show him that the man was cruel and vindictive. He felt a stab of guilt at having left her in compromising circumstances and he prayed that she had not suffered too much on his behalf. Daniel had been deeply fond of Bérénice and would have been drawn to her even if she had not been the neglected wife of a French general.

All thought of her was abruptly suspended when he heard soldiers, yelling above the tumult and demanding to know if anyone had seen a man fleeing down the road. There were loud complaints from the crowd as the troops forced a way through to conduct their search. Daniel risked a peep out of his hiding place and caught sight of bayonets glinting in the sun. They were being used to probe under tables, into stalls, into piles of hay and anywhere else where a fugitive might conceivably lurk. Slowed down by the sheer number of people, the soldiers were nevertheless methodical and painstaking. It would not be long before they explored the area behind the stalls.

Shrinking back behind the carpets, Daniel turned sideways so that he presented less of a target for an intrusive bayonet. Protests in the square grew louder still as more soldiers joined in the search and elbowed people roughly aside. Daniel braced himself. Hearing orders being barked in German, he knew that Bavarian soldiers were leading the search. The tramp of feet and the guttural commands got closer and closer. Daniel picked out a snatch of conversation.

'He won't get far,' said one soldier.

'All the gates will have been closed by now,' said another.

'He's trapped in the city and everyone's looking for him.'

'We'll roast him alive when we catch him.'

'He can have my bayonet up his arse.'

At the moment he made the threat, the soldier thrust his bayonet into the stack of carpets and missed Daniel by less than an inch. Before the man could repeat the exercise, the carpet dealer rushed around in a panic from the front of the stall and begged him not to damage any more of his ware. When the soldier relented and moved on, Daniel dared to breathe properly again. Had it made contact, the bayonet would have ripped him apart and the dealer would never have been able to sell a carpet that was sliced open and soaked with blood. The hunt continued but it was slowly moving away from Daniel. For the time being at least, he was safe.

When news of the victory at Donauworth reached the Imperial capital, there was delight and celebration. Vienna toasted the success of the Confederate army and gave thanks to God for their deliverance from a menacing foe. The tidings were received with more muted enthusiasm in The Hague. While the States-General appreciated the significance of the victory, they were horrified by the high number of casualties in the battle and felt that the captain-general should have protected his troops more carefully instead of sacrificing them to enemy fire.

The Dutch, however, decided to mark the event by casting a victory medal. On the obverse side was an image of Louis, Margrave of Baden. A Latin inscription adorned the other side. In translation, it read: "The enemy defeated and put to flight and their camp plundered at Schellenberg near Donauworth." There was no reference whatsoever to the Duke of Marlborough, who had planned and achieved the signal victory. It was almost as if he had taken no part whatsoever in the engagement. The medal was a calculated insult to him.

Unaware of the snub that awaited him, Marlborough amused himself by reading out the letter sent to him by Leopold, Emperor of Austria. It was written in Leopold's own hand, an honour reserved only for an exceptional situation. When it had been translated, Adam Cardonnel was interested to hear the full text of the letter, filled, as it was, with an extravagance of expression totally at odds with the prosaic despatches from the Dutch.

'*Illustrious, Sincerely Beloved,*' Marlborough read. '*Your desert towards me, my house, and the common cause, are great and many, and the singular application, care and diligence, which you have expressed, in bringing up and hastening the powerful succours, which the most serene and potent Queen of Great Britain and the States-General of the United Netherlands, have sent me to the Danube, are not to be ranked in the last place; but nothing can be more glorious than what you have done, after the conjunction of your army with mine, in the most speedy and vigorous attack and forcing of the enemy's camp at Donawert, the second of this month; since my generals themselves, and ministers, declare that the success of that enterprise (which is more acceptable and advantageous to me, in the present time, than almost anything else that could befall me) is chiefly owing to your counsels, prudence and execution, and the wonderful bravery and constancy of the troops, who fought under your command. This will be an eternal trophy to your most serene Queen in Upper Germany, whither the victorious arms of the English nation have never penetrated since the memory of man.'*

Though diverted by the flowery language, Marlborough was very touched. It proved that his arduous efforts had been given full recognition by someone. Cardonnel raised a mischievous eyebrow.

'Should we send a copy of the letter to The Hague?' he asked.

'They would denounce it as a forgery, Adam.'

'How would it be received in England?'

'Parliament would revile any praise of me.'

'You won a notable victory – what more do they want?'

'A miracle,' said Marlborough. 'Both Parliament and the States General want a battle in which the enemy suffers casualties while our troops survive miraculously without even soiling their uniforms.'

'They do not even give you credit for having come this far, Your Grace. To complete such a remarkable march and then to have such a triumph at the end of it, is an extraordinary achievement. It's a peal of bells that will ring down the centuries.'

'Now, now, Adam,' cautioned Marlborough. 'Let's not smile at the Emperor's exaggeration then indulge in some of our own. Instead of speculating about our place in history, we must simply look ahead a few days at the time. As for Emperor Leopold,' he added, 'instead of writing a letter, I would have much preferred him to send me the heavy guns that he promised. All I have from him is the mixed blessing of the Margrave of Baden.'

'Baden is wondering what our next move will be.'

'Ideally, I would either like to entice the Elector out of Augsburg so that we can fight another battle against his depleted forces. Or,' said Marlborough, 'I would like to persuade him that he should abandon his alliance with the French.'

'I foresee difficulties, Your Grace,' said Cardonnel with a frown. 'To achieve either objective, you'd need to lay waste to the Bavarian countryside. Only when he heard that his pretty towns and villages have been burnt to the ground, would the Elector be forced to fight or sue for peace.'

'On past experience, he may do neither.'

'His correspondence is markedly less hostile than it has been.'

'I fancy he is trying to woo us into the belief that he may join us,' said Marlborough, 'while still holding firmly to the French. If and when Tallard appears on the horizon, the Elector's letters may take on a different tone.'

'Tallard is still crossing the Black Forest mountains.'

'It's the second time this year he's done that, Adam. The scenery will begin to bore him. He came through the forest in May to deliver reinforcements to Marshal Marsin and the Elector. Tallard will be shocked to learn how many of those troops we killed.'

Their discussion was interrupted by a British lieutenant. After announcing his arrival, he was invited into the tent. Over his arm was a long red coat with the insignia of a captain on it. In his other hand, he carried a tricorn hat covered in dust. He exchanged greetings then held up the two items.

'I led a patrol earlier today, Your Grace,' he said, 'and we found these discarded on the plain.'

Marlborough winced. 'Did they belong to Captain Rawson?'

'I fear that they did.'

'Is there any blood on the coat?'

'None at all,' replied the lieutenant.

'Then there's still a faint hope.'

'Why should Captain Rawson have taken off his coat and hat?' asked Cardonnel. 'Were they left there as some sort of signal?'

'We may never know,' said Marlborough sadly. He took the coat and held it with almost reverential care. 'No man wore his uniform with more

296

pride and gallantry than Daniel Rawson. If he is no longer alive – and we must accept that grim possibility – he leaves a gap in our army that will never be filled.'

Though the hunt had moved on from the market square, Daniel knew that he could not remain indefinitely in his hiding place. When the dealer finished trading for the day and loaded his carpets on to his wagon, he would find the fugitive and call for help. Sooner or later, Daniel had to get away. His problem was that he was too conspicuous and he could not always conceal himself in a crowd. Having lost his coat and hat by necessity, he was wearing a shirt, a waistcoat, a cravat, breeches and a pair of boots. The cravat was untied at once. Now that he had a moment to inspect the flesh wound in his arm, he was able to bind it with the cravat and stop the blood trickling down his arm.

Daniel needed a disguise. The soldiers involved in the search were looking for a British officer bereft of his coat and hat. They would have been given a rough description of his appearance. It had to be changed. Behind the adjacent stall were some sacks that had been emptied of the fruit and vegetables they had contained. Making sure that nobody saw him, Daniel crept over to grab one of the sacks, tearing a hole in one end and in both sides so that he could slip it over his head and put his arms through. When he rolled up his sleeves, he had already transformed himself into a countryman in a smock.

His boots, however, were too expensive for any

rustic to wear yet he could hardly abandon them. Picking up a second sack, he tore it into strips and tied them around his boots like cross-gartering. Since the sack had been filled with potatoes, it had a liberal supply of earth in it as well. Daniel used it to rub on his face and on the sleeves of his shirt. Having no cap, he retrieved a wooden box from the ground and hoisted it up on to his shoulder, thus obscuring the side of his face. He felt confident enough to put his disguise to the test.

Stepping between the stalls, he joined the crowd in the square. By leaning forward, hunching his shoulders and adopting a limp, he looked very different from the tall, striking, virile Captain Rawson. One or two people tossed him a curious glance but nobody stopped to question him, still less to hail the search party. He was dismissed by those who noticed him as a slow-witted country bumpkin who had drifted into the city on market day like so many from the surrounding area. It was a long time since he had last eaten. To stave off hunger, he bought a hunk of bread then drank water from the chained iron cup beside the pump. He felt restored.

Daniel realised that his disguise had limited use. It might deceive the casual observer in a crowd but it would not pass the more searching scrutiny of the guards at the various gates. If he tried to walk past them, Daniel would probably be arrested, and none of the people returning to their farms would be taken in by him. Close to, they would recognise him as an impostor. His hands were strong but they had not been mottled and hardened by work on the land. While his face might be dirty, his hair was still too well-groomed and had no resemblance to the unkempt thatch of a labourer.

Making use of the crowds, Daniel took the opportunity to get his bearings, noting which road led to the main gate and which to the other gates that pierced the city wall. He passed a group of Bavarian soldiers at one point and they ignored him completely. Hours slipped by and the first shadows of evening began to creep across Augsburg. Vendors dismantled their stalls and loaded their unsold wares on to wagons and carts. The last customers started to leave the marketplace. Deprived of his cover, Daniel sneaked off down a foul-smelling alleyway, still carrying the box on his shoulder and avoiding the gaze of anyone who went by in the opposite direction. He felt more vulnerable now, worried that he might encounter a patrol and be stopped for questioning.

General Salignac would not abandon the search. As long as Daniel was in the city, he was in grave danger. Having no weapon, his disguise was his only means of defence. When he came to a corner where two donkeys were tethered, he sat against the wall beside them to consider his next move. The animals shielded him from the gaze of the occasional passerby and enabled him to have his first proper rest since the exertions of the duel. With light fading out of the sky, he turned his thoughts to Abigail Piper and to the two men who had abducted her. On her behalf, Daniel had been able to kill Frédéric Seurel and he hoped that he would one day be in a position to dispose of Charles Catto as well. It was Catto who had kidnapped Abigail and kept her in a state of terror. Daniel wanted him dead.

General Armand Salignac was still shaking with fury. As he paced the floor of his quarters, he rid himself of a whole series of expletives before rounding on Charles Catto.

'Why did you let him get away like that?' he demanded.

'I was too busy helping my friend, General.'

'You should have gone after the rogue.'

'Frédéric had been run through,' said Catto reasonably. 'I could hardly race off and leave him there in that condition. He and I have endured many misadventures these past couple of months. Captain Rawson has been an elusive quarry.'

'I want him caught and brought here!' roared Salignac.

'I'm sure that he will be – in time.'

'What's taking them so long?'

'Augsburg is a big place, General. It has lots of hiding places.'

'I want every one of them searched. I said from the start that we should have sent French soldiers after him. These mutton-headed Bavarians are as blind as bats.'

'They *know* the city,' Catto told him. 'Our soldiers do not. While we are waiting – and it will not be a long wait, God willing – you may wish to decide on a suitable death for Captain Rawson.'

'I'll have him hanged and left to rot.'

'Would you not prefer to take him on in a duel

again? You are far superior as a swordsman and drew the first blood.'

'My wrist is still sore,' said the other, rubbing it gently with the other hand. 'When my sword hit that wall, it sprained my wrist and jolted my arm. Captain Rawson was very fortunate in that duel. He'll have no such luck next time.'

'I'm sorry that Frédéric will not be there to see him die.'

'There's someone else I would like to have been present at his execution,' said Salignac, thinking of his wife.

'I kept a full reckoning of our expenses,' said Catto, taking some papers from his pocket. 'Is this a convenient time to give them to you?'

'No, it's not!'

'You told me to keep an accurate record, General Salignac.'

'What I told you to do was to kill Captain Rawson.'

'I felt that *you* would enjoy that more than either of us.'

'And I would have done,' said Salignac, 'had he not slipped through my fingers like that. On balance, it would have been better if you had obeyed the orders you were given.'

'Catching him alive was more difficult than killing him.'

'But you've not caught him,' said Salignac. 'The man is at large.'

'That was an accident, General.' He held up the papers. 'As for my reckoning...'

'Don't bother me with that now, Charles!'

'You promised to pay our expenses and give us

a large reward.'

'The money has to be earned first. Until Captain Rawson has been captured and put to death, you'll get nothing. Put your papers away,' shouted Salignac, knocking them from his hand and sending them floating to the floor, 'and stop bothering me!'

Charles Catto controlled his indignation. 'I'll join the search,' he said and went swiftly out of the room.

While darkness made it easier for Daniel Rawson to hide, it also intensified the hunt. More people were involved in the search and the Bavarians had been joined by French soldiers. Carrying torches, they went down every road, street and alleyway, banging on doors, storming into taverns and respecting nobody's privacy. Even the brothels were invaded and inspected. It took all of Daniel's speed and agility to keep ahead of the pack. When he was not diving into dark corners or lying flat behind a water trough, he was taking evasive action of another kind. At one point, with soldiers approaching him from both ends of a street, his only means of escape was to climb up the side of a house and spread-eagle himself on the roof.

It turned out to be his salvation. When the soldiers had finally marched past and the acrid smell of their torches had been dissipated by the cool night air, Daniel was able to take a cautious look across the city. Blazing light told him that he was surrounded by search parties but they all seemed to be moving away from him. The street below was deserted. Before he could climb down, however, he heard the clatter of hooves and saw a rider coming out of the gloom. Daniel obeyed instinct. As the soldier arrived below him, he hurled himself down the roof and landed on the man's back, knocking him from the saddle and staying on top of him as they dropped to the ground.

The soldier was stunned by force of the impact. Though he tried to defend himself, he was no match for Daniel, who pinned him down and got both hands to his neck. Life was slowly squeezed out of the man and he went limp. It was only when he had throttled him that Daniel realised he had killed a French soldier. Of equal importance was the fact that he had just acquired a horse. Startled by the attack, the animal had been too well-trained to bolt and had simply trotted a little way along the street. Daniel soon retrieved it. When he had tethered the horse, he dragged the corpse into a lane and began to strip it of the uniform. He was glad to possess a sword once more.

He could have wished for a bigger man but he took what he had with gratitude. Shedding his own rough garb, he put on the coat, hat and breeches of a soldier in a French cavalry regiment, using the sacking to cover part of the dead body. As he mounted the horse, he realised how tight the uniform was on him but nobody would observe sartorial deficiencies in the dark. Anxious to be out of the city before the dead body was discovered, Daniel headed for the main gate. By the light of the torches, he saw to his relief that Bavarians were on guard duty. Talking his way past French soldiers, while wearing an ill-fitting uniform, might have posed more problems.

Digging in his heels, he cantered along the road to give a sense of urgency then drew the horse in a semi-circle as he came to a halt.

'Open the gates!' he said, speaking in German.

'Why?' asked one of the guards.

'I have despatches for Versailles and must leave post haste.'

'Show us your pass.'

'I'm acting on the authority of General Salignac,' said Daniel impatiently. 'If you insist on holding me up, you'll answer to him.' The guards hesitated. 'Very well,' he went on, turning his horse, 'I'll fetch the general in person and he'll have you all flogged.'

'Wait!' called the guard.

'You are obstructing a royal courier.'

'I am sorry, my friend. We were told to stop everyone. There's a fugitive in the city and nobody must be allowed to leave.'

'The fellow has been caught,' said Daniel. 'When you Bavarians failed to capture him, some sharp-eyed French carabiniers tracked him down. I saw the man being dragged off to General Salignac. Well?' he challenged. 'Do you want to suffer the same fate as the fugitive?'

'Open the gate,' said the guard and two men rushed to obey. 'I owe you an apology, my friend. Take your despatches to Versailles.'

'I will,' said Daniel. 'I bid you all good night!'

Without waiting to hear their farewells, he kicked his horse and went swiftly out through the half-open gate. The city of Augsburg remained full of noise and intrusion as the search continued but the fugitive was never found. Daniel Rawson was riding hell for leather through the night.

Having crossed the Danube, the Confederate army established a camp from which it could range into the whole of Bavaria. British soldiers were now further away from home than they had ever been during the war and one of them in particular found it irksome. Henry Welbeck had been drilling his men under the watchful eye of Charles, Lord Churchill. When it was all over, the sergeant sought information.

'How much farther do we have to go, my lord?' asked Henry Welbeck, his face a study in displeasure. 'We've been marching for months now.'

'We may have to continue for a few months more yet,' replied Churchill. 'This is a long campaign, Sergeant. It will be autumn before we can think of returning to England.'

'Some will never return.'

'That's true, alas. Our losses have been severe and the one prediction we can make is that several other names will be added to the list before we're done.'

'At least, *she* won't be there to see it happen.'

'Who?'

'Miss Abigail Piper,' said Welbeck. 'The young lady is on her way back home and I, for one, was glad to see her go.'

'I suspect that most of us were,' said Churchill evenly. 'Miss Piper was a charming addition to the camp but an army on the march has no need of such charm and beauty. Most of us would prefer to meet someone like Miss Piper at a ball in London.'

'Not me, my lord.'

'Are you not a dancing man, Sergeant?'

'Only when I have to dodge the enemy's fire,' said Welbeck. 'I can dance like a dervish then. As for female company, I shun it in and outside the army. It always leads to mishap.'

'That's not true at all.'

'I speak as I find, my lord.'

'Then you have clearly never found the right woman to grace your life. I daresay that you have never even looked for one but most of our troops have been fortunate in that regard. Marriage can be a great comfort, even when you are apart from your wife.'

'I get my comfort from staying apart from *all* women.'

Churchill laughed. 'Then you are a real oddity.'

'I've seen the harm they can bring,' said Welbeck soulfully. 'Take that Miss Piper, my lord. She caused a real stir when she first arrived in camp. There was crude gossip about her among my men and the flash of her skirt will have brought out the jokers in other regiments as well. Worst of all, she distracted Captain Rawson.'

'Yes,' said Churchill sorrowfully. 'That was a bad business.'

'I rode with him when the young lady was held hostage. I felt as if I was taking him to the scaffold. It's not right, my lord.'

'Captain Rawson is a brave man. He saved her life.'

'And lost his own in return,' snapped Welbeck,

letting his anger show. 'I'm sorry, my lord,' he continued, speaking more calmly, 'but I held the captain in the highest respect. If there's fighting ahead, he's the sort of officer we need most.'

'I couldn't agree more,' said Churchill, 'but all may not be lost. I refuse to believe that Daniel Rawson is dead until I have clear proof of the fact. He's had amazing escapes before. Who knows? He may yet have survived this latest crisis.'

Lips pursed, Welbeck shook his head. 'He's gone, sir. Not even Captain Rawson will come through this,' he decided. 'He surrendered to a man who'd already tried to kill him twice – and he did so in order to save a silly young woman. That's not bravery, my lord, it's sheer bloody madness.'

Daniel Rawson did not slow down until he was well clear of Augsburg. If the dead soldier was discovered, and if it transpired that someone had left by the main gate in a uniform taken from the corpse, there would definitely be a chase. Daniel was still deep behind enemy lines and he could not afford to relax. At the same time, he could not over-tax his horse by pushing him too hard. Stopping at the first village, he went into a tavern to take directions from the landlord, knowing that he would be leaving a clue for any pursuit but needing to ensure that he was on the right road. Once out of the village, he proceeded due north at a steady canter.

Daniel still had the best part of twenty miles to go through the Bavarian countryside. Rain began to fall and he was soon drenched. His uniform felt tighter than ever, pinching him under his arms and climbing a couple of inches above his wrist. Yet he dared not discard it in case he met an enemy patrol. It was well past midnight when he reached the next village and it was in total darkness. Skirting the houses, he rejoined the road on the other side of the little community. An hour later, when the rain had stopped, he felt able to stop in order to rest his horse and allow the animal to drink from a stream and crop some grass. Slipping off his hat and coat, Daniel scooped up handfuls of water to wipe the dirt from his face.

It was only now that he was free at last that he realised how weary he was. From the moment when he had been taken captive, he had not had a wink of sleep and had been in a state of continuous tension. Daniel had to fight to stay awake. Looking to the future, he hoped that Abigail Piper would have departed from the camp. Though he had rescued her from the clutches of her captors, he did not relish the prospect of being showered with her apologies and overwhelmed by her gratitude. Daniel yearned for a long passage of time before he and Abigail ever met again.

In spite of his efforts to keep his eyes open, he eventually dozed off for a while, waking with a start and scolding himself for falling asleep. He put on his hat and coat again and untied his horse. Resuming his ride, he kept to the road as it meandered through a thick forest before straightening when it met open country. A first finger of light pointed to the approach of dawn. Daniel found the silence comforting and, after a period of captivity in a boisterous city, the sense of being completely alone was a positive tonic.

It did not last long. From somewhere ahead of him came the sound of many hooves clacking on the surface of the road. Daniel turned his own mount off the track and hid behind a stand of trees nearby. Minutes later, a troop of cavalry went past in the direction of Augsburg. He could not see the colour of their uniforms but they were clearly going to reinforce the garrison. Daniel's immediate fear was that, on the way, they might meet riders pursuing the fugitive and join in the chase. It made him urge his horse into a gallop.

The blanket of darkness gradually lifted to reveal a beautiful landscape that Daniel had no time to enjoy. Intent on putting as much distance as possible between himself and any pursuit, he pressed on until he reached a range of hills. The peak of the first hill commanded a view that stretched back for miles. Nobody was following him and he was, in any case, well over halfway to his destination. Daniel allowed himself and his horse a longer rest this time before pressing on. His dash for freedom had succeeded and he could maintain a less frantic pace from now on. He was even able to notice the rural splendour of his surroundings. Arriving at a hamlet, he chose to ride straight through it, wondering what the inhabitants would make of a French trooper in a uniform that was visibly too small for him.

The miles rolled steadily by. When he stopped to speak to a farmer, he was offered food and drink in return for news of what was happening in the war. His horse appreciated a mouthful of hay and the chance to dip his nose in the water trough. Donauworth was now less than five miles away and he guessed that the camp would be even closer than that by now. Daniel continued on his way until he came to a wooded rise that looked tranquil in the sunshine. It was an illusion. Almost as soon as he entered the trees, a shot was fired and his horse buckled underneath him.

Daniel's reactions were swift. Jerking his feet from the stirrups, he rolled clear of the animal as it hit the ground with a thud and neighed in distress. He then darted for the nearest cover, pulling out his sword as he did so. He could hear muffled voices approaching. Seeing some large bushes behind him, he plunged deeper into the undergrowth and hid behind them, straining his ears for telltale sounds. The snap of bracken warned him that someone was close and the first thing that came into view was a musket. With one swish of the sword, Daniel knocked it to the ground, jumping out to confront the soldier who had been holding it, only to find that he was face to face with a corporal from his own regiment.

'What the devil are you doing, Reynolds?' he demanded.

The corporal blinked. 'Is that *you*, Captain Rawson?'

'Of course, it is, man!'

'We took you for a French soldier, sir.'

'Then you should have tried to capture me. All you've done is to lose us a valuable cavalry horse.' Sheathing his word, Daniel picked up the musket. 'Listen to the poor animal. Let's put him out of his misery – and call off the others.'

'Hold your fire!' yelled the corporal. 'It's Captain Rawson!'

Daniel went back to the road where the horse was still convulsed in pain. The musket ball had shattered a hind leg and it was unable to stand. Its head was flailing about and its eyes rolling fearfully. Daniel put the musket to its head and fired the ball into its brain. After quivering violently for a few moments, it lay dead. The other members of the foraging party came out of the trees to stare in wonder at their captain. The corporal spoke for all of them.

'Why are you dressed like that, sir?' he asked.

Daylight exposed the ugly truth in Augsburg. The discovery of the dead trooper was linked with the news of a courier who left the city at night by the main gate. It fell to Charles Catto to pass on the tidings and they brought a fresh explosion from General Salignac.

'He's *escaped?*' he bellowed.

'So it would appear, General.'

'How on earth could he escape from a whole army? Is every soldier in the city a complete imbecile?'

'The guards on duty at the main gate are being punished,' said Catto. 'It was they who foolishly let him out.'

'Has pursuit been organised?'

'There's no point in it, General Salignac. He has been gone over eight hours. They could never catch up with Captain Rawson.'

'Someone must do so.'

'I know,' agreed Catto, teeth clenched, 'and the

311

task must be mine. He belongs to me. I'll set off at once.'

'Make no mistakes this time,' said Salignac, jabbing a finger at him. 'Captain Rawson must be killed. Don't come back unless you bring un-equivocal proof of his death.'

CHAPTER FIFTEEN

Unable to tempt the Elector out of the safety of Augsburg, the Duke of Marlborough adopted a policy of wholesale destruction. Farms, hamlets and villages were razed to the ground in various parts of Bavaria and thousands of refugees fled in terror to the cities. There was no respite. As one raiding party returned, another took its place. Their orders were to leave a scene of devastation behind them. It was over sixty years since Bavaria had last seen warfare within its borders and it was appalled by the atrocities committed. The Mar-grave of Baden had protested strongly against the policy and there were those in the British army who objected to what was happening.

'It's a disgrace,' said Daniel Rawson. 'I yield to none in my admiration of our captain-general but I do believe he's conducting a mistaken cam-paign.'

'Have you told him that, Dan?'

'He's not interested in my opinions.'

'They're shared by a lot of people,' said Henry Welbeck. 'None of my men would take any pleasure in setting fire to thatched cottages and seeing whole families put to flight with children in their arms. I'm grateful that we're not involved in such work.'

'But we can see the hideous results of it. When I escaped from Augsburg,' Daniel recalled, 'I was given food and drink at a little farmhouse. I had to watch as it went up in smoke. This is no way to fight a war, Henry. Our job is to kill enemy soldiers, not to put the fear of death into innocent civilians.'

'Yet the policy might work.'

'It's not done so yet.'

'Give it time, Dan.'

'We've already had too much of it,' complained Daniel, 'without any real effect. Because we lack a proper siege train, it took us the best part of a week to bring Rain to its knees and, even then, the garrison did not capitulate. They were accorded the friendliest of terms of surrender and marched off to join the Elector. What kind of a war is this,' he wondered, 'when we harass ordinary people and let the enemy soldiers go free?'

'Everyone suffers in a war,' said Welbeck lugubriously. 'It's not like a game with set of rules that we all obey.'

'It should be, Henry.'

'Can you imagine the French abiding by rules of warfare?'

'As a matter of fact, I can,' said Daniel. 'There was a time when King Louis tried to constrain his armies from pillage and the taking of hostages. He wanted a levy exacted from a defeated town or province, and the amount was to be no

313

greater than the figure paid in tax by the inhabitants to their overlord. Do you see what he was trying to do?' he said. 'He was trying to instil civilised values into French soldiers.'

'Then he failed.'

'Not entirely.'

'You should talk to some of the veterans from the Dutch army,' said Welbeck. 'They remember the brutal way the French behaved during the Dutch Wars. And it's less than twenty years since these Frenchies wiped cities like Mannheim, Worms and Speyer off the map. There was no sign of any civilised values then.'

'I still believe that we need rules of engagement.'

'What we need is peace, Dan – years and years of it.'

'We'll get none till we've defeated France for good,' said Daniel levelly, 'and putting the torch to Bavaria is not the best way to do it.'

'It might flush the Elector out of his hiding place.'

'He's too secure in Augsburg. I've seen the fortifications there.'

'What about his estates?'

'He'll have sent men out to defend those against attack.'

'Then he'll have weakened his army,' said Welbeck, 'so the Duke's plan will have achieved something useful. We'll have fewer of those flat-faced Bavarians to fight.'

They were in Daniel's tent. Though they might disagree with some of the orders they were given, they obeyed them to the letter. Unless invited to give his opinion, Daniel would never openly criticise decisions taken by superior officers. Welbeck never stopped criticising them but only when he was alone with his friend. It was weeks since Daniel's escape from Augsburg and he was enjoying the unalloyed pleasure of a blunt interchange of views with the sergeant. Daniel had been hurt and saddened by the policy of ravaging Bavaria and it had deepened Welbeck's melancholy.

'Is it true that the Duke is ill?' asked Welbeck.

'He suffers from severe headaches,' replied Daniel, 'and hasn't left his quarters for three days.'

'I've had a severe headache since the day I joined the army.'

'Nonsense – you're one of the healthiest men I know.'

'My brain feels like a red hot cannon ball.'

'That's because you drink too much, Henry.'

'Nobody would allow *me* to retire to my quarters.'

'We need you ready for action,' said Daniel. 'Now that Marshal Tallard has reached Augsburg with the reinforcements, there'll be another battle before long.'

'There was a time when commanders had the sense to avoid battles,' said Welbeck, striking a wistful note. 'Skirmishes and sieges were the order of the day then. That kept the losses down. More of our troops stayed alive. It's not easy to replace dead soldiers and damaged equipment, Dan. I vote for a siege every time.'

'Then you should have ridden off with the Margrave of Baden,' said Daniel. 'He's going to invest Ingolstadt. We must have a second crossing over the Danube in case the one at Donauworth comes under threat. Ingolstadt will be battered until resistance crumbles.'

'If there's going to be a battle, we need the Austrians with us.'

'We'll have Prince Eugene of Savoy instead.'

'Baden's men fought like tigers at the Schellenberg.'

'Yes,' said Daniel, 'and he's been claiming credit for the victory ever since. That's an insult to the British and Dutch soldiers who gave their lives that day. Baden, alas, has not yet grasped the concept of a shared triumph. He wants all the glory. No,' he concluded, 'I'll wager that Prince Eugene will prove a better ally in combat.'

Prince Eugene of Savoy was delighted to have been reunited with the main army. While the majority of troops had now crossed the river with Marlborough, the Italians remained on the north bank to observe enemy movements and to guard Donauworth from possible attack. The pontoon bridges allowed easy access between the two sections of the Confederate army. With some urgency, Prince Eugene used one of them to join Marlborough for a council of war. Charles, Lord Churchill and Adam Cardonnel were also present.

'The French are on the move,' Eugene reported. 'They have crossed to the north bank of the Danube at Lauingen and seem intent on bringing their whole army there. The plain of Dillingen is crowded with troops.'

'I did not expect so decisive a move,' admitted Marlborough.

'I had a good position from which to observe them, Your Grace, but I dared not stay the night there. With only eighteen battalions, I was hopelessly outnumbered.'

'Where are your troops now, Prince Eugene?'

'At our camp near Donauworth,' said the other. 'We fell back there. May I please impress upon you the importance of not being trapped between the mountains and the Danube?'

'There's no need to do that,' Marlborough told him. 'I appreciate it all too clearly. Well,' he added, looking around his companions, 'this is troubling news. Marshal Tallard clearly wishes to threaten our supply lines running back through Nordlingen.'

'If he cuts through those,' said Churchill, 'we'll be isolated.'

'He'll not do so, John. We'll stop Tallard dead.'

'Where?'

'It will have to be at Hochstadt,' said Eugene. 'That's the last open ground where a battle could be fought before the mountains close in on the river.'

'Then that's where it must be,' decreed Marlborough, looking at the map laid out on the table before him. His index finger found the spot. 'We'll meet him here – close to the village of Blenheim.'

'That will surprise Tallard,' said Cardonnel. 'He won't expect us to resist. His army contains some of the finest and most feared regiments in Europe. He'll think he's outmanoeuvred us and

317

that we'll be too weak to offer battle.'

'We'll cross the river at once and unite with Prince Eugene's army at Munster,' said Marlborough firmly. 'Tallard will soon learn that we are eager to take him on. Is everyone agreed?'

The others gave their consent with a nod. Prince Eugene left to return to his camp and Churchill went off to issue marching orders. Marlborough was left alone with Cardonnel. Both men were excited by the promise that the crucial battle they had sought against the French would take place at last. Years of waiting, training and planning would finally come to fruition.

'It's a pity we cannot call upon Baden,' said Cardonnel. 'I know he would probably want to steal all the glory but his forces would have been invaluable.'

'Securing another crossing of the Danube was vital, Adam,' said Marlborough. 'That's why I sent Baden to Ingolstadt. I also sent him a further ten squadrons and we'll most certainly miss those when we take on the French. But I remain confident,' he went on, rubbing his hands together. 'In taking the action he has done, Tallard has revealed his complacency. He thinks his army invincible and that we'll quail before it. We'll make him regret his mistake.'

'Yes, Your Grace.'

He gathered up his map. 'We must be away.'

'Before we go,' said Cardonnel, raising a hand, 'I need to remind you about the French deserters who came in yesterday.'

'They can tell us nothing that Prince Eugene has not already told us. Besides, so many of these so-called deserters are no more than French spies, planted on us to gather intelligence.'

'That may be so in some cases, Your Grace. All the men are interrogated to make sure that they are genuine deserters. One of them at least deserved to be heard.'

'Why is that, Adam?'

'He was a member of General Salignac's staff,' said Cardonnel. 'He's not some frightened man from the ranks. He's a senior officer who might well have useful information for us.'

'Then let's hear the fellow. What's his name?'

'Frédéric Seurel.'

'Bring him in.'

Cardonnel lifted the flap of the tent and beckoned a man outside. He stepped back so that the deserter could enter. Wearing the uniform of a captain in the French army, Charles Catto came boldly into the tent.

On August 13, 1704, the Confederate army began its march at three o'clock in the morning. Preceded by an advance guard of Horse, eight columns marched through the darkness along routes that had been chosen so that there was no danger of one body of men impeding another. The infantry tramped ruinously over standing crops in the fields, leaving the road free for the teams of horses pulling the cannon, ammunition wagons and the pontoon train. In total, over 50,000 men were on the move. Not all of them were happy about the situation.

'I hate night marches,' grumbled Henry Welbeck as he trod on a stone that made him stumble. 'I like to see where I'm going.'

'Console yourself with the thought that we'll catch them off guard,' said Daniel, riding beside him. 'The French and the Bavarians will still be fast asleep.'

'Lucky buggers!'

'We're the lucky ones, Henry. This is a day of destiny.'

Welbeck was sceptical. 'It doesn't feel like it to me, Dan.'

'I don't believe that. You have the same tingle that I always have before a battle. You have the same fluttering in your stomach and the same buzzing inside your head. You know that today is special.'

'What's special about losing more of my men?' retorted the other. 'What's special about being deafened by the sound of enemy cannon, charged at by their cavalry and shot at by their infantry?'

'You could end the battle as a hero.'

'I'm more likely to end it in an unmarked grave.'

'We've never lost an important battle under the Duke,' Daniel reminded him. 'I'd always back him to outwit Marshal Tallard.'

'Which is the bigger army?'

'Theirs.'

'Then stop telling me it's a day of destiny for us.'

'Superior numbers don't always win.'

'But it's always encouraging to have them on your side,' said Welbeck, looking up at him. 'I've never shirked a fight but I do prefer it when it's a fair one.'

They had been marching for a couple of hours and tiny specks of light were starting to appear in the black canvas of night, only to be lost from time to time in a swirling mist. Daniel was optimistic. It had been six weeks since the hostilities at the Schellenberg. All that the Confederate army had done since then was to raid a series of Bavarian settlements and leave them in flames. Much to his relief, Daniel had not been directly involved in the wanton destruction. What he wanted was a full-scale confrontation with the enemy and it was now about to take place. Nothing else mattered. He had forgotten about Abigail Piper, about his escape from Augsburg and about all the other events in the past few months. The future of the war could be determined on a plain near the village of Blenheim.

Pulsing with energy, Daniel was ready to do everything in his power to achieve the victory he felt was within their grasp, and he knew that Henry Welbeck would fight with the same resolve. Hidden behind the sergeant's characteristic moans lay the wholehearted commitment of a professional soldier. When battle was joined, Henry Welbeck would not hold back. Like his friend, he would wish to be involved in the fiercest action.

Daniel emitted a sudden laugh. 'I was just thinking,' he said. 'How nice it would be to see the look on Marshal Tallard's face when he realises we are coming!'

During his time as French ambassador at the Court of St James's, Camille d'Hostun, Comte de

Tallard, had been immensely popular in England. He was known for his lavish hospitality, for the opulence with which he surrounded himself and for his diplomatic skills. He and Marlborough had met a number of times at social events and got on well together. Now that he held a marshal's baton, however, he accorded his rival no more than a cold respect. Even on a campaign, he liked to eat the best food and drink the finest wines. As a man who enjoyed his sleep, he was not pleased to be roused from his comfortable bed with the news that the enemy was approaching.

Notwithstanding his reputation as a diplomat and as a soldier, Tallard was not an imposing figure and his shortsightedness was so bad that it was joked about behind his back. Even with a telescope, he could not discern the true meaning in the approach of the Confederate cavalry. He believed that the show of force was merely a distraction to allow the main Allied army to creep away to safety with its tail between its legs. The despatch he dashed off to Louis XIV confirmed this belief – *They can now be seen drawn up at the head of their camp, and it appears they will march today. Word in the country is that they are going to Nordlingen. If that is so, they will leave us between them and the Danube, and consequently they will have difficulty in sustaining the places that they have taken in Bavaria.'*

Shortly after his messenger had ridden off, Tallard was forced to realise his blunder. It was barely seven o'clock when he received reports that the entire enemy army was heading in his direction. He was stunned. Summoning Marshal

Marsin and the Elector of Bavaria, he led them up the church tower in Blenheim so that they could get a better view of the enemy's movements. The three commanders tried to divine the significance of what they saw. Having underestimated Marlborough's boldness, Tallard now went on to misinterpret it.

'He must have acquired reinforcements,' he concluded. 'Even in his rashest moment, the Duke of Marlborough would not contemplate an attack on us unless he had greater numbers at his disposal. And there's another worrying development,' he went on. 'There are rumours that the Margrave of Baden is on his way here to add his support. That would markedly strengthen the enemy and we know to our cost what a fearless general Baden is. No, gentlemen, only one course is open to us. We must fight a defensive action.'

His companions agreed with his decision. They understood the importance of holding both flanks of the Franco-Bavarian lines. No matter how large the enemy forces, they had faith in their strong defensive positions. One of them was around the village of Blenheim.

When they were two miles from Blenheim, the Confederate army split into two wings. With 36,000 troops, Marlborough intended to attack on the left against a French army under Tallard of almost equal size. Prince Eugene of Savoy, at the head of 16,000 men, was ordered to attack on the right against the forces of Marshal Marsin and the Elector. He was thus taking on a combined army of 24,000. Unknown to Tallard, he had far more men in the field than Marlborough. Where the Allied army did have clear superiority was in the number of their cavalry squadrons.

As in most battles, the opening shots were fired by the artillery. The French right wing discharged the first cannon balls and a British soldier was the initial casualty. Colonel Blood, the artillery commander, was told by Marlborough to choose his counter-batteries. When these had been inspected and approved by the Duke, the bombardment began with a vengeance, cannon booming on both sides for the best part of four hours. The thunderous exchange of fire was so earsplitting that, it was later learnt, the Margrave of Baden could hear it forty miles away in Ingolstadt.

Daniel Rawson was proud of his battalion. They had to wait patiently for hours until Prince Eugene and his men had looped around to the position from which they could attack. Throughout this time, the French bombardment continued with unceasing ferocity. Like all the other battalions, Daniel's had been ordered to sit or lie on the ground to escape the worst of the deafening cannonade. They were motionless targets but they did not flinch or run as the cannonballs and howitzer shells rained upon them. They had been schooled by men like Sergeant Welbeck to obey orders under fire. Daniel noted with gratification that even when some were killed outright or received critical injuries the soldiers around them did not lose their nerve.

There was another cause for delay. Before they could close with the enemy, the Confederate army had to cross the Nebel stream, a tributary of the Danube. There were few places where soldiers could cross in numbers. While the brigades waited, therefore, pioneers went on ahead to level the banks of the stream, to build causeways out of fascines, to repair the old stone bridge torn down by the French and to erect new bridges made of tin pontoons. It was well after noon when the order was finally given and the infantry rose to their feet and moved forward with their bayonets fixed.

Daniel's battalion was under the command of Brigadier-General Rowe who had warned his men that no shot should be fired until he had struck the enemy barricade with his sword. By one o'clock, they began to wade across the Nebel, aided by the fact that the ground fell slightly from around Blenheim, giving them protection to re-form their ranks before marching towards the village. When they were 300 yards away, they lay down to await the arrival of the Hessians under Major-General Wilkes, and a pair of guns. As soon as the cannon were in position, they pounded the French barricades.

Marching on foot, Archibald, Lord Rowe, led his men forward in the teeth of unrelenting artillery fire. When they got within thirty yards of the palisade, they were hit by a first volley from French musketeers. British soldiers crashed to the ground on every side but the drums kept beating and the battalions held their shape as they moved inexorably forward in their serried ranks. Rowe reached the outer palisade, but, as he struck it with his sword, he was shot from close range. The lieutenant-colonel and major who ran to his aid were also cut down by enemy fire.

The fusillade was returned by the advancing brigade, their flintlock muskets popping across a wide front before being reloaded for a second discharge. Though many French soldiers were hit by the onslaught, they still outnumbered the attackers and they were shooting from behind barricades at unprotected targets. Having lost their commander and under withering fire, the first line of Rowe's brigade eventually fell back. The French cavalry posted to the left of Blenheim were quick to exploit the signs of disarray. General Zurlauben led out three squadrons of the Gens d'Armes of the Royal Household cavalry.

They charged at the exposed flank of Rowe's own regiment and, as it struggled to form a square, they fired their pistols then used their flashing swords to hack a way through the disordered red uniforms. To the horror of the British soldiers, their regimental colours were seized. Elated by their success, the horsemen continued to slash and stab at will. They were so confident of success that they did not notice the Hessians being deployed to their flank and rear. It was only when deadly volleys rang out that they realised the danger they were in.

Driving the Gens d'Armes before them, the disciplined ranks of Hessians spread confusion among the cavalry. Some horses bolted, many crashed to the ground as they were hit by musket balls or gored with bayonets, and an endless succession of riders were toppled from their saddles. The unthinkable had happened. Elite French cavalry squadrons had been trounced by Hessian infantry. Daniel Rawson's battalion swiftly rallied and joined in the attack. Fighting on foot, he used his sword to cut and thrust. When a French blade whistled down at him, he parried it expertly then reached up quickly with his other hand to haul the rider from his mount. Before the man could even begin to defend himself, Daniel had stabbed him through the stomach.

Pulling his sword out, he left his victim writhing in agony and ran across to the riderless horse now looking around in bewilderment amid the mêlée. Within a second, Daniel was in the saddle, turning the animal in a circle until he saw what he wanted. He dug in his heels and rode towards the plundered regimental colours that were being held high by a French cavalry officer. It was a humiliation that could not be borne. Daniel had to kill two more riders and wound a third before he got close to the captured colours. Though Hessian soldiers converged on the man holding his trophy to block his escape, Daniel got to him first.

He was enraged that a Frenchman should be brandishing the colours of a British regiment. It was an unforgivable insult. There was a furious clash of blades as the man tried to defend himself but Daniel's assault was irresistible. With a final sweep of his sword, he almost cut his adversary's face in half, leaving him crazed by pain and blinded by blood. Before the man tumbled to the ground, Daniel snatched the colours from him and carried them aloft to the remnants of Rowe's regiment whose honour had been retrieved.

The battle continued for hour after gruelling hour. The Confederate army had successes and reverses, breaking through at some points while being strongly repulsed at others. As the afternoon wore on, the deficiencies of the French defence became more apparent. Marshal Tallard had drawn up his men in and around Blenheim, keeping them separate from those under the command of Marshal Marsin and the Elector of Bavaria. The latter had built their respective barricades around Oberglau and Lutzingen. While the two flanks of the Franco-Bavarian forces were therefore well-defended, the long centre ground between the two had nothing like the same strength and organisation.

Marlborough was alert to the gaps in the enemy dispositions. There was a patent lack of unity. It made him wonder if Marsin and the Elector felt aggrieved that, having been beaten by the Allied armies, they had to rely on Tallard to rescue them. Both commanders were trying to vindicate their reputations now. As Prince Eugene of Savoy led an attack on the right flank, he was met with such stern resistance from Bavarian soldiers that he was forced to retire. A second assault also ended with a hasty retreat and heavy losses.

It was on the left flank that the seeds of victory were sown. When the illustrious squadrons of Gens d'Armes were put to flight by the Hessians and by supporting British Horse and Dragoons, the brigades of Foot re-formed for a second attack. Inside Blenheim, meanwhile, there was considerable alarm. Until that moment, it was inconceivable that the finest cavalry in France could be defeated in battle. When he saw them limping back, one of the generals inside the village resorted to panic and called up the reserve.

A small settlement of some 300 houses was suddenly flooded by French infantry, packed so tightly together that they got in each others' way. When the Confederate army attacked, there was hand to hand fighting at the barricades but the defence of Blenheim was grossly impeded by the masses of men and equipment clogging up its streets. Marlborough did not need to capture the town. Once it was contained, it could offer no support to centre or to the right flank. He was able to concentrate his attention on those areas.

Help was most needed on the right flank where Prince Eugene's men had been driven back for the third time, incurring even more casualties. Some of them despaired of ever making headway against the superior numbers of Bavarians. Deserters began to flee. Prince Eugene was so disgusted that his soldiers were running from a fight that he shot two of them dead with his own pistol. He then sent urgent messages to Marlborough, requesting support. When the relief came, it was led by the commander-in-chief himself. With fresh troops at his back, Prince Eugene was at last able to make incisive raids on the right flank. The Bavarians cowered behind their defences.

With Blenheim and Lutzingen now effectively contained, both flanks were under control. It was possible for Marlborough to move the main body of his army across the Nebel to advance on the French centre. Seeing the enemy's intention,

Marshal Marsin launched a counter-offensive from his position in Oberglau and the Confederate army was put under intense pressure. Though it buckled, it did not break and brisk redeployment gave it back the advantage it had lost. The steady advance continued into evening, the Allied cavalry retiring behind the infantry when under extreme pressure from the French cavalry, and supported by batteries of artillery that were brought forward.

What turned the battle were the superior tactical skills of the Duke of Marlborough. He knew when and where to strike and how to respond instantly to any reversal. Stuck inside Blenheim, Tallard was simply not in a position to control an army stretched tight across a wide front and lacking any real coordination. For a man of his talent and experience in the field, it was maddening. He was always reacting to situations he could not anticipate. Instead of being able to relieve his allies by attacking the enemy flank, he was bottled up in a village that was bursting at the seams with French soldiers.

Total defeat was only a matter of time. At seven o'clock that evening, Marshal Marsin and the Elector accepted the fact and began to withdraw their forces in an orderly fashion. So exhausted were Prince Eugene and his men that they had no strength to pursue them. Tallard was not allowed the dignity of a retreat. Failing to escape from Blenheim, he surrendered along with most of his staff. For the French and for the Bavarians, it was a shattering defeat from which they would never fully recover. For the Confederate army, it was a triumph that would reverberate throughout Europe.

Daniel Rawson had played no small part in it. Having helped to recapture the colours of Rowe's regiment, he had been fully engaged in the later assaults on Blenheim, fighting on bravely after collecting a range of minor injuries and inspiring his men with his wholehearted commitment. He only quit the field for a short while when he carried the wounded Henry Welbeck through the chaos of the fray to relative safety. Leaving his friend in the hands of a surgeon, Daniel had hurried back to rejoin the battle.

Now that it was all over, he was able to visit the field hospital to check on Welbeck's condition. The sergeant had been very fortunate. A bullet had pierced his thigh but missed the bone. While he had lost a lot of blood, he was in no danger of sacrificing a limb. Despite being surrounded by wounded soldiers, Welbeck was almost cheerful.

'We beat them,' he said, grinning. 'We beat the bastards.'

'We did more than that, Henry. It's too early to give the full numbers yet but, according to what I've heard, we captured Marshal Tallard and his generals, over 1000 officers and almost all the soldiers left in Blenheim.'

'What about our casualties, Dan?'

'There could be as many as 12,000 killed or injured,' said Daniel sadly, 'and they included some good friends. But we accounted for over three times that number in the enemy ranks. We achieved a famous victory. Even you must be pleased to be part of it.'

'I was, Dan. Our men gave of their best.'

'That's what they were trained to do.'

'When the news reaches France, the King will fill his breeches.'

'I don't think they'll be in a hurry to tell him the truth of what happened here today. They'll delay the messengers as long as they can. Bad news upsets King Louis and this news is disastrous.' He studied his friend. 'You're looking better already. You've got some colour back in your face. What you need now is a long rest.'

'Does that mean you'll wait on me hand and foot?'

'I'd be glad to if I was here, Henry,' said Daniel, chuckling, 'but I'll be on my way back to England. I'll be helping to take the good news back home. They may be keeping the result of the battle from King Louis but Her Majesty will rejoice to hear it. I wanted to call on you before I left.'

'Thanks, Dan. I appreciate it.'

'I'll see you when I return.'

'I may have retired from the army by then.'

'People like you *never* retire,' said Daniel, clapping him on the shoulder. 'Without the Sergeant Welbecks of this world, there'd be no such thing as a British army. You're part of its very backbone.'

'Then why don't they pay me more?' challenged Welbeck.

Daniel laughed. 'I'll take the matter up with His Grace when I see him,' he joked. 'A review of sergeants' pay must be a priority. I'm sure he has nothing else to worry about just now.'

Charles Catto had been utterly frustrated by the turn of events. Having tricked his way into the Confederate camp for the third time, he hoped that he simply had to wait until an opportunity arose to kill Daniel Rawson. Instead of that, the whole camp had suddenly erupted into action with the promise of a battle. All that Catto could do was to trail impotently in its wake. Primed by General Salignac, he had been able to provide Marlborough with information that, while not giving away too much, had been accurate and useful. It had established his credibility. Catto had shaved off his beard but left a neat moustache on his face. In uniform, and by adopting a strong French accent, he was a convincing impostor.

Yet his role as a deserter would be meaningless if it not enable him to fulfil his commitment. Catto's fear was that the battle of Blenheim would rob him of his prize and that Daniel would have been mown down with so many other British soldiers during the attack on the village. Having come so far, and taken such enormous pains along the way, he felt that it would be cruel to have Daniel snatched away from him by a nameless French musketeer. Catto was no longer working for General Salignac. When he heard that Blenheim had fallen, he knew that the general would have been taken prisoner and would therefore be inaccessible. Salignac's war was over.

Catto was on his own now. What drove him on was sheer hatred. Daniel Rawson had killed Frédéric Seurel, and, in escaping from Augsburg, he had exposed Catto to the full wrath of Armand Salignac. Deprived of a large financial reward, Catto was fired by a sense of personal mission. He wanted to avenge the death of his friend and had taken on Seurel's name in order to do so. But his plans were shattered by the battle and he was in despair at the British victory. Before he had left Augsburg, Catto had seen Marshal Tallard arrive at the head of an army that was unmatched for its brilliance and its record of success in the field. Yet that same proud army had now been soundly defeated by a smaller force.

It was clear that Daniel Rawson would have contributed to that defeat and – were he still alive – he would thereby have given Catto an additional reason to kill him. The would-be assassin could not destroy an entire army but he could murder a man who, in his febrile mind, symbolised it. As he watched Confederate soldiers trudging back into camp, and as he saw orderlies carrying in the wounded, he prayed that Daniel would be among the survivors and not be one of the many thousands that littered the battlefield.

The first person with whom the Duke of Marlborough had wanted to share news of the triumph was his wife. Borrowing an old tavern bill from a member of his staff, he scrawled a message in pencil.

I have not time to say more, but to beg you will give my duty to the Queen and let her know that her army had this day a glorious victory. M. Tallard and two other generals are in my coach and I am pursuing the rest. The bearer, my aide de camp, Colonel Parke, will give her an account of what has passed and I shall do it in a day or so, by another, more at large.

It was on the following day that Daniel Rawson was summoned to Marlborough's quarters and entrusted with letters that gave a fuller account of the action and its consequences. After the long and intense battle, Daniel was still weary and the superficial wounds he had picked up still smarted. The honour of acting as a courier, however, was the perfect balm. From the moment he was given the despatches, his aches and pains seemed to fade away.

'Ride hard, Daniel,' said Marlborough. 'By the time you reach England, the Queen and Secretary Harley will know only the fact of our victory and be desperate for detail.'

'What about the Dutch, Your Grace?'

'Even they will rejoice at the news though I'll no doubt be pilloried for the scale of our losses. In Vienna, at least, there'll be no carping – except perhaps from the Margrave of Baden.'

'He'll be aggrieved that he was not here,' said Daniel.

'As it happens, we managed without him though our task would have been made easier by the presence of his men. But you must forgive me,' said Marlborough as a memory nudged him. 'I've not congratulated you properly on rescuing the colours of General Rowe's regiment from the enemy.'

Daniel was modest. 'That's nothing,' he said.

'All I captured were regimental colours – you captured a marshal's baton.'

'That was satisfying, I must admit.'

'What will happen to Marshal Tallard?'

'He'll be taken back to England with other prisoners of war.'

'You don't intend to exchange him, then?'

'Oh, no,' said Marlborough with conviction. 'I'm not letting him loose to threaten us again. The marshal has fought his last battle against us.'

'That's good to hear.'

'King Louis might not find it so pleasing.'

'I fancy not,' said Daniel. He patted the leather pouch containing the despatches. 'I'll deliver these in England.'

'Enjoy some rest while you're there. You've deserved it.'

'Thank you, Your Grace.'

'Do you intend to call at the Piper household?'

Marlborough's question had a studied casualness but it hit Daniel like a blow between the eyes. All that he could think about was carrying news of their victory back to England. Decisions about what happened afterwards had never even entered his mind. He was shocked to realise how easily he had forgotten Abigail Piper, and how irrelevant his friendship with her now seemed. On the other hand, he owed her consideration for the way she had followed him all the way into Germany. Daniel had obligations.

'Yes, Your Grace,' he replied. 'I will be calling at the house.'

The sight revived Catto's spirits at once. When he

336

saw Daniel leaving on horseback with two companions, he knew that they must be acting as couriers. Catto's vigil outside Marlborough's quarters had been repaid. He not only discovered that Daniel was still alive but that he was leaving the protection of the camp altogether. It would be much easier to track and kill him on the open road. Though nominally still under guard, Catto had been able to move quite freely around the camp. Leaving it might be more problematic. He needed a change of clothing, a fast horse and an element of luck. The main thing was that Daniel had survived. It was a portent.

The clothing was easily acquired. Catto stole it from a washing line strung between two wagons owned by camp followers. It was too large for him but suitably nondescript. When he filched a hat from the inside of another wagon, he was able to complete the metamorphosis from a French captain into a Dutch civilian. The horse was taken from the stable area where the animals were tethered in long lines. Many of them had collected cuts and gashes during cavalry charges. Catto was careful to choose a horse that had come unharmed through the battle. When nobody was watching, he led his mount quietly away and was almost clear when he was challenged.

The soldier was no more than seventeen but the hardship of army life had added years to his face. Catto gave him a plausible excuse for taking the horse but the soldier was suspicious. When he turned to call for help, he had a hand clasped over his mouth and a dagger inserted into his back. Catto hid the dead body under a pile of hay. It would be some time before it was discovered. As a result of the battle, the camp was in a state of relative disorder and its ranks had been noticeably thinned. Picking his spot, Catto was able to slip past the sentries without being seen.

He was confident of being able to follow Daniel. If the latter were carrying despatches, he would be going to England or The Hague. Whichever his destination, he would take the speediest way north. Catto simply had to stay on the main road and maintain a good pace. Seven miles or so from the camp, he met a farmer who told him that three British soldiers had galloped past him earlier on. Now that his guess about Daniel's route had been confirmed, Catto rode on with renewed zest, speculating on how he could best kill a man who had caused him so much trouble.

It was evening before he finally caught up with them. Daniel and the two subalterns had stopped at an inn to rest their horses and refresh themselves. Catto approached slowly, entering the courtyard with his hat pulled down over his forehead. After tethering his horse, he peeped into the taproom and saw the two subalterns sitting at a table with a drink in their hands. Daniel was not there. When he walked around the outside of the inn, Catto understood why. Instead of drinking with his companions, Daniel had strolled down to the edge of a stream nearby and unbuttoned his uniform to let the breeze cool him down after the sweaty ride.

Sensing that he might never get a better chance, Catto moved with deliberation towards his victim. Under his coat, he was gripping the handle of the dagger that had already killed one British soldier that day. It was about to claim a more important life. Daniel was gazing into the water, seemingly oblivious to all else. In fact, it was the stream that alerted him to sudden danger. The ground sloped sharply downward to the edge of the stream and, as Catto strode purposefully on, his reflection appeared on the surface of the water.

It was only there for a split-second but it was enough to goad Daniel into action. Spinning around, he saw his attacker coming at him with the dagger raised to strike. As Catto closed in on him and stabbed with his weapon, Daniel grabbed his wrist and held it tight. The point of the dagger was only inches from his chest but it did not get any closer. As the two men wrestled violently on the bank, Daniel knocked off his attacker's hat and recognised him. It made him fight even more strenuously. He had a score to settle with Charles Catto.

They were well-matched. Daniel was the stronger of the two but Catto was the more guileful. At the height of the struggle, he stuck out a foot and tripped Daniel up. Though he fell backwards with Catto on top of him, Daniel did not release his grip on the wrist. As he hit the ground, he twisted his hand as sharply as he could then pulled the wrist towards him, embedding the dagger inches into the grass. Before he could pull it out again, Catto was punched so hard in the face that he was forced to release his weapon.

He replied by punching Daniel and by trying to gouge his eye with a thumb. Then he got both hands to Daniel's neck but he did not hold them there for long. Using all his strength, Daniel heaved him off then rolled down the incline with him until both men toppled into the water. It was a fight to the death now as they grappled, punched, kicked and sought for any advantage. The two of them vanished beneath the water, threshing about madly and creating a wide circle of ripples. Catto drew on the memory of what had happened to Frédéric Seurel and had a surge of energy. He began to get the upper hand.

Daniel, however, had his own memories on which to call. He remembered the brutal death of Lieutenant Hopwood, the abduction of Abigail Piper and the duel that was heavily weighted in favour of General Salignac. He remembered the way that Catto had taunted him while he was their captive. The man Daniel was fighting was a traitor, an Englishman in league with the French. Catto was despicable. Stirred by these thoughts as they flashed across his mind, Daniel felt an uprush of power reinforced by a fierce pride. He was on his way to deliver important despatches to Queen and to Parliament. Nobody was going to deprive him of that honour.

Swinging Catto over so that his back was on the bed of the stream, Daniel lifted his own head above the surface and gulped in air before submerging again. The struggle continued but Catto was weakening with every second. His lungs were on fire, his body was aching from the punches he had taken and his limbs were no longer under control. Daniel held him down firmly for another couple of minutes. After one final, desperate attempt to break free, Catto went limp. It was all over. Daniel surfaced and gasped in more air. As he looked down at Catto, he gave a weary smile of celebration. He had finally got rid of the man who had been hired to kill him.

When she returned home, Abigail Piper had begun to see her wild adventure in a different light. Infatuated with Daniel Rawson and buoyed up by the hope of seeing him, she had somehow coped with all the adversity that beset her and Emily Greene. Once back in England, however, the full danger of what she had done became much clearer. Abigail was terrified by her own wilfulness. She had put not only her own life at risk but that of her maid as well. Worst of all, she had been responsible for handing Daniel over to his enemies and she could never forgive herself for that. Viewed objectively, her visit to Germany had bordered on catastrophe.

Her despair had first manifested itself in a physical illness. Having held up gamely all the way back, she had collapsed once she crossed the threshold of her home. A fortnight in bed and regular attendance by a physician had eventually recovered her but there was no cure for the demons in her mind. Weeks after she was back on her feet again, Abigail was still obsessed with her folly. As she sat in the garden with a book in her lap, she was not reading the poetry it contained. She was still agonising over what had happened.

Her sister, Dorothy, recognised the now familiar signs.

'You must not keep blaming yourself, Abigail,'

she said.

'But I did something terrible.'

'It was not intentional.'

'That does not excuse it, Dorothy. I went hundreds of miles to see Daniel then ended up by leading him to his death.'

'You don't know that.'

'I do,' insisted Abigail. 'Those men told me they'd been paid to kill him. They used me to lure Daniel into their hands. Had I not been there, they could not have done that.'

'Then they'd have found some other way.'

'He sacrificed himself for me.'

'I'd expect nothing less of Captain Rawson,' said Dorothy softly.

It was one of the few improvements to come out of the whole business. Abigail and her elder sister had been brought closer. When she first heard that Dorothy had written to Daniel, having earlier talked her out of doing so, Abigail had resolved to take her sister to task. As it was, she had neither the strength nor the urge to do so. During her sickness, she had been touched by the way that Dorothy had cared for her. She had never once reprimanded her younger sister or tried to coax details of her escapades from her. Dorothy had been a model of sympathy and support. It was the reason Abigail felt able to confide in her. There was no competition over Daniel any more.

'Will I ever learn what happened to him?' Abigail wondered.

'It might be better if you did not,' said Dorothy considerately, 'and I'm sure that His Grace will keep any unsavoury details from you.'

'But I'm involved. I'm entitled to the truth.'

'The truth is that you were a young, headstrong girl who made a mistake in following your heart. We've all done that, Abigail.'

'Not with such disastrous consequences.'

'Stop fearing the worst all the time.'

'What else can I do?'

Glancing down at her book, Abigail closed it shut and stood up. It was a beautiful day to sit in the garden but her mind was in turmoil and she could take pleasure from nothing. She was about to go back into the house when a servant came out.

'Captain Rawson has called,' he said.

Abigail almost fainted. 'Captain *Daniel* Rawson?'

Dorothy helped her sister to resume her seat on the garden bench then she looked up at the servant. 'We'll see Captain Rawson out here,' she said.

After giving an obedient nod, the man retired. Abigail was dazed. Instead of feeling joy and relief, she went completely numb. Seeing her sister's confusion, Dorothy sat down and put an arm around her.

'Bear up, Abigail,' she said happily, 'it's wonderful news.'

'Yes... Yes, I suppose it is.'

'There's no supposition about it. Captain Rawson is alive. You won't have his death on your conscience any more.'

'That's true,' agreed Abigail, realising it for the first time and letting a cautious smile break through. 'Daniel is *alive*.' The smile was replaced by a chevron of concern. 'But what if he's badly injured? What if those two men inflicted terrible wounds on him? *That* would be my fault.'

'Don't rush to embrace a problem that may not be there.'

'I'm scared.'

'There's no need to be.'

'What am I to say to him, Dorothy?'

'Oh,' said her sister, squeezing her shoulder affectionately before releasing her, 'I think you'll find the right words somehow.'

They had a moment to compose themselves before Daniel was shown out. He gave a formal bow and they rose from the bench by way of acknowledgement. Daniel was wearing a smart new uniform. Abigail searched for indications of terrible injury but found none. Apart from a couple of lingering scars on his face, he seemed to be in rude health. She gave a strained laugh.

'I thought that you were dead,' she admitted.

'There were a few moments when I came close to death,' he said affably, 'but heaven is not yet ready to receive me.'

'What about those two men?'

'They are no longer a threat to me.'

Abigail was startled. 'Do you mean that you...?'

'Forget about them,' he advised. 'They belong in the past.'

'What brings you back to England?' asked Dorothy. 'I thought the campaign would go on for months yet.'

'You've obviously not heard the good tidings,' he said, 'and why should you? I've only just come from delivering despatches to Her Majesty the Queen, to the Earl of Godolphin and to Secretary Harley.' He spread his arms. 'We fought the enemy at Blenheim and achieved a stunning victory. The whole of London will soon resound with the news.' Dorothy let out a spontaneous cry of pleasure. Abigail clapped her hands. 'Marshal Tallard is a prisoner of war and the French army has been routed. Pardon me if I am still a little out of breath,' he went on, a hand to his chest, 'but it took me eight days to get back to England and I had little rest on the way.'

'Then we are all the more grateful that you found the time to call on us,' said Abigail. 'It was excessively kind of you.'

'I wanted to make sure that you got back home safely.'

'Abigail has told me what you did for her, Captain Rawson,' said Dorothy, 'and it was the act of a true gentleman. I offer you profound thanks on behalf of the whole family. However,' she added, looking first at Abigail then back at Daniel, 'at this moment, I suspect that the only person you really wish to see is my sister. Please excuse me.'

Dorothy went back into the house and left them alone together. There was a prolonged silence. Since she had never envisaged such a meeting taking place, Abigail was hopelessly unprepared for it. For his part, Daniel had had neither time nor inclination to rehearse any speech. Until he had handed over his dispatches, Abigail Piper had not really existed. A blend of guilt, affection and curiosity had guided his footsteps to her door. Yet both of them were certain about one thing. Instead of being brought together by Abigail's pursuit of him, they had been driven apart.

'Will you be staying in London for long?' she asked at length.

'No, Abigail, I have to ride to Somerset.'

'Are you going to call on relatives?'

'I'll be visiting my father's grave,' he told her. 'It's something I always do when I return to England. I owe him a great debt. It was because of my father that I joined the army.'

'That's your world, isn't it, Daniel?'

'It always will be.'

'I'm sorry that I embarrassed you by stumbling into it.'

'You caused no embarrassment, Abigail,' he said with a forgiving smile, 'and, if anyone should be apologising, it's me. I'm sorry that I was not able to spend more time with you in Germany but, as you saw, I was somewhat preoccupied.'

'I can't believe that I was so reckless,' she said.

He was tactful. 'I think we both profited from the experience.'

'I learnt a lot about myself, Daniel, I know that. And it frightened me more than I can say. I'd never *dream* of doing anything as selfish and irresponsible as that again.'

'I hope that it wasn't entirely a cause for regret,' he said gently. 'There must have been some happy moments for you.'

'Oh, there were – lots of them. Each one of them is faithfully recorded in my diary.'

'Good.'

'And now they'll be treasured,' she said. 'When

I thought that you'd been killed because of me, all that I could do was to grieve and rebuke myself. I didn't have the heart even to open my diary and read about our time together. I was wasting away with anguish. Now that you've come back, now that I've seen you with my own eyes, a huge weight has been lifted from me. I can cherish fond memories again.'

'I'll do the same, Abigail.'

It was the moment for a chaste kiss of farewell but it never came. Abigail was too nervous to invite it and Daniel too afraid that it might be misconstrued. They settled for a polite handshake.

'Will you be returning here from Somerset?' she asked.

'Only to take ship to Holland,' he replied. 'I have to rejoin my regiment. We may have won a mighty battle but the war will continue. The French army will be back again before too long.'

'And Captain Daniel Rawson will be there to fight them.'

'I have to be. It's my vocation.'

'I discovered that when I came to Germany.'

'Your friendship has been a delight to me, and, in a perverse way, I admire you for what you did. It showed courage and madness. Those are the very qualities that drove me into the army so we have an affinity. As you found out, however,' he said with a shrug, 'I can never be more than a friend. You must take me as I am, Abigail.'

'And what is that?'

'A soldier of fortune.'

The publishers hope that this book has given you enjoyable reading. Large Print Books are especially designed to be as easy to see and hold as possible. If you wish a complete list of our books please ask at your local library or write directly to:

Magna Large Print Books
Magna House, Long Preston,
Skipton, North Yorkshire.
BD23 4ND

This Large Print Book for the partially sighted, who cannot read normal print, is published under the auspices of

THE ULVERSCROFT FOUNDATION

THE ULVERSCROFT FOUNDATION

... we hope that you have enjoyed this Large Print Book. Please think for a moment about those people who have worse eyesight problems than you ... and are unable to even read or enjoy Large Print, without great difficulty.

You can help them by sending a donation, large or small to:

**The Ulverscroft Foundation,
1, The Green, Bradgate Road,
Anstey, Leicestershire, LE7 7FU,
England.**
or request a copy of our brochure for more details.

The Foundation will use all your help to assist those people who are handicapped by various sight problems and need special attention.

Thank you very much for your help.